CW00496380

Broken Light

— J. K. DENNING —

Sacristy
Press

Sacristy Press
PO Box 612, Durham, DH1 9HT

www.sacristy.co.uk

First published in 2024 by Sacristy Press, Durham

Copyright © J. K. Denning 2024
The moral rights of the author have been asserted.

All rights reserved, no part of this publication may be reproduced
or transmitted in any form or by any means, electronic,
mechanical photocopying, documentary, film or in any other
format without prior written permission of the publisher.

Scripture quotations, unless otherwise stated, are from the
New King James Version®. Copyright © 1982 by Thomas
Nelson. Used by permission. All rights reserved.

Every reasonable effort has been made to trace the copyright holders
of material reproduced in this book, but if any have been inadvertently
overlooked the publisher would be glad to hear from them.

Sacristy Limited, registered in England & Wales, number 7565667

British Library Cataloguing-in-Publication Data
A catalogue record for the book is available from the British Library

ISBN 978-1-78959-352-5

Life, like a dome of many-coloured glass,
Stains the white radiance of Eternity,
Until Death tramples it to fragments.
Percy Bysshe Shelley, Adonais

Numberless are we, all and each speak we, sounding in concert,
One on his own remains voiceless; black but we play upon white fields,
Though we converse on high things, no sound beats on the ear drum;
Speak we the past and the now, foretell many things in the future.
Seventh-century Northumbrian Riddle

. . . if I were called upon to write a book . . . I should prefer
to write it in such a way that a reader could find re-echoed
in my words whatever truths he was able to apprehend. I
would rather write in this way than impose a single true
meaning so explicitly that it would exclude all others . . .
Augustine, Confessions. *Book XII, 31*

Preface

Several years ago, I visited the National Glass Centre in Sunderland for the first time. Hovering, translucent, on the edge of the Wear estuary, it is an uplifting, inspiring place. My imagination was instantly captured by the mesmerizing displays of molten glassblowing, the kaleidoscopic exhibitions and by discovering the fascinating, and long, history of glass making in the Northeast. It was remarkable to learn that lying in St Peter's Church, just a stone's throw away, were fragments of coloured glass from the seventh century, and that in the twin monastery church of St Paul's, a little further up the coast, was arguably the oldest stained-glass window in the world.

The story of the Anglo-Saxon bishop Benedict Biscop's journey to engage Gaulish glaziers to reteach the natives of Britain the lost art of stained-glass continued to fascinate me. I have returned many times to the Glass Centre to try my hand at various courses, visited St Peter's, Monkwearmouth and St Paul's, Jarrow, and read what I could find about the period, including of course from Bede's *History of the English Church and People* and his *Lives of the First Five Abbots of Wearmouth and Jarrow*.

Back in the 1990s, when I was studying for my English Literature degree at York University, my paper on the Romantic period was prefixed by a short quotation from Shelley's *Adonais*. I have also used it at the beginning of this novel. The idea of "life", in all its broken beauty, staining the "white radiance of eternity", has stayed with me, along with the vivid memory of a visit to Lincoln Cathedral during the same time period, where I was struck by the physical effect of the "many-coloured" light falling through stained-glass windows onto the pale stone floor. This impression has been reinforced during subsequent visits to Durham Cathedral and indeed in the many wonderful church buildings up and down the country, including St Peter's and St Paul's. Over time, the image became the germ for my novel, growing as it combined with my interest in the art of glass making and its history and significance for the Northeast. It seems to me a powerful metaphor for our human experience in a fallen world, where there is so much goodness and beauty and yet also so much corruption and pain. I see the ultimate expression of this in the rainbow, created through sunshine and rain: God's covenant promise to a fallen world.

In this novel, I have attempted to explore something of this mixed nature of our lived experience and how, in every age, God speaks both to us, and through us, in our human creativity and in our loves. In *Broken Light*, I want to affirm that although fallen and broken, our lives and our art can have enduring significance through relationship with Him.

I wanted the book to encompass two very different and disparate times, that of the seventh century and of my own student era of the 1990s, to illustrate that the big questions of our human existence and our fundamental needs have not changed. I am also fascinated by the way that art, visual, oral and written, can create a dialogue across time and speak truth into the world in a way that is ageless, taking on meaning beyond itself.

The protagonist Adam's inner, spiritual journey, set in the mid-1990s, is mirrored by co-protagonist Alwin's physical travels, as he accompanies his bishop, Benedict Biscop, on his pilgrimage to the continent in AD 679. All of the characters in this novel are entirely fictional, apart from, of course, Benedict Biscop, with whom I must confess I have taken some liberties, as it is difficult to find much information on the real personalities of people from so long ago. Many of the places in the novel are also real places, or based on real places, but in an imagined form.

Adam's story is told in straightforward prose. Alwin's story, however, presented something of a challenge, being set in such a distant past. While I was experimenting with the best way to tackle this, I happened to listen to J. R. R. Tolkien's wonderful retelling of the medieval *Sir Gawain and the Green Knight*, another favourite from university. This struck me with sudden inspiration, and having always loved poetry, I decided to tell the seventh-century part of my tale in alliterative verse. Thus, Alwin and Biscop's tale is recounted as a fourteenth- or fifteenth-century narrative poem, penned by an unknown scribe, about the even earlier Anglo-Saxon period. To weave the two stories together, and allow them to inform one another naturally, Adam, a specialist in medieval literature, is translating the verse into contemporary English. My poetic account draws significantly on Bede, Augustine and the Bible.

It was important to me that both journeys towards self-understanding and the rediscovery of lost knowledge should begin and end against the sea-haunted backdrop of Northumbria. The Northeast has a long and distinguished spiritual and creative heritage. I have been privileged to live in Durham for the last years and have grown to love the region's deep but unassuming sense of history and the strange juxtaposition of heavy industry and wild natural beauty, particularly evident along the miles of coastline. I hope something of this distinct and unique sense of place comes through in this tale of loss, creativity, love and redemption.

I was very sad to read recently that the National Glass Centre is set to be closed by the University of Sunderland due to its structure being broken beyond affordable repair. There have been promises that it will be relocated, but the loss of that jewel of a building will be keenly felt, I am sure, as another blow to a region that has suffered so much loss, neglect and betrayal in recent decades. In one sense, nothing in this world lasts for ever, but things of value do point to a higher and greater reality. The Northeast has bequeathed us so much beauty, wealth and wisdom, and it deserves a better fate than that of recent times. I hope that the phoenix will rise again from the ashes. But even so, the legacy we have inherited continues to speak in voices that mingle with the many multitudes of other voices from across the world and down through history, all attesting to the truth that how we live now—what we do and how we love; what we say and write and create—really matters and has lasting, even eternal, significance.

I will leave the last word to another Romantic poet, John Keats, whose tragically early death Shelley is elegizing in *Adonais*. In the ultimate sense I believe he is right:

> *A thing of beauty is a joy for ever:*
> *Its loveliness increases; it will never*
> *Pass into nothingness.*

Jennifer Denning
Durham, 2024

Acknowledgements

I am indebted to Peter Hunter Blair's book Northumbria in the Days of Bede for helping the Anglo-Saxon era come alive for me. Also to Micheal Reeves' The Breeze of the Centuries, in his whole approach but particularly his excellent chapter on Augustine. To C. S. Lewis, from whom Reeves has taken his title, in every way. And to Malcolm Guite's little book The Word within the Words, which has enriched my appreciation of and wonder at the divine gift of human language.

I would like to thank all those who have helped and encouraged me while I have been writing this book, especially my husband John for his constant love and support and my dad Mike who began my love for stories by reading to me when I was small, writing his own books and letting me into his secret, that when it's hard to know where to start, it doesn't have to be at the beginning! Also the many other friends, including members of my dad's writing group, the North Pens, who have read, made suggestions and generally helped me improve the narrative and encouraged me to keep going. In particular, my thanks go to Marie McHugh and Brenda Norton who have spent many hours painstakingly reading and checking for me. I am also grateful to Natalie and Richard at Sacristy Press for believing in the story and turning it into a reality that can be held in the hand, and to Claire Clark of Apostle Designs and my daughter Joanna who, with their gifted artwork, have transformed it into a thing of beauty. Whether the contents live up to their cover or whether the light is too broken, the reader must judge for themselves.

A sparrow in winter

When the wintry winds whirl
Around the bleak wilderness of this world
And snow swirls in the stormy sky,
Beating and battering the beleaguered hall,
That one small human refuge
From the hostile rage of ravening nature,
A single sparrow might soar
From that outer darkness
Into this pinprick of light,
With which the prudent may compare
This present little life of man upon the earth
When viewed next to the vast
And trackless waste of eternity,
That void into which all vanish,
And from whence
All unknowing and unknown
We unwittingly proceed.
This swift sparrow's flight
Through the momentary safety
And warmth of the firelight
Is as our fate:
The banqueting hall of a great king
Sitting in his splendour on a winter's day,
With counsellor and thane,
Warmed by his fire, whilst without
The storms of snow and rain are raging wild.
This small sparrow flies swiftly
In through one door and out the other;
While inside, he feels safe from winter storms
For a few fleeting seconds
But after these moments of comfort

And maybe even mirth by flame and hearth,
He vanishes again from view
Into that wintry world from whence he came,
And his place knows him no more.

Numinous

November. Dregs of another year. The dark comes on early now. That indeterminable time between day and night when the greyness is tangible, almost alive. A wind and rainswept pier in the bleak, industrial Port of Tyne. At first indistinguishable from the icy rain and howling gale, a lone man in a long grey coat leans over the end rail staring down into the surging waves beneath, a cigarette in his mouth and an inscrutable look in his eyes. Shielding from the world an impotent, biting rage and sorrow, he is cradled in the arms of that wild fury, embraced by it, as it carries him with empathy, spitting out unspeakable curses. The relief was in the recklessness of that driving water all around and the harsh burnt-out scrag end of the day. There was nowhere on earth he would rather be. Where humanity had abandoned him, nature in its otherness, in its utter lack of hypocrisy, stood by him in solidarity, like a ferocious but loyal dog. He noted it with vague surprise. There was some comfort in this.

He had no idea how long he had stood there, with the darkness closing around him. At length the cold wildness of the weather became too much even for his current lack of care for physical comfort. The water poured off his nose and bedraggled hair into his eyes and streamed in icy rivulets down his neck, soaking his clothes inside his coat. The skies and seas that had driven him outside for catharsis now drove him to find refuge from their purging fury. Man, he thought grimly, can only commune with the elements for so long. In a battle of endurance, we always lose. Although that was nothing new. He always lost everything, and even here he must concede his ground.

Grinding the useless cigarette end beneath his foot, he fought his way off the pier, grabbing at the rusty rails at intervals to steady himself and at length found himself, head bent, striding along the path of the river, which was in full spate. The concrete blocks of the Ministry of Transport were behind him by the estuary and the regimented rows of new Nissan cars lined up endlessly away to his left, like monstrous, perfectly disciplined legions of shiny insects. Hardly aware of his surroundings, his feet forced him inland, away from the pitiless rain now driving from behind, past the farm, past the parkland and the closed coffee shop until he found himself amongst the ruins of the monastery. *Alwin's monastery*, he thought vaguely. St Paul's. Strange. He had not ended up here intentionally.

Although the rain was unforgiving, above the sky was cracked with sudden threads of gold, and slanting low through the rain and clouds a rare late-afternoon beam of sunlight pierced the grey landscape and fingered the ancient stone walls that rose up before him, offering sanctuary. Desperate now for respite, he grasped the iron ring and stumbled through the door into the old stone church. As he slammed it shut against the gale, there was immediate and absolute silence, as if someone had turned off a switch.

At first the contrast confused him. He was stunned and dazed by the quiet and warmth. It did not feel entirely natural. Yet it also offered relief— strangely but perfectly balanced with that brought by the wild weather. Golden and oddly warm, the sudden rays streamed through the tiny leaded panes and fragments of ancient glass, to be broken and recast into jewels of liquid light. Just standing there, absorbing that light and warmth and colour was reviving. His body and soul which he had turned over to the elements to be torn and shredded now felt, inexplicably, the merest hint of a healing he could endure without contempt. The invisible physic that infused the place filled him too, like silent hands skilfully reordering the shattered fragments of his soul, drawing order and coherence from his chaos and turmoil. With slow deliberation he placed his feet on the pale reflected rainbow patches scattered on the smooth stone flags and followed their path, his eyes half shut, trancelike, and for once, at peace. When he reached the base of the window, he raised his eyes to its radiance: at first just a jumble of splendour but gradually beginning to take shape. Sublime. Panoramic. All-embracing. In that transfiguring moment it seemed to him to draw all things into a great pattern of wondrous, complex completeness. And yet his overwhelming impression was that of the harmony of perfect simplicity.

Suddenly and terribly, he became aware that he was not alone, that he was in the presence of something or someone wholly Other, that eclipsed his own mind and senses. It was utterly unlike anything he had before experienced or could have imagined. The furthest fibres of his innermost being were touched and trembled before this great Other, reverberating, shuddering, quivering, like the strings of a harp thrilling to the hand which had strung and tuned it. And he felt himself to be a profane nothingness; a nothingness in the presence of that which is All. He stood in blank wonder, in dumb and absolute awe. He saw himself in antithesis, no longer the centre of his carefully constructed little world. Instead, he became as an infinitesimal grain of dust in the beam of that infinite gaze as it swept the vast reaches of an immense, sublime universe. And he wept. Bathed in that kaleidoscopic light, he experienced for a single moment the utter euphoria of un-making, of relief and release from the appalling tyranny of his own being.

Outside, although he did not know it, a real rainbow arched above him.

In kind simple am I nor gain from anywhere wisdom,
But now each man of wisdom always traces my footsteps.
Habiting now broad earth, high heav'n I formerly wandered;
Though I am seen to be white, I leave black traces behind me.

An Abbot of Jarrow

Adam

He sat down at his favourite desk in front of the large diamond-paned window and with a deliberate movement picked up his pen. He, Adam Hunter, always worked with pen and paper first. He had never mastered the art of typing thought straight into a computer. If he was honest, he rather despised them, and anyhow, new habits are hard to form. He needed to feel the ink flowing from his pen onto the page. It seemed to open up a more direct path to the brain and allow creativity and ideas to flow too. In this instance it felt even more important in order to harness the right contemporary words to convey those distant words and thoughts of men so far removed in time.

He thought of the goose quills and the vellum, the nameless scribe selecting, then cutting, then dipping the newly sharpened point into the precious pigment, of the momentous first stroke. Surely that must have always been accompanied by a little apprehension and anticipation as he began to weave the magic art of letters.

He always used the same pen himself, a gold-nibbed Parker, and his preference was for unlined paper, ideally of a fairly heavy weight and with a little texture to hold the ink. He unscrewed the top carefully and held the pen poised above the paper, in that limbo between thought and the commitment of words.

Today was no different, and yet it was. Everything had changed.

After his crazed flight up to the sea-savaged pier, his strange epiphany in the church and his quiet and reflective drive home, he knew that for better or worse a page in his own life had been turned and that nothing would ever be the same again. There was no way back to the old life.

Of course the externals carried on as usual: the hurried breakfast, the takeaway coffee en route, the walk through the tree-lined paths by the ever flowing Wear and then up to Palace Green Library, the flocks of sleepy undergraduates, the few dogged red-faced cyclists (who in their right mind would try to cycle up that hill?), the distant clattering from Castle kitchens, and wafting through the thin morning air the smell of the remnants of breakfast already mingling with the mince and cabbage for lunch, the old metal-studded door, the smooth winding stone steps, worn by centuries of feet, the shouted greetings to colleagues, the sound of the birds as they wheeled and called round the cathedral towers, the sunlight and the shadows. But inside, everything was changed, and he felt he was observing these familiar things with the eyes of a stranger.

Never mind, there was work to be done and he must do it. It was the only thing left. But how to begin . . . Well, perhaps at the beginning. He adjusted the clean, new piece of paper so it was squarely in front of him, laid the facsimile where he could see it clearly with his annotations and notes, gripped his pen firmly and in his beautiful cursive hand wrote the title and underlined it with a flourish. A working title, he thought to himself. It would do for now.

Beginnings (AD 674)

By Britain's bright shores,
Which before bore the name Albion,
Where ancient Arthur
Performed acts of acclaim and renown,
In this white land—this land well-watered
With springs both salt and hot
And lavishly laced with lead
And many marvellous metals besides,
Vast veins of copper, iron and silver,
Vibrant and vital, and fine jet,
Black jewel wrought in Jurassic times
Which when fired fights off snakes with its flame
And when warmed by friction
Holds fast firmly as amber;
Abounding in grain and grass,
Peaceful plentiful pasture,
Trees for timber, cultivated vines,
Various birds of land and sea,
Springing streams of salmon,
Eels, dolphins and seals,
Wondrous whales and smallest shellfish,
Scallops, shrimp, mussels,
Wherein wealth and riches may be found,
Pearls of greatest price
And whelks from which may wrested be
Wonderful dye of deepest hue,
Unfading scarlet for the wise and regal wearer,
Like wine with age more fine,
Bathed in both milk and honey pure,
Made into mead of golden hue,
Where winter's bite

The bleaker strikes in daytime dark
And summer's light still lingers
In northern nights so near
That 'twixt twilight and dawn the sun
Scarcely sinks beneath the shining sea—
In this blessed and sceptred isle,
In Northumbria's regal realm,
Before he fell from his high calling,
King Ecgfrith, inspired by heaven and his holiness,
His excellence and enthusiasm
To endow the English church with grace,
Endeavouring to following that fair path
Of enlightenment rekindled by great Edwin,
Bestowed upon Bishop Benedict Biscop
A bounteous gift of land to build,
Twice blessed, two abbeys
Where abundance of all good things might thrive,
Dedicated to Peter and to Paul,
Those peerless predecessors in proclaiming
The gracious gospel of Jesus Christ,
Good news to Gentile and to Jew.
The abbeys, after these Apostles named,
Were to abound with marvels,
And as time would tell,
The prize most praised would prove to be
A priceless pearl, that man most venerable,
The virtuous Bede, Jarrow's gentlest jewel
Set in our coveted country's crown
Whose worth in weaving words would greater be
Than all the treasures
That the five-times-travelled world would yield;
Yet still this sacred sanctuary of saintly fame
Would by and by boast
Many marvels made with matchless hands

And here would counted worthy be
All various and virtuous craft
As well as diverse doctrinal discourse,
For from far shores this fervent bishop
Fain would furnish his holy house
With sacred store, valuable volumes
Of ecclesiastical elegance and holy pictures
Painted purposefully to point to the Passion of our Lord.
And from France, when the work was well-nigh finished,
He would send for gifted glaziers
To make a glass so glorious
It might lift the gaze to heavenly grace
And nurture our natives in the nature of their trade
To fashion forms of beauty and facility,
For it was an art that from our own fair shores had fled,
Lost in the long and languishing dusk,
Which made us strangers to many sacred skills.
As at the first that quickening Word-made-flesh
Had voiced form from out the formless void,
So sought he eagerly to entreat those excellent hands
To teach us how to trace again the precious pattern
Of paradise and peace
And coherent creation from chaos
Cause to be re-cast anew;
His earnest vision, that the excellencies
Of this edifice would to the expectant eye exhibit
One whole and holy scene
Of man's most high and heavenly hope;
Richest redemption;
Whereupon the broken, humble heart
Might melt with gratitude and love,
Bathed and re-born in beauty and in truth;
Most blessed mystery of grace divine.

Translation

He had been working frenetically for hours. Lunch had been forgotten. Discarded sheets of paper covered in multiple corrections and crossings-out lay littered all around him. In front of him the sheets were filling with his own distinctive script, even and beautiful, the odd correction here and there, where he had thought of a better word, neatly amended. He had been desperately trying to keep his own thoughts out and fill his mind instead with the thoughts and words of those other men, trying to render them faithfully for the modern ear but without losing the poetry. But there was no escape. He found to his horror that their thoughts and his own began to run alongside and weave in and out of one another, mingling and finally converging on the image which had haunted his mind ever since he had stood before it the previous afternoon—that "glorious glass", the window. This was appalling. Was he going mad? Were the ancient words on the manuscript shifting and reforming to match the pattern in his own frenzied brain?

With a great effort he tried to calm himself. He gathered together and turned over the sheets of paper he had been working on and with a decisive act of will put them in a pile on the far corner of the desk. He would have a break from this section and check through the earlier fragments he had already translated. He delved into his bag and removed the foolscap folder, opening it in front of him and spreading out the contents. Although it was still early in the afternoon the light was dull and dim. He turned on the comforting library lamp and the gentle green glass shade was illuminated, casting a warm pool of yellow light over his papers.

Although he could refer to the precious manuscripts, he was mainly working from facsimiles of the original text, but they were still beautiful. His own annotations were carefully noted in the wide margins. The sharp white paper that contained his own translation looked somehow sterile and lifeless in comparison.

A few months before there had been much excitement in certain circles over the discovery of a previously unknown manuscript dating to somewhere between the end of the fourteenth and the middle of the fifteenth century and written in Middle English alliterative verse, similar to that of *Sir Gawain* or the slightly earlier *Piers Plowman*. It had been discovered when a later volume of ecclesiastical writings, part of a series, had been taken for rebinding. As was so often the case in bygone days with the rarity of materials being what it was, the earlier manuscript had been repurposed and used in the strengthening of the spine and cover of the larger book. On closer examination other volumes of the collection were discovered to contain more fragments of the text by the same scribe, who, not unusually for the period, was unnamed. What was more unusual were the early Reformation overtones. Perhaps that was another reason it had been repurposed. Bit by bit the scholars had pieced together a fairly coherent narrative, although it was unclear whether absolutely all of the original manuscript had been found.

What was particularly interesting to Adam was that it turned out to be a Middle English narrative poem about an even earlier age, telling the tale of Alwin, a seventh-century novice monk, as he journeyed from his native Northumbria in the company of his famous companion and mentor, the Anglo-Saxon abbot and founder of the Monkwearmouth-Jarrow Priories, Benedict Biscop. Adam's specialism was medieval alliterative poetry, and although he was less familiar with the earlier period this poem dealt with, and although his taste ran more to the chivalric than the ecclesiastical, he had nonetheless been tasked with the translating of the Middle English text into contemporary language for publication. He had already achieved some acclaim for his translations of other bits and pieces from the period that he had worked on alongside his lecturing, having a good ear for the texture and flow of the language. It was a challenge he relished. He had always nursed a secret desire to write his own poetry; however, the right words seemed to elude him, like the fruitless chasing of a dropped parking ticket on a windy day. And so he had poured his poetic desire instead into the translating of older texts, making them accessible for a new generation of readers, trying to remain faithful enough to the original while at the same time retaining as far as it was possible the older alliterative form. It seemed odd to him that most people thought poetry should rhyme.

Although that form had in the end triumphed to become definitive in the English language, it was his opinion that alliterative verse offered another experience to be embraced and was particularly suited to the telling of long narrative tales, helping the flow of the language through its emphasis on recurring consonant sounds. At times the form had to be sacrificed to retain the meaning. It did not really work the other way round he had found, while experimenting. Whatever theory one might hold of language, in the practical matter of his translating he had found form must be subservient to meaning. Naturally it was absolutely joyful when the two came together like a perfect marriage. Those experiences were, however, few and far between.

He began to read through his rendering of an earlier, more introductory part of the tale. The text was heavily reliant on Bede, although of course slightly anachronistically, as Biscop and Alwin had predated him by a number of years. Even so, the later writer had woven poetic descriptions of Britain at around that time and earlier, drawing from Bede's famous Latin prose *A History of the English Church and People*. Adam had found himself also succumbing occasionally to the temptation of anachronism, so this did not trouble him in the least; in fact he welcomed it. When your mind is resonating with the words and phrases of so many great writers from throughout the ages, it is difficult not to appropriate them to new or even older contexts. That was one of the joys of working with English literature: the great wealth of expression and beauty building on itself through the centuries, each new layer enriching and elucidating those that had come before. At least that's how it should work, he thought. And so he justified the reading back into older texts as much as the reading out of newer ones. They were all part of the same tapestry of words. The more they were woven back and forth the more beauty and complexity they achieved. To real, absolute meaning he had never given a lot of thought. He had simply succumbed to their beauty. But now he was beginning to wonder. Was it probable that things of such power, such beauty as words could exist somehow untethered from a greater and more substantial reality?

He turned to the section he had finished a few days before which was setting the scene for the mission and journey of Alwin and Biscop by connecting it with the foundations laid by the even earlier Edwin, foundations that had themselves been traced back to a time before the Romans had fled in AD 410, snatching away, so it was supposed, the light of truth and learning from the shores of Britannia.

He had begun his translation with a short fragment, which had appeared to be the first part of the lost manuscript, opening the tale with the iconic Anglo-Saxon motif of the sparrow in the hall. Then followed the famous response of King Edwin and his pagan high priest. This appropriately set the scene for the unfolding tale of the light of truth and learning being rekindled, a defiant blaze of glory bursting back into the pagan darkness. When he had first written the opening lines, he had never imagined how they would so soon come to mirror his own plight of uncharted flight through the bleak wasteland his life had become.

Rekindling (AD 627)

"And so is our human plight
Like the sparrow in winter
When we know not God nor his gospel of grace
And grope in darkness, cold, lost and afraid
Without hope and without help in the world."

And when good king Edwin heard his counsellors
Urging him thus to carefully consider the new way
Which gave more certain knowledge—
And in fulfilment of his vow made
When visited by a divine vision that vouchsafed
His life and victory over his enemies—
He promised that he and his people would pursue
The proclamation of Paulinus
And urging of Pope Boniface to embrace
The True faith, together with his principal advisors
And even Coifi the pagan priest,
Who openly professed that he perceived
The old religion to be valueless and powerless
And publicly renounced the worthless superstitions
And idols he had formally worshipped,
Begging the king for arms and the royal stallion
Upon which to ride to rid the land of its abominations.
And reaching the temple of his former gods,
He thrust in the spear and profaned the false sanctuary,
Ordering his companions to burn with fire
This hideous place of Beelzebul's bondage,
Desecrating and destroying the altars that he himself
Had dedicated in his former darkness, now full of joy
In his knowledge of the worship of the one true God,
Father, Son and Spirit; inseparable Trinity.

And so, by God's gracious providence in the matters of men,
It could thus be said that He rekindled the flame of truth
That was for a while withdrawn from our lamenting land,
Left woeful and wretched with little light,
And lost knowledge once again was sought and found
And nurtured upon our blessed shores.

*   *   *

Even rereading this earlier passage had an unnerving effect on Adam as he sat in the half light of that dreary afternoon. The words seemed to have taken on a new and menacing significance. They almost seemed to be goading him, pricking at the edges of his mind. He gazed unseeing out of the window. Another sensation at that moment broke in upon his consciousness; the great cathedral bells had begun to toll.

"Mene, Mene, Tekel, Upharsin"

"You have been weighed in the balances and found wanting." The writing on the wall. *"Weighed and found wanting—You!"* The words echoed round and round in his head.

Why had he gone to that service? Why break the habit of a lifetime? Why invite torment? But perhaps he had thought it might bring comfort, or maybe some insight. Of course, it was because of what he had seen in that window yesterday and read in his own words today. He had heard the bells ringing as he had sat in the library gazing out of the window at the fading light and the black silhouettes sharpening against the pale winter sunset, while the birds darted back and forth around the towers. It was as if they were summoning him. Before he had really known what he was doing he had laid down his pen, bundled his things into his bag and was down the stairs, striding across the Green, the cold air making his eyes smart and his nose tingle. The beautiful windows were lit up from inside, the whole structure of the cathedral from without. The ancient building looked weightless, like a giant paper lantern floating high above the silver ribbon of the river running silently below. As he entered, melodious choral singing warned him the service had already started. He slipped into a pew near the back and sat down.

He fumbled with the Book of Common Prayer for a while, finding he was not able to make head nor tail of it, a slightly embarrassing admission for an English Literature lecturer and somewhat surprising given he had been forced to attend chapel on a regular basis at school. His habit, however, had been to try to sneak in a book of his own and slip it inside his prayer book or alternatively to gaze at the young and rather pretty music teacher, so perhaps it wasn't really so surprising after all! He quietly put it down and began to look around. Obviously he had been in here, or rather through here, many times before, sometimes for concerts but mainly as a short cut to the convenient parking on the other side of Prebends' Bridge on the days he wanted to go straight to the library and had a heavy bag. He had always appreciated the beauty, but he was now looking at it differently.

Did this place really hold any answers? He had always dismissed it all as childish nonsense before, albeit in some quarters with a pleasing aesthetic. The beauty and sheer size were quite overwhelming, particularly as he looked up to the soaring buttresses overhead. It did realign human preoccupations with a sense of a greater reality. Put frivolity in its place, kept the serfs humble, he thought cynically to himself.

The lighting and the music and the atmosphere were certainly conducive to a kind of peace. But it felt rather surface-deep. The singing began again. It was soothing. He saw or felt nothing though that resonated with his experience yesterday afternoon, that overwhelming sense of smallness in the face of an immense peace and cohesion. In fact, on the contrary, the service seemed rather fragmented and incoherent. Beautiful bits of chanting and singing, responses from the congregation in which, he realized with slight embarrassment, he was meant to be participating, and seemingly unconnected Scripture readings. It all stirred vague memories of school services, but as with the Prayer Book, he had never taken much notice at the time, being usually more agreeably preoccupied with his own fantasies, one way or another.

And then it had happened. He was suddenly hearing those famous words from *Belshazzar's Feast* in some ancient tongue. He was familiar with the cantata, and vaguely aware of the biblical text it was taken from, but he had never really paid any attention to the words beyond their lyricism and cathartic power. Whatever he did in practice when translating, could he really believe words had a true meaning? Fluidity was the zeitgeist. But now it was as though he was hearing them for the first time, as clearly and as concretely as coffin nails being struck one by one into his consciousness. They were being spoken directly to him and everyone in that service knew he was the condemned man in their midst. "*You! You, Adam Hunter, have been weighed in the balances, and found wanting.*" It was utterly devastating. In every balance, by every standard, he was found wanting, lacking, deficient, defective, flawed, faulty, inadequate, insufficient . . . His command of language, his knowledge of the thesaurus hardly helped him now. The words flowed relentlessly on in a long black list, marching from the white page of his mind like an overwhelming tide or invading army.

The image of a large and terrifying pointing finger filled his consciousness, as in Michelangelo's famous painting, but in his nightmare vision reaching out to accuse and condemn. Not to create but to obliterate. "*You!*" But he found he had nothing to say in his defence. In fact, he couldn't speak at all.

Oblivious to those around him he had stumbled up the aisle and out of the door into the bitter night air of the cloisters. The moon had now risen and shed silver light through the shadowy Romanesque arches onto the stone floor as he staggered along, retching. He made it outside, to the entrance of the stone tunnel and was violently sick by the wall.

He was vaguely aware of two elderly ladies tutting at a distance—"Fancy being drunk already at this time of evening, and at his age! Worse than the students!"—one was saying.

He had somehow managed to lurch home and the combination of emotional exhaustion and whisky had finally drawn him into the temporary mercies of a fitful sleep.

Alwin (AD 660)

What makes for a Saint?
A noble birth and notable name?
Fame for sanctity in life?
A reputation for renowned miracles
Worked by revered relics after death?
Can a few bones or fragments of cloth
Cause the cleansing of ills
Or the cure of ailments
Or delivery from curses fell?
Who can delve into these mysteries of the past,
Perceive with unclouded eyes and hear
With ears attuned to different harmonies?
But even across this vast gulf,
Through these impenetrable mists,
Some radiant shards illuminate
Occasional gleams of gold
And distant melodies murmur upon the balmy air,
Bringing half-forgotten sounds to our straining ears.
If we will, we may pause a while
By the shores of the sundering sea
And let the breeze of the centuries
Breathe upon our upturned faces,
And gently lift our hair,
As we gaze with open hearts and half-closed eyes
Upon that distant horizon;
For who but God writes mysteries in the sand
Or amongst the starry hosts of heaven?

To love and trust the Lord
And lean only upon his lovely name,
To come in nothing of our own

And recognize our righteous acts are but filthy rags
Compared to His pure holiness,
To cast ourselves upon his glorious grace
And clothe ourselves in His clean garments
Gifted to cover our grating poverty;
This washing of our sin in His precious blood,
Poured out freely, shed for us, must be enough!
For Paul, to his beloved fellow saints,
Does write thus in his urgent epistles,
Commending them to keep the faith
And cling to that fellowship of truth and love;
The vast multitude innumerable,
Like sand upon the shores of time,
The golden chain that stretches back to all beginnings,
Forwards towards all ends; alpha and omega
Linked by fiery stars flung across the firmament;
By myriad upon myriad of ordinary saints.

And so, as laid our Lord his lovely infant head
Upon the lowly cattle's crib, here too a comely child
Of our own country is cradled by a humble hearth.
And lying on his back on bed of sheepskin and straw,
Stirred from sweet slumber, he gazes upon
A stream of sunlight straying through the silvery thatch,
The fine particles of dust dancing in its broken beam,
Glancing golden on his gentle mother
As she sleeps silently beside him.
He hears the washing of the waves
Upon the watery shore a stone's throw hence
And smells the wholesome scent
Of beasts and salt and spray.
It is very early on one of those endless summer days
Of earth and elderflower, where wonder weaves
Its dewy web of dawn, and even duties are delight;

This his earliest earthly memory, ephemeral
And yet seeming to him, an echo from eternity.

It is six hundred and sixty summers
Since the gracious nativity of our Saviour
And this Alwin, son of sea and salt and sand,
Is second born to Saewine and Kendra. His sister,
Eostre, is seventeen cycles of the moon his senior
And in time he will fleetingly find four sisters more,
But not hold fast, for death will winnow three of six
Before sixteen summers scarce have flown.
But they are a family bounteously blessed
To bring three babes to be full grown
And tears and grief are sown with seed into the soil
In hope for souls now sailed,
That they may be received at last upon that shore
Of rest where all redeemed reside; that blessed land
Where there will be no more weeping and woe
And Time's terrible tyranny
Is thwarted and overthrown.

This child of lowly hearth will hallowed be,
And as Hannah her son Samuel did commit
Unto the service of the Lord,
So Alwin is set apart to serve,
And is received into that holy house
Hard by his humble home from tender years,
To be taught the trade of word and sign and soul.

Revelations

Adam had only managed to complete a short section by lunchtime the next day. It was the part that introduced the main protagonist, Alwin. He thought vaguely how very different the experience of life must have been back then, in those distant days. "*Solitary, poore, nasty, brutish and short*"—the words of Thomas Hobbes floated into his mind. But according to his unknown poet there was light too, and beauty. Perhaps he had fallen into the trap beloved of writers of every age of romanticizing the past. Perhaps his poet felt the need to look back from his own more complex later medieval world to a time when he imagined faith was simpler and more pure? Perhaps we humans are always chasing the memory of some imagined golden age to help us better endure our own? Or maybe it is even because we all know, somehow, deep down, that things are not the way they are meant to be, and so are always straining, even subconsciously, to return to some lost Eden?

Unsurprisingly after the occurrences of the evening before, Adam's head was pounding and he felt very on edge as these new thoughts ran round his mind. As he sat in his office on Elvet trying to round off the section on Alwin's birth and dedication, he suddenly had the strangest sensation of someone watching him, of a presence in the room with him. He turned round quickly, certain one of his colleagues must have come in unheard. There was no one there. The sensation grew. It was as if someone, or something, just beyond his perception, was overshadowing him. It was a heavy, oppressive shadow that weighed on his whole being right to the core. It was, in a way, the polar opposite of his sensation the other day in the church.

Whether it was what he had been translating unconsciously striking a chord, or the sensation of the presence, or both, he didn't know but he was suddenly filled with an overwhelming compulsion.

I must talk to Lucy!

An image of her simultaneously flooded his mind. He tried, and failed, to push her out and found he had already slid his chair back, stood up and was making for the door. Where did that come from? Why couldn't he get her out of his head?

Lucy. She hovered inexplicably in his mind like a beacon of hope, all bright white and gold, maybe like the angels he had seen in medieval paintings, those fearful visions with their intense, jewel-like colours and luminosity, while everything else, all the normal familiar things and people seemed to have faded and retreated, become as flimsy and insubstantial as wraiths, or as smoke twisting from chimneys on winter days. It was as if the whole familiar old world kept rolling in sepia, while he was suddenly aware of a much greater, horrifyingly vivid reality running not only alongside but above and below too, and Lucy seemed to be the only other fully flesh-and-blood character in the play, full of vibrant colour and life . . . Bloody hell, he really must be going mad! Lucy. Saint Lucy!

He had hardly given her a serious second thought before, other than when the fun of tormenting her had filled the odd half hour of boredom. Or had he? If he was honest with himself, hadn't she been haunting the fringes of his mind like a harbinger of doom ever since he had met her, like the half-perceived shadow of some monstrous force, the incessant beating of whose dark wings against the edges of his consciousness was a horror to be kept at bay, to be resisted at all costs? And before her, hadn't there always been something or someone else, however small, snagging at the threads of his perception, like a piece of grit in a shoe?

He had always shut his mind to that madness before and kept the busy bright lights and dazzle of his world determinedly in focus. Now the defences were utterly broken down. Everything had turned on its head and his soul was unfurling, helplessly unravelling to himself, revealing layer upon layer like an oriental puzzle box. What mystery lay hidden at the centre? Or did he already know? Some long-forgotten seed of knowledge that really all people carry but cannot recall with their brittle, hardened minds? And Lucy suddenly seemed the key to the lock of the forgotten innermost box. She was the only bright point in a world that had gone suddenly and brutally dark. Must he really let himself go, slip over the edge of his safely constructed reality and fall into that unknown space towards her light? What had before felt like a shadow cast over his identity now seemed the first pin prick of light in that flimsy shroud. Instead of repelling her he now felt compelled to seek her out.

He passed a hand over his clammy forehead. Perhaps he was thinking in this crazy way just because he knew she was into spiritual stuff, he tried to rationalize to himself. But was it even spiritual? It felt so physical too, as if for the first time he was properly awake. But to confide in Lucy? After how he'd treated her too . . . It was awkward to say the least, after all that pitiless teasing and mocking and harassment, his cruelty. He had been vile to her; he could see that now with such clarity that he shuddered inwardly. In fact he had been vile altogether to everyone. Why hadn't he seen it before?

No wonder Cynthia had left him, although she was hardly a saint herself. If Lucy needed a foil, it was his sophisticated, unfaithful wife. Even in appearance. An image of her tanned, half naked, wrapped in the arms of another man, a younger man, her raven hair falling in damp ringlets around her elegant face, flashed into his mind. Memory of the old life was still savagely vivid, even though the present had strangely retreated. He had known really, but actually seeing it was excruciating. He ground his teeth.

When she'd seen they'd been caught out, what did she do? A frantic snatching of clothing, disentanglement, implorings, tears? No, she'd laughed. Seared into his memory, her beautiful dark eyes full of malice, laughing at him over the shoulder of her lover . . . Hadn't he even said he would come home for lunch that day? He pressed his fingernails into the palms of his hands until they bled . . . He had slammed the door, charged down the stairs and out into the pouring rain, got into his Mazda MX-5, with the roof still down and driven like something possessed, northwards, heedless of the speed limit, not knowing or caring where he was going. The rain poured down, soaking him, the car, the landscape with icy, relentless water. He didn't care. His mind still felt on fire. And eventually, abandoning the car in a layby, he had found himself by the sea, at the end of a pier, drawn like a magnet by its inhuman ferocity, wanting to lose himself in its boiling fury . . .

But himself: the flirtations, the affairs, the drinking, the bitter rows and hurtful riposte—he was masterful at that. No, the only surprising thing was that she hadn't done it sooner. I suppose it was because of the kids, he thought with another pang. The image of their faces, so young and beautiful and vulnerable, even though they were well into their teens, with their sad, accusing eyes watching him, flashed before him and he felt his stomach twist with shame. He was a disgrace to the name of father, to the name of man. He had had every opportunity: money, education, intelligence, influence; and how had he used it? To mercilessly tear other people down, to use and abuse them for his own ends and sometimes just for the hell of it. He hadn't lost anything; he'd squandered it and tossed it aside with all the profligacy of an ancient tyrant. He had neglected and betrayed his nearest and dearest, and been betrayed in his turn. As he walked, the thoughts and memories of his past life became an avalanche of shame, each one a knife, shredding pitilessly through his carefully constructed ego; so long in the making, so quickly torn to pieces. By the time he reached the other side of the building he was struggling to keep upright. He felt as if he'd been repeatedly punched in the stomach.

He hauled himself up the stairs and hesitated outside Lucy's office. He knocked tentatively. There was no reply, but the door, which wasn't properly shut, swung open, revealing an empty room, small and dingy. He walked in and crumpled into a chair. He must wait for her. He could do nothing else. He must speak with her.

*   *   *

He didn't have to wait long, but as he sat there, mingling with his troubled, haunted thoughts, scenes of previous interactions with the quiet, self-effacing girl swam before his eyes. He groaned and put his head in his hands.

Christmas party last year, too much to drink. He and Robert leering all over anything in a skirt ... His unreasonable annoyance as she'd backed away from him, with thinly veiled disgust in her eyes. She'd had

27

the misfortune to be sitting next to him. Cynthia watching him from another table . . .

"Come on, Saint Lucy, can't you have a night off being holy? You look like you could do with a bit of fun; you're so damned uptight. Have another drink!"

"She doesn't want anything to do with two old, hardened sinners like us, Adam!" Robert had scoffed. "She'll need a bit more encouragement! Do have another drink, sweetheart; it's on me!"

With mock chivalry he had poured a large glass of champagne and shoved it towards her. Adam, with a clumsy flourish, had tried to pick it up and push it towards her lips, but instead ended up spilling it down the front of her dress.

"Shit!" Laughing he had leant across trying to dab her soaking chest with a napkin, and with mock courtesy, "Do forgive me, fair lady!"

She had backed away and stood up abruptly, knocking over the chair. He'd laughed scornfully, slightly menacing now.

"Would do you good to know a bit more about the world. Think you're too good for the rest of us, don't you! Your kind are always so judgmental, such killjoys!"

"You know what happened to the real Saint Lucy, don't you, Adam?" sneered Robert. "Something about a brothel and a knife . . . She wouldn't play ball either!"

He'd laughed again, contemptuously. "Maybe that's what she needs to loosen her up, right time of year too. Although perhaps a few elocution lessons first might also improve things! Or else tie up her tongue and bring her silently!"

He had lurched towards her, laughing at his own wit. He remembered vividly the tears in her beautiful blue eyes, her wide, frightened, sorrowful, liquid eyes, as she'd turned and run from the room. How he had hated the look in those eyes at the time, how they had maddened him. Now, how the memory of them shamed him, made him feel nauseous with horror at himself.

And then there was that other time. He had felt so self-righteous, taken such complacent pleasure in the disciplinary process . . . How censorious he had been. What delight he'd taken in escalating the incident to the highest level within his power. He was a champion of the liberal minded, who would not tolerate such inappropriate, unprofessional behaviour in his staff.

Had it really after all been about revenging himself on her for making him feel bad at the party, making him feel uneasy altogether? He mused. He was seeing everything from the other side now. It was disconcerting, like the familiar yet back-to-front reality you see in a mirror.

A student had complained to Robert about her. Apparently, the girl had been crying outside a lecture theatre one day, just after the beginning of term. Lucy had happened to walk past. She'd stopped and tried to comfort her, bought her a coffee, sat with her. The girl had poured out her heart: her parents' divorce, her boyfriend who'd just dumped her over the phone, her work which was so overdue and in such a mess. Lucy was not a professional counsellor; she was only admin, bloody hell, who did she think she was, little do-gooder, thinking she could fix the world! She should have referred the girl on to her own tutor, himself in fact, or another appropriate person.

What did she do instead? She had chatted to her about everything, even the girl's work, and then shared about her own faith, about a holy God who loved her, sin, wrath, forgiveness, grace . . . Offered to pray with her! How dare she? Lucy had obviously taken advantage of her vulnerability, preyed upon her insecurity and exploited her when she was too down to act rationally, trying to win a convert no doubt, easy game, to her own bigoted sect of weirdos; not even C of E but some dubious type of non-conformists, probably of the drab kind with no art, no beauty, who seem to think ugliness and dullness are a kind of virtue.

When she'd come to her senses, not surprisingly the girl was furious and lodged a complaint with the head of department, Robert Du Prey. As Lucy's direct line manager Adam had been involved in the disciplinary case, which resulted in a reprimand and caution. If such unprofessionalism and inappropriate behaviour happened again, she was out.

Inappropriate? Unprofessional? The brutal mirror that was relentlessly inverting his life taunted him again with his own tawdry truth. If he had got to the weeping girl before Lucy, what then? What would he have done? Probably given her alcohol, not coffee, and been very sympathetic. A shoulder to cry on often eased the way nicely in his experience; both consenting adults anyway, the narrative ran, and words are cold comfort. Mutually agreeable and affirming and casual because of course that was a much more acceptable exploitation even now, even in this year of grace 1996. People may disapprove, but they wouldn't be afraid, because a sin of the flesh is so much easier to forgive than a sin of the spirit. He'd have put her in touch with the official counsellor too, of course. The right boxes would have been ticked on the meaningless piece of paper.

He remembered how he had silently gloated over Lucy after his victory. How deflated she was, how timid and biddable she had become, how cowed when he breezed into her office demanding this and that. What had rejoiced his heart then pierced him now as he sat there in her office desperate to pour out his own soul to her. What a turning of the tables. What humiliating poetic justice the gods were dishing out to him.

*   *   *

"*Sin, wrath, holiness, forgiveness, grace . . .* " such strange words. They belonged to this ancient, new world. He did not have the tools to decipher these words, these signs. How to reach the substance? How to understand and to grasp what lay hidden within those brittle shells of sound? Maybe they didn't have any real meaning at all and were just bogeymen fashioned to frighten and control the ignorant and weak-minded of yesterday. We have new words, signs and symbols for that today; he was well aware of that. He was practised in using them to full effect. Words, and knowing how to use them, most certainly gave one power and he had been using them expertly for years.

They also had an independent power of their own though, as he was now beginning to realize. They would not all bend to accommodate him and his desires. Rather the opposite, unbidden they were beginning to bend him, bend his mind, slip away from him, elude him, betray him, and like his unwritten poetry taunt him with his inability to grasp and hold the deep things, the things that matter. He had found himself unequal to this holding-on in both words and life, unworthy to be entrusted with such precious gifts. He must make do with other, better people's words. How could it be with all their lack of knowledge that those men of distant times could yet seem to understand more about the important things of life, the big questions, while his own, with all its technological advances didn't seem able anymore to even discern what was really important or urgent, or even know what questions needed to be asked?

One thousand, three hundred and thirty-six years since Alwin was born. So very long ago. Even distant history to his Middle English poet. And yet this story was beginning to seem more real to him than his own. Or rather he seemed to have entered into that distant world, which had become so vivid in his mind, while his own world was falling away from him, like a landslide. There was no solid foothold, no hand to grab—*unless perhaps Lucy? This was madness!*

His world was falling around him. Perhaps the world had always been falling. Perhaps his was only a little microcosm after all. The self-satisfied West was falling. What a propensity our society has, he reflected, to be ever inflating our bloated sense of self-importance while at the same time gnawing, preying upon our own foundations, whittling them needle-thin whilst the great, tottering monstrosity sways giddily, intoxicated, grotesque and impossible, over the abyss of its own ruin. How like himself too. This impending doom of a spent and unsustainable way of life, an untenable and decaying civilization, he had been vaguely aware of for some time if he had cared to think of it, as so many educated others are vaguely and lethargically aware, but it hadn't really troubled him. *Why hadn't it troubled him?*

But this was nothing new. Civilization had fallen before, many times, and been rebuilt. Yes, in blood and sweat and tears, but rising again none-the-less, like a phoenix. Alwin knew something of that. So did his poet. So did every age in its own way. Was it not possible that it should happen again? Was it not possible it could even happen for him?

The prophets change but the message remains:

"Wake up! Before it is too late! Flee from the wrath to come!"

The reckoning. Was there still time to heed the signs, the warnings? The loud prophets of today might be the environmental scientists but they too warned, even if using different words, of the cataclysmic disaster facing our human race as we merrily, blithely, blindly stumble, sated and dulled by our own greed and complacency, towards a new dark age, Armageddon, annihilation. And there is no mercy at the hands of an impersonal science of despair. The poor and the vulnerable would go down first, but no one would escape the inevitable shipwreck of our doomed civilization, our plundered and ravaged world.

Better, perhaps even to face an angry God? But our world is saturated with spilled blood, injustice, violence. It is not just the physical fibres of this world that are fraying but the moral fibres too. He could suddenly see it. It is defiled and it cries out for judgement and justice, just as his own life was defiled and was ripe for a reckoning. A society living on borrowed time. A man living on borrowed time. Despite the enormity of his ego, he had to submit to the idea that he was only a small part of the rot. This was both comforting and humbling.

"Our sins will find us out!" We know it. He knew it instinctively. Yet in spite of all this, whatever else we humans are bad at, he reflected, we excel in refusing to face reality. Maybe, he thought, we've all been ignoring the signs since Eden, right from the dawn of time, silencing the prophets and refining and perfecting our refusal to decipher, in ever increasing sophistication and cunning, the signs of coming ruin, the groanings and birth pangs of a creation, a universe, subject to futility. Wars, and rumours of wars, earthquakes and epidemics, famines and floods. Water and fire and blood. A broken, decaying world, broken by broken, decaying people. It was unspeakably bleak, so dark. The horror of that great darkness closed around him, enveloping his mind. He felt its stealthy, relentless creep, imagining it like a terminal cancer, multiplying, invading his flesh and bones, unstoppable, spreading through body and soul. He felt his whole being groan under the weight of it.

How had he been so effectively beguiled by the phantom lights before? The will-o'-the-wisps playing over the swamp of a dying age. The real lights had all gone out; well, almost all. But they had gone out before.

Many times. Was there not a shred of hope in this? Was there still time for another rekindling? Another renaissance? Another reformation? Another revival? He supposed at some point that time would run out and the point of no return would be reached. Was there still time or was the damage now irreparable? Was there any way back to the light for the world, for him?

He suddenly had a glimpse, an insight, into that alien word "sin". A kind of sickness, a kind of madness, a kind of moral blindness. A refusal to see what is staring us in the face. Or if we do see it, a failure to act accordingly. A persistent failure to live in the light. A rebellion of darkness in the face of truth.

But truth. What is truth? The perennial question. How hard to say or even think without a cynical twist of the voice. Strange how little he had cared about it before, even though he loved words, the signs and symbols of the educated man's ostensible pursuit of knowledge.

Can words really convey truth? This new idea seemed on an endless loop in his brain. Could not the meanings of words shift over time? Yes. That much seemed evident. But could the concepts really change just by changing, re-defining the words, reorienting the signposts? And did those concepts really have any substance anyway, and if so, could even the substance be changed, shifted, eroded gradually until there was nothing left?

Nothing now seemed to have substance apart from the window, and the ancient words . . . and Lucy.

Lucy

When Lucy entered her office, the first thing she saw was Adam slumped in a chair. She started with surprise. He had his head in his hands. He looked up as she came in. He looked terrible, like she'd never seen him before; great dark circles and a haunted look in his eyes.

"What on earth is the matter, Adam?" she exclaimed, sitting down next to him and putting her hand on his arm awkwardly. This was so different from the Adam she knew, was a little afraid of and, if she was honest, disliked intensely. There was something about him that disturbed her and she had always had a vague sense of uneasiness in the pit of her stomach when he was around, even before the disciplinary incident.

"She's left me, Lucy," he said, his voice totally flat and expressionless. "My wife, she's finally done it. Wants a divorce. Found herself a nice new man."

As he spoke his voice sharpened and he tried, and failed, to laugh sardonically.

"Well, in fact *I* found *them*, in my own bloody bed . . . Not that I'm exactly clear in that department myself, but not in our own fucking bed!"

He was shocked by the rawness of his own fury. He realized he was almost shouting, clenching his fists.

"And the damn kids, taking her part of course, following her like lambs to the slaughter . . . "

He could feel the angry tears pricking his eyes. The pain was overwhelming. How could it have gone from zero to a hundred like this in 30 seconds, ripping through the ceiling of his consciousness like a rocket?

Why was he telling her, of all people, these things? Did he want some justification for his own behaviour—he knew immediately that if that was the case, he wouldn't get it, particularly not from her. But why was he hedging the main issue? The reason he'd come! It was easier to talk even about this than the other thing.

"Oh, I'm so sorry . . . " she faltered, confused and very uncomfortable. She did not know his family very well, had only seen them once or twice at faculty functions. What was he doing here? She gingerly removed her hand from his arm and stood up awkwardly looking at him.

"I'm not," he said, "I hate her, and she hates me. It's exactly what I deserve. It's what she deserves too—we both deserve all the bloody mess that's coming to us, but the kids, it's not fair on them. I feel so crap, so soiled, such a failure."

Normally so erudite, even his ability to articulate seemed to be failing him.

She moved across the room. "I'll put the kettle on."

He leant back in the chair and looked at the ceiling. "I know you don't have any sympathy for me," he smiled weakly, "and are right not to! That's why I'm here, and not somewhere else I suppose! I don't want sympathy and I don't deserve it."

She didn't say anything, just clattered maybe louder than necessary with the tea things.

"Here you are." She shoved a large mug of strong tea into his hands. "Biscuit?"

"It would make me sick, but thanks!"

"But what can *I* do to help you, Adam?" she said, sitting down opposite looking at him in her old, quiet but uncompromising way, the way he used to hate, before he had tried to break her spirit. He used to think it was arrogance. He could see now it was simply honesty. And what greater respect can we afford another human being than to look them honestly in the eye and not flinch or recoil?

He looked away.

"I don't know," his voice faltered again, fighting back tears. "I just need to know if there is any way, oh I don't know, but any way *back*?"

Why were these things coming out of his mouth?

She shifted uneasily in her chair. Was this genuine or a trap?

"We can never go back," she said slowly. "We have no choice but to go forwards, but I suppose that can be forwards upwards, a journey towards the light rather than downwards to more darkness, if you know what I mean. You can't erase the past, but you can help untangle it, try to understand . . . To state the obvious, you can say sorry!"

"I know I need to say sorry to you!" he mumbled. "I've been vile, I'm disgusted with myself when I think of the things I've said, done . . . " His voice cracked. "I have no right to be here, to even speak, I know!"

"It's ok!" She leant across and put her hand on his arm again. This felt so strange, like some alternative reality. He put his undrunk cup down on the desk and tried to light a cigarette, but his hands were shaking too much. After a moment's futile fumbling he dropped the cigarette packet and lighter on the table hopelessly and stared down at them.

"It's not ok. But what can I do? Lucy, what can I do?" His fingers gripped her hand on his arm until the knuckles turned white.

"I want to feel clean again," he spoke quietly, avoiding her eyes. "I know, umm, people are afraid to speak of their beliefs these days, and, oh Lucy, God knows, I've got a lot to answer for on that front, but I know you believe, believe in hope and the possibility of forgiveness, cleansing, God . . . "

He paused and took a deep breath, and then with a rush:

"Something strange happened to me the other day. I haven't told anyone. It seems crazy, but it feels like it was the turning point of my life, a kind of epiphany. I've tried to explain it away in every way I can think of, but I can't. I saw something, felt something, that spoke into the very depths of my being. And since then, after that moment of almost complete peace, I feel like I'm being hunted . . . "

He passed his hand over his eyes. His voice dropped almost to a whisper; it seemed to be working ahead of his conscious mind.

"It sounds so mad, I know. I can get no rest, day or night. I feel like I'm being pursued to within an inch of my life. Oh Lucy, I'm so afraid, so lost! I don't know where I'm going, but I can't stop. Please, please help me if you can. Be my light!"

Before he knew what he was doing he had grasped both her hands in his with such force that she winced. For a brief moment his eyes looked desperately, pleadingly straight into her own and then releasing his grip just as suddenly, he dashed from the room.

She stared after him, stunned. It was the first time he'd ever actually touched her and yet the first time also he had not been either mockingly flirtatious or contemptuous and disdainful. He had been deadly, painfully serious.

Commission (AD 679)

Now nineteen summers have well-nigh passed,
Six hundred and seventy since our Lord's saving epiphany,
And Alwin, with his new-tonsured golden hair and handsome face
Is grown full-height. He stands in the stone archway
Bathed in a bright beam of spring sunshine, shyness forgot,
Hands clasped in his homespun habit, his face uplifted to the light,
His clear blue eyes animated with excitement and energy,
With joy, vivacity and life. He is speaking with his Bishop,
That blessed Benedict Biscop before acclaimed,
Great acquirer of artefacts and beauty from learned antiquity.

"Father, what I hear rejoices my heart,
For I have greatly longed to see the holy city
And the many wonders that there surely are in this wide world!"

Beaming benevolently upon his young novice
Biscop beckons him near:
"Then surely, my son you shall share with me this journey,
Join in my joy and bear my burden.
For there is indeed a wealth of wonders in this world
And much of beauty to behold and claim. They help us
Better to reflect upon the righteous glories of heaven
And the redeemed riches of renewed Creation
That shall be when Christ returns, as revealed
To Saint John on Patmos Isle, when as poor prisoner
He lifted up his eyes from his earth-bound state
And in the Spirit pierced the veil to perceive
The precious promised truths of paradise regained,
And in this seventh heaven saw Christ's victory
Over sin and death and hell, with all his holy hosts,
The lamb and lion of Judah now enthroned on high,

The peerless potentate of all eternity in majesty arrayed,
Pronouncing peace to his people and judgement just.
But in this vale of tears where we now walk,
We fain would not forget that worldly wonders
Are but patterns of perfect paradise
And while they may point the way,
We must not mistake them for the thing itself,
The real reality and true truth
Towards which we strain with every sinew in our souls,
Seeking solace in shadows and signs.

Never forget, my son, what I have said,
For you, I see, struggle in the same vein as I myself,
Though your appearance belie belief of it,
Looking as you do like an angel of light!
And we must ever both be vigilant
Against the vicious vice of idolatry,
Shunning the voice of false beguiling beauty,
That as Delilah betrayed Samson to his doom,
Lest like the firstborn of ancient Egypt we fall prey
To the avenging angel, the scourge and destroyer
Of the disobedient in the desert,
Even amongst the chosen race,
Whose faithless corpses fell in the wilderness
For failing to fix their faces from sin,
Favouring instead Aaron's golden calf, idolatrous image,
Liking to look upon its lifeless form they despised
The saving serpent of bronze held aloft
By matchless Moses, called God's friend;
Those who stubbornly turned their faces to the wall,
Eschewing life, lest they should look and live.

Let us then not be of that number who fall prey
To Satan's schemes, that serpent of old,

Who in the beginning beguiled our first parents
To believe his lie over God's good truth
And exchange what is genuine for what is false and fleeting,
But follow instead the fair path and heed the pointers
That will by and by lead us to peace and perfection,
Guarding one another's hearts in holy fear
As faithful companions and friends,
Patient pilgrims who for a season must forego
Their native shore and be as exiles upon the earth.
For I believe, nay feel within, that this will be
The last mortal journey I will walk
Before that last and greatest pilgrimage
That all manner of men must make.

Our holy houses will be well tended by
Our trusted Eosterwine and Ceolfrid in our absence,
Faithful shepherds and fathers to their flock,
While we tread the perilous and weary way,
Beset with many dangers, toils and snares
As well as strewn with wonders and delights.
We must arm ourselves with the weapons and word of God
Wherein we will find wisdom to contend
With the world, the flesh and the devil,
Whose devices we must needs combat at every corner.
But, remember this, the greatest enemy we encounter
Is always our own errant heart
From which no exile can extricate us.
We may fly to the ends of the earth and by no means escape
The deadly foe that dogs our feet,
And returning, find it curled like a cur upon our own hearth,
Entwining our sinful souls like a bitter root.
But through the saving grace of our Lord, we will strive
Against Satan and the flesh abroad and will prevail,
The better to prepare us to repair to our own cloister

To confront and conquer this last and foulest of foes,
The faithless, ferocious fiend and enemy within.
We all have battles we must fight,
And none so deadly as with our own selves,
Yet fight we must unto the end, for no soul thrives
On ease and peace in this fleeting, fallen world."

*   *   *

Adam could not bear to return to the haunted atmosphere of his office that dreary afternoon. He had unconsciously stuffed the sheets he had been working on into his pocket as he had left the room to go in search of Lucy. And then, when having found her and poured out his soul, he had suddenly found he could no longer bear to sit under her gaze; felt like some creeping thing of darkness that must scuttle back under its rock. Where could he go? He would do his editing in the bar. He must continue to work somehow. At least he would not be alone there, and the presence of other human beings may help steady his mind, which seemed to be becoming unhinged.

As he looked over what he had written he found himself envying the companionship of the two men as he sat, pen in hand, and yet mind straying again to that faraway scene. He desired now, above all things, a faithful companion to help guard and guide his heart. And yet he had driven away any upon whom he might before have had a claim. He had broken faith and found himself now justly alone and bereft. And his own company had become a horror to him. He now understood something of what had before seemed bizarre: "*the enemy within*".

The crisp white sheets had become dog-eared and were now stained with the ring of his whisky glass. This was so out of character for him. He hated his work to be tainted by the debris of life, but it no longer seemed possible to keep them separate. He looked ruefully over the creased, soiled sheets spread before him and in disgust shoved them back into his pocket.

Mirror

Should she call Robert? It seemed that Adam was having some sort of breakdown. Was he a danger to himself? Was it correct protocol to call someone in this sort of situation? And yet Adam had sought her out, confided in her. She had not stumbled across him. Lucy sat with the telephone receiver in one hand, with the dialling tone buzzing in her ear finally becoming an insistent drone. She suddenly made up her mind and put it down. What was the point in believing in anything at all if when actually confronted with the reality of one's beliefs, the possibility of the supernatural breaking into the natural, the divine into the human, one simply tried to give it a naturalistic cause and remedy, follow procedures to protect oneself but did nothing to actually help the one in need? *Why was it so hard to believe, living in our brittle, materialistic modern culture?* Why, "believer" though she was, did the idea of divine intervention seem almost indecent to her late twentieth-century Western mind? Whatever it actually meant, something had happened to Adam that had shaken him to the core. To believe in God but then not believe that perhaps He had acted—surely that would be the greatest folly of all.

Feeling nervous but resolved, she picked up the packet of cigarettes and the lighter Adam had left on her desk and set off to find him.

She found him eventually, slumped in a corner of the bar, elbows on the table, with a number of empty glasses in front of him and a still half-full glass of whisky.

"I've brought you these back," she said hesitantly, walking over to him and putting them on the table.

"Thanks," he muttered, keeping his eyes down.

She hesitated a moment and then said tentatively, "Can I join you?"

He waved an arm morosely indicating the chair opposite.

She sat down and after a pause said rather awkwardly, "Are you ok? I, I thought I should just come and check . . . " Her words trailed off.

"I don't know," he said after a pause. Then he raised his eyes and embraced the discomfort. It was better than being alone with only his own terrors for company. He looked intently at her for a few seconds. "I feel as if . . . like someone who's just had the rug pulled out from under them, like everything that seemed substantial is actually as flimsy as a dream and the things I thought were fantasy are perhaps after all the real things, the real reality. I don't know, perhaps I'm just going mad, having a breakdown or some sort of midlife crisis, but somehow, in another way I feel more sane now than I ever have before, as if I can suddenly see. More sane and inexpressibly more miserable!" He smiled bitterly.

"But," he continued thoughtfully, looking at her, "I think you maybe know what I'm talking about. You're the only person I know who does. I used to think you were some strange relic from an obsolete and, quite frankly, ignorant and childish age. But now you seem the only person who is properly alive! Somehow you seem part of this madness, or sanity, or whatever it is.

"It's all an illusion, isn't it? If nothing else, I feel this. This idea that we can exert any control over our own destinies? We are driven on by an invisible hand, even against our own will and seeming rationality, hunted and harried towards an inevitable doom, but I never knew it until now."

He leaned gloomily towards her across the sticky-ringed veneer of the table. She could smell the peaty tang of whisky on his breath.

"However hard I fight, I am wrestling against an irresistible force that will not let me rest, that forces me, almost taunts me, to face my own tawdry, redundant *brokenness*, drives me on, towards trying to understand, strangely, towards you!

"I suppose I've fought all my life, fought so hard, spent all I had, poured my soul into building myself, my ego, making it impenetrable, a self-begotten triumph, I felt lord of my world, which gave back my own image, glorious, successful, untouchable and then, then it all started to crumble, like an avalanche, uncontrollable, and within hours, literally hours, the whole carefully constructed myth of myself was in pieces around me. And then it happened—when I had nothing and no one, when my whole self was like a crazed and broken mirror, then I saw it, that vision of, of *completeness*."

Vision

"In dreams and virtuous visions of the night
Vouchsafed to my kindled mind,
I see some shadow of that which I am striving,
With God's grace, to make manifest;
To bring forth in bodily form the insubstantial wraiths
That now lie naked and nascent within my teeming breast,
To clothe with matter and light the concepts that collect
And hover in my heaving head, my mind on fire with glory.
And yet my hands are at a loss to learn how to loosen
These cerebral visions from their ethereal bondage
And bring to birth in marvellous matter,
Fix in sublime substance, these beautiful,
Swirling shapes that transfix my soul, to capture
One moment of glory in a form of eternal worth,
To work grace and speak truth
Into a broken but beautiful world,
To bring holy healing to the heart and be
A gateway to the gracious path that leads to Him;
To Him who is the author and perfecter,
The beginning and the end, the alpha and the omega;
To Him who though being in very nature God
Did not consider equality with God
Something to be grasped and clasped,
But emptying Himself of all but love,
He took upon Himself a human form.
Being born in likeness of broken man, the Eternal Son
Was even Himself clothed with flesh, the incarnate Word,
And in His great epiphany, brought forth into our Time
A human child to crush the corrupting serpent's head."

Thus spoke good Benedict to his young companion
As they conversed concerning their great and glorious task.

"I will entrust this great enterprise to you, my son,
And entreat you to engage the finest craftsmen to create
A wondrous window for our holy house
Wherein all the weight of glory may be beheld
By those with eyes to see,
Whilst I too must be seeking many things
Of beauty, wisdom and worth with which
To endow our blessed twin sanctuaries.
For when two work together they have
A better reward for their labour, and when two
Travel the weary road, they bear each other up,
And when two lie down to rest upon the way
They shall be warm and safer
From the pestilence that stalks the dusk.
But as we walk, we know we're not alone,
For the Lord himself goes with us wheresoever we tread,
Our ever-present companion through
All the weary ways of this world, who has walked
All paths before and knows our frail frame. He even
Bears us in His arms if we should stumble, faint and fall,
As the tender shepherd with a straying, stupid sheep,
And bless with His speed all those who ever seek
To serve and glorify His name. He is our strength
And within His providence our purposes shall prosper,
For a threefold cord is not easily torn."

*   *   *

As if to taunt his sense of abandonment and solitary state, Adam found himself over the following days writing again and again of the blessings and comforts of companionship. But he had severed the cord, the lifeline that bound him to other people. They had all been sacrificed on the altar of his ego, his broken idol. There was no one left with whom to share his soul-sorrow, no one upon whom he had a legitimate claim. No one who would understand. No one but Lucy. And how ridiculous that was. He had the least claim of all upon her; she upon whom he had vented much of the worst of his bile. She whom he had despised, rejected, humiliated, again and again. And yet, he had no choice. He was driven towards her. Her co-existence in this new and terrifying narrative was the only foothold he had. It was either to cling there, in the teeth of all his pride and her discomfort, or to fall. And the survival instinct is remarkably strong.

"More things in heaven and earth . . . "

"What did you make of what I told you the other day?"

Lucy frowned. "Well," she said dubiously after a long pause, "it wouldn't be considered a very orthodox means of, well, revelation, I suppose, for want of a better word."

She looked at him hard, trying to work out if he was messing about with her or not. "What exactly do you think you saw?"

"I don't *think* I saw, I did see," he said impatiently, lighting another cigarette. "But it was so complex and somehow multi-dimensional it's almost impossible to describe. I'll just have to take you there, then you'll understand."

"But Adam," she said haltingly, almost in a whisper, "I, I looked into it a little bit—that window, umm, well, it says it was destroyed during the Reformation. What's there now are just the old, rediscovered fragments of glass randomly arranged."

He stared at her blankly for a moment and then frowned, the glowing end of the cigarette slowly creeping towards his hand.

"I know what I saw. You must be confusing it with a different place."

She reached for the folder where she had put the photocopies she had taken from the large hardback encyclopaedia in the library. It lay under some loose papers that had been folded hastily as he had entered the room.

"I can show you what I found . . . " she began tentatively.

"No!"

Striding towards her he slammed the folder shut with such force, only just missing her fingers, that it made her jump violently. He clenched his free fist and, forcing his voice to a more measured tone, hastily continued, with a mirthless attempt at a smile.

"I refuse to have my experiences reduced to the content of an Encyclopaedia Britannica entry!"

He walked across to her small office window and looked out across the roof tops to the birds wheeling around the chimneys. Breathing out a slow cloud of smoke, he inwardly wrestled with his confusion. As he stood in limbo, he caught sight of her reflection staring at him intently, slightly fearfully. He turned round abruptly, forcing a laugh.

"'*There are more things in Heaven and Earth, Horatio, than are dreamt of in your philosophy* . . . ' Of course I may just be going mad, but in that case surely I deserve your sympathy. Oh, and by the way, has anybody ever told you how beautiful you look when you're serious?"

Was this deflection or was the whole thing some silly joke?

"I can see some things never change!" she retorted with slight irritation. She didn't know whether to feel amused, worried or angry. "I think I should be getting on with my work, don't you?"

"Come on," he was momentarily back to his old self again, "let's have a trip over there and I'll show you, and tell you what, I'll treat you to dinner afterwards! What do you say?"

His charm was entirely wasted on Lucy. She looked at him sceptically.

"Are you kidding? Not a chance man! I'm not being dragged through miles of boggy fields to see something that isn't there. Nice try!"

He grinned and stubbed out the cigarette in an obliging mug. At least she'd stopped behaving like a frightened mouse and her old spirit had been partially restored. As he opened the door, he turned towards the perplexed, half irritated, half amused girl behind the desk with mock seriousness, attempting to mask his own inner perturbation.

"I'll get you there one day, one way or another, even if I have to drag you the whole way! Then you can be the judge of whether I'm telling the absolute truth or am in fact completely mad."

Lucy had to resist a sudden, almost overpowering urge to throw the pen in her hand at his irritating, grinning face as he left the room. How maddening he was! She could not tell when he was being serious and when he was just being annoying. Probably it was a mixture of both. She didn't even know if this strange new Adam was preferable to the old hostile, contemptuous one. At least she knew where she was with that version. Anyway, she didn't intend to lose her job over him either way.

*   *   *

In reality, Adam found he could concentrate on nothing beyond his own terrors except his translation. His lecturing had become atrocious and was beginning to attract comment and complaint. This was out of character, as he had previously been a popular lecturer. He loved a captive audience and was good at playing to a crowd. In fact, he fed off the sensation of a room of young, eager people hanging on his words. He was a good and entertaining speaker and knew his subject well. Where he had failed to prepare properly, he was always able to wing it and if necessary, fall back on charisma and charm. These abilities had all, however, like everything else, deserted him. He now found himself standing there at the front of that sea of inquiring faces, gradually shifting from anticipation, to confusion, to concern, to boredom, to disgust as he stumbled through his previously prepared notes. It would have been utterly mortifying if he had not been so preoccupied with his own troubled thoughts. Even so he felt it enough. At the end of each of these unhappy occasions he would slink off as quickly as possible, trying to shut his ears to the murmurs of discontent around him. Not surprisingly his audiences dwindled as the days went by, until only the most devout braved his incoherent ramblings, most preferring an extra hour in bed and no doubt finding it more profitable.

His one main preoccupation had become getting back to the old church by the sea, to stand once again before the window, to try to recreate the feelings that had been awakened there, to bathe again in that overwhelming vision of peace and coherence. He knew what he had felt, what he had seen, didn't he? It was a memory burnt into all his senses. He could not have imagined it all, could he? Surely his imagination did not contain the raw materials for such a creation without some outside agency? How could such light and radiance have been drawn out of his own darkness? No, he was sure he must have been responding to someone else's creation, seeing their vision bodied forth in glass and stone, hearing their voice. But for all his obsessive preoccupation, he dared not go alone. He did not know exactly why, other than that it mattered too much. He had both a great longing and a great fear of revisiting this momentous place. Lucy's unwanted research had disturbed him further and had left him with an agony of doubt.

He had the absurd feeling of someone preparing for a great pilgrimage, which would prove to be the defining journey of a lifetime. *It's only a few miles up the A19*, he kept telling himself in an attempt to speak some reason into his mind. *I could be there again in half an hour!*

Half an hour or half a lifetime? Distance is not only calculated in miles. He was not ready to face alone whatever he found when he reached his destination. He needed a companion, a confessor, another human being, Lucy, in fact, to steady him, to reassure him he was not mad, and yet he feared when it came to it, thus it would prove to be. He also wanted to justify himself, prove himself to her, that he was not just messing around, playing silly games. But above all he just needed her. This journey was too great to travel alone and unprovided. As Biscop took his young companion as a help on their great journey, and to Alwin acted as a guide, so Adam, as he immersed himself in translating their preparations, knew he too needed a guide. Did not even Dante have Virgil as a guide when compelled to walk the circles of hell? Even if he deserved such a dark path, would he really be expected to walk alone? He would have loved to have shared in Alwin's eager and youthful anticipation of pilgrimage in springtime instead of feeling it as a burden, a heavy commission or quest laid upon him by an unknown hand in the dark days of winter. Nonetheless he found some relief in entering into that other journey as a sort of proxy for his own that he knew, sooner or later, he must make. There was nowhere and no one else he knew of to look to for instruction, so this ancient tale must provide his pattern until such time as he could persuade his own guide to light his way and face alongside him whatever perils lay in store.

My colour ever changes as I flee,
And leave behind me heaven and earth; no home
Have I upon the earth, nor in the skies.
No mortal fears an exile hard as mine,
Yet I with soaking drops make green the world.

Aldhelm

Setting out

And so, before beginning on their quest,
Needful provisions are provided and prepared:
Clothing, food for man and beast, and gold
With which to gain the treasures that they sought
Of both holy artefacts and skills of gifted men,
To glorify their great and honourable houses
And point to that greater glory of the gracious realm,
Wherein our Lord sits enthroned.

Alwin, heart abrim with excitement and not a little awe,
Readies himself for the road ahead, and amidst
The astounding beauties of a spring morning they set out
With the song of youth sounding in his ears;
The crisp grass still sparkling with early frost
And the tiny buds of the trees beginning to burst.
A watery sun leaks a pale light from low in a luminous sky
And birds are soaring, as is Alwin's spirit in his breast,
And the spring in his step betrays a soul spreading its wings,
A strong boyish body on the brink of manhood,
Flexing muscles and mind.
Biscop smiles to himself as he regards
His young companion teetering on the cusp of life,
Whereas he draws towards its close; an old man
Spent in the pursuit of wisdom, worship and beauty
And now near his final rest.
He prays for strength and physical power
To complete his purpose and finish his course.

First a great tract of their own territory must be traversed,
From their native Northumbria in the far-flung north
Down the eastern edge. Leaving familiar shores and friends

They wend their winding way,
Seeking shelter where they may,
And often exposed to the extremity of the elements,
The bitterness of frost and snow and hail,
That cruellest and coldest of corn;
To the hills which harbour, it is whispered,
Robbers and wild and wicked beasts;
The dangers of the dragons which rove
The mist-shrouded heaths when not foretelling
In fiery flight, the portents of horrors to come.
Then the haunts of the fenland demons must be braved,
As hermits tell, where the devils multiply
Amid the poisonous vapours, tormenting Christian souls
And the grey wolf roams in the gloaming,
And the black raven swoops on the fallen dead.

Theirs for a time the fate of the forlorn cloud,
Fellow of neither heaven nor earth,
But chased back and forth restlessly between the two,
Colour changing as it flees. No mortal though
Fears a fate as fell as the hapless cloud,
For even these pilgrims on the path
Can look ahead to temporary respite and homely hearth
And, if Heaven wills, a journey's end.
But as the cloud with soaking drops the world makes green,
So the great hope in these gracious hearts:
That their endeavours will by and by
Bring bounteous blessing to men and glory to God.

The dream

For the next few days Adam persisted in his attempts to persuade Lucy to go with him back to the window. He was a man used to getting his own way and he was not going to let it rest. It was becoming wearing and she felt increasingly out of her depth. She was trying to quickly eat her lunch after minuting a meeting that had endlessly overrun, tired and hungry, when he was there again. She pre-empted the question.

"I will come with you one day, maybe, Adam, but not yet. I'm not ready and this is all too strange, too sudden, too intense, and to be honest I just don't know what to make of it . . . of you. I know that sounds awful, but there it is, that's the truth."

"What do you want me to do then?" he snapped impatiently. "You won't believe me. You won't let me prove it to you. You don't even trust my intentions. Bloody hell, you're impossible!"

This was becoming intolerable.

"Excuse me! I never asked for any of this, I never invited you to dump your life's problems and revelations on me," she retorted angrily. "I just want you to leave me alone and leave me out of it. For all I know you're just playing one of your games with me, trying to trap me, like before, and then the next thing I know I'll be hauled over the coals, or worse . . . "

"Is that really what you think of me?" He was angry now too.

He slammed his hand down on the desk.

She flinched.

"Well, what do you expect?" Her voice was shaking with indignation. "With your track record? Your bullying, your aggression? You frighten me!"

If her job was on the line, so be it. There was only so much of this she was prepared to put up with. She inhaled slowly, trying to regain some calm, eyeing him warily. How would he respond?

He visibly deflated. "You're completely right," he muttered. "I have no right."

Humility did not come easily to him. This was so hard. Did he have to unlearn a whole lifetime of being? Painfully unpick all his patterns, discard all those familiar internal maps, tutor himself to master himself? It felt impossible. He was a driven man, part of the key to his success. *Success? On whose criteria?* He felt like a force of nature, just pushing on relentlessly over anything and anyone to achieve his end, meet his needs, satisfy his desire. He had been proud of his force of character, but now he despised himself with all the loathing of regret and self-awakening, seeing only destruction in his wake. He was now afraid of the untamed, undisciplined force inside himself. He had given it full sway and now it drove him. He had lost control, only realizing what was really at the helm when it seemed too late to claw it back.

He threw up his hands in a gesture of despair.

"I'll not take any more of your time!" he snapped ungraciously and slammed the door behind him.

Lucy sank down in her chair and felt the tears starting to run down her cheeks. *What was going on? What did he want from her? What did God want from her?* She could not help it; despite everything she was beginning to care for him in some strange and confusing way. But what a man! He could not be more different from her ideals and dreams of what a man should be. And he was so totally messed up, so untrustworthy and such a bully, capable of such brutality and cruelty. Could even God really change such a man?

Her head told her to keep well clear. But her heart moved towards him in compassion and somehow, deep within her being, her soul stirred with recognition, a still small voice urging her on.

She did not know how long she sat there, gazing blankly out of the window. It was dark by the time she stirred herself and she felt stiff and cold and drained. She simply could not do any more work now. Anyway, she had those documents and folders Adam had told her to drop back to Palace Green Library.

She got up, put on her coat, turned off the light and locked the door. She trudged down the corridor and the stairs and out into the twilight, feeling a slight twinge of resentment that she was always the one lugging heavy bags of books and folders around. Crossing Kingsgate Bridge, she headed up the cobbled Bailey, gratefully unburdening herself at the library desk and then headed through the narrow gap towards the river path. It had begun to drizzle and was very cold. She pulled up her hood.

She felt a jolt in the pit of her stomach. There he was again, sitting on a bench looking at the water flowing slowly past, completely oblivious to her presence and the rain falling on his bare head. His thick dark wet hair curled a little around his temples, ears and at the nape of his neck. It needed cutting, and with an inexplicable rush of tenderness she noticed it was beginning to grey. She was in a horrible dilemma. Should she try to slip past without him noticing or should she speak to him?

He was lit by the beam from a lamppost, shimmering through the gently falling rain like a silver mist. This made the shadows outside of its circle denser. She quietly walked to the far side of the path and managed to slip by unnoticed in the dark. Almost immediately her heart smote her. She believed he was suffering, but she had walked by, tried to not get involved. Images from the "Good Samaritan" sprang up in her mind. Was she like the Pharisee? It was too late now in any case. She waited numbly at the freezing bus stop for what felt like for ever, and then finally, after a cramped but lonely journey, hurried home. Fumbling with her keys in the dingy stairwell, she was finally able to shut the door on the world.

It was a cheerless flat, one of a number over a small row of shops, not much more than a bedsit really, although she had done her best with it despite her endless struggle with mess and encroaching chaos. Moving a pile of clothes onto a chair she plonked herself wearily down on the bed and put her head in her hands. What a day. It was cold and dark. Could she afford to put the heating on? She got up reluctantly and moved towards the thermostat. Normally she would have just put on an extra jumper and pair of socks, but tonight she gave in and flicked the switch for an hour's warmth, glancing anxiously at the balance on the coin-operated meter.

She started to slowly get her tea together—boiling the kettle to pour on the dried pasta in the pan and heating a tin of tomatoes in a small bowl in the microwave. She smiled wanly. At least if she accepted one of Adam's offers of dinner, she'd get a fancy meal. She knew he certainly wasn't short of money, whatever else his deficiencies. She immediately felt guilty for such a mercenary thought. Mechanically grating some cheese on top of her pasta she sat down at her small table to eat her tea. Normally she would have had a shower, maybe watched the telly for a bit, or even worked on some of her own secret writing after eating if she didn't have anything else on, but tonight she felt so wrung out she flopped down on the bed and laid her aching head on the pillow. She'd just have five minutes, then she'd get ready for bed.

The next thing she knew the pale dawn light was peeping through the undrawn curtains. It was still early. She was cold, despite her clothes, from having lain on top of the covers. She rolled over and looked at the clock. No point in putting pyjamas on now. She should be getting up soon anyway, but just a few more minutes . . . She pulled the covers over herself and sank back into a light but troubled sleep.

She was running down a long dark tunnel where the walls seemed to be made of immense banked up mountains of water, with their menacing foamy tips looking as though they were at any moment going to crash down upon her. She was running with all her strength towards a bright light at the far end. It seemed to get further away the more she strained towards it. As she ran, she became aware of someone running behind her, calling her name. It was Adam, he was calling for her to wait for him, to help him, or was he laughing, trying to pull her back into the watery darkness? She half turned and saw him reaching out towards her, but she just kept on running as fast as she could. She could see the door now, or was it a window, from which the light was emitting. She was through and she slammed it shut behind her. Adam's cries, or was it laughter, gradually receded, as if he were being pulled back into the darkness as the great waters engulfed him . . .

She woke with a start in a cold sweat. She was shaking and her heart was racing. For a moment she didn't know where she was, then gradually the familiar surroundings took shape. She lay completely still for a while staring at the patch of light on the ceiling while she tried to reorientate her thoughts. What a horrible dream. She tried to pray, but she couldn't get the image of Adam, reaching out towards her from the dark waves, out of her mind. This was terrible. She heaved herself out of bed and put the kettle on. She was still shaking. She plunged into the shower and let the warm water pour all over her head and body. The cold stiffness that had taken possession of her gradually ebbed away. She stood there, with her eyes tight closed and prayed simply, "*Help me! Protect me! Give me wisdom, give me grace. Show me the way . . .*" She started to feel just a little bit better. She turned off the shower, wrapped herself in her old towelling dressing gown and made herself a cup of strong tea. The horrible vividness of the dream was beginning to fade, but its atmosphere stayed with her all that day and even afterwards, haunting the edges of her mind.

Compelled by fate that likewise rules the sea,
I roll out month-long periods of time
In sure-returning cycles. As the light
Of glorious beauty slowly leaves my face,
So does the ocean, flowing from the shore,
Lose its increase of water in the deep.

Aldhelm

The wide expanse of the sea

They come at last to great Canterbury,
Then Barham, then the channel coast
And at Dover board the ship that will bear them
Across the sundering sea: a great open boat,
Clinker-built, blunt stern and many benches
That can be driven by man's muscle work at the oar
Or, when the winds are fair, a square loose-footed sail
Will harness the speed of the skies,
Steered by a single starboard oar, close to the stern.
Stern and stem posts sweep upwards, soaring towards the sun,
Sculpted with wondrous skilled carvings of marvellous beasts,
The like of which Alwin has never before beheld;
Maybe appearing as Job's Leviathan,
That fell and fearsome lizard that frolicked in the waters
At the dawn of time, sire of serpents and dragons,
Enough to strike terror into the heart of any who see
Its terrible head come riding in upon the rising tide,
But wonderful none-the-less as it takes flight,
Skimming seas and mounting waves, snowy topped.
This brave vessel is guided by sun and stars
And the ebb and flow of tides, enticed by the moon,
As she draws the wild waters back and forth at her whim,
Waxing and waning, sometimes smiling
On the shimmering face of the deep and sometimes
Hiding her haughty beauty behind the fleeing clouds
As they hurry across the heavens;
This fragile craft her plaything, either rocked and cradled
In temperate arms or tempest tossed,
As her capricious mood and phase ordains;
This wandering home, this lodging for all times and places,
The glad companion of the calling curlew and gannet,

Mewing gull and icy-feathered tern,
Eerily answered even by the white-tailed eagle,
Dewy-winged, screeching overhead.

Alwin has heard wondrous, horrifying tales
Of the creatures of the deep, one inspiring
His imagination above the rest, intriguing and appalling
In equal part: that of the island whale Jasconius,
Upon whose broad back, bare of sand, blessed Brendan
Celebrated Easter mass with his companions
And after lit a fire to cook their frugal meal,
But warned by the unexpected heaving of their refuge,
They regained their boat rapidly and in relief,
Witnessing in awe their floating island swim away to sea,
Fire still flaming on its rugged back,
And thanked in prayer and song the God of heaven
That they did not share the fate of those hapless sailors
Deceived by the dreadful Fastitocalon,
Of whom Alwin has heard whispered fables;
That deceitful harbour, of land that is no true land,
That wicked whale to whose welcoming, beguiling flanks
Grateful sailors fasten their high-prowed ships,
Set up their camp, light fires and rejoice in kindly weather
Until the false friend, the rock which is no real rock,
Treacherous terrain, plunges them down suddenly
To their doom; to the watery embrace of death
On the silty-soft bed of the sea,
Drowning them in the dreadful deep,
Just as man finds himself, Biscop reminds Alwin,
So easily ensnared by the deceitful devices of the devil.

For the brothers regard their temporary home
With awed eyes accustomed to allegory:
This laden boat and bearer of burdens as it tosses and turns,

Plunging on the foam-tipped waves, raising
Perilous plumes of spray, pressed less from storms above
Than by the hideous horrors that hide beneath,
The teeming terrors that haunt the murky dungeons
And watery chambers of the deep;
And contemplate how they themselves are like
Such fragile barks borne before the storms of life,
Tempest-tossed as Saint Paul and his companions
Driven terribly back and forth across the Adriatic Sea,
And how their monastery home, bearing his name,
And now left far behind, is like a haven of hope,
A safe harbour from the shipwreck and catastrophe
Of this present life, where man is ceaselessly tossed
By waves of care, beguiled by the snares of Satan,
Lurking like a legion of leviathans
Beneath the glassy skin, bent on luring him down;
Thus, the godly man must be ever seeking
Safe refuge for his storm-beleaguered soul,
Like a ship dragging its anchor before the rising storm
And wild and perilous weather of this world,
Straining with all his fibres towards the promised port,
Chasing the friendly star that will surely guide
To safe haven and to home.

*   *   *

Strangely cathartic, Adam was almost enjoying translating the fragment of the tale that dealt with the channel crossing. It was an exhilarating task, not just a compulsion today.

To get on the Eurostar and nip across to France for a day's shopping was not uncommon these days, particularly for those living in the south where he had grown up. How incomprehensibly different embarking on that crossing would have been all those centuries ago.

Although the original text had no section or chapter titles, he had taken the liberty of adding his own wherever there was a natural pause or a change of scene or theme. He felt it made it more accessible for the modern reader and helped break up the long narrative into more manageable chunks. He particularly liked his title for this section: *The wide expanse of the sea.* It had the feeling of freedom about it, of adventure and of spreading wings and soaring away, escaping from the terrors and troubles of home with one's face set towards the shining horizon. He loved the description of the birds, the sounds of their calling echoing in his mind, the carved head of the boat, the big square sail, the splash of the waves, the prow skimming the frothy sea, the capricious moon, the creeping tides.

He had always loved riddles, and the ancient Northumbrian ones that his poet had made use of, mainly attributed to Aldhelm, were particularly beautiful. He was also fascinated by the strange Anglo-Saxon tales of saints and fishermen mistaking whales for firm land and even setting up camp on them. The vivid picture of Jasconius swimming off with a campfire on his rugged back and the wicked Fasticalon suddenly plunging the sailors to the murky depths, having lured them into a treacherous false haven, thrilled his mind. He loved the great and mythical beasts of legend. Maybe they had indeed existed. The ancients wrote of such things with such clarity and assurance. It was a feast for the imagination, a feast for the modern Western mind, starved and stretched thin by the relentless tide of facts and figures and data and materialism. So practical, so unimaginative, so dreary. Perhaps we are no longer able to see the mythical and marvellous surrounding us, he thought, the allegories and the pictures of the past, because we have shut our eyes to marvels, our ears to the heavenly harmonies and our hearts to awe and wonder. Just as the typed page is such a poor descendant of the illuminated manuscript, we have lost the colour from that old world of wonder, and limp on in black and white and shades of grey, for all our technological advances, numbing our senses to beauty and the deeper things of life. Adam mused on these things as he looked at the beautiful facsimile he was working on. Even in comparison to his own, well-formed handwriting on the crisp white paper, this ancestor was in every way superior, except for accessibility.

But as he went on, he became increasingly drawn into the terrors also involved in such an endeavour. It was no small thing for men of that era to take to the sea. No lifeboats and helicopters if things went wrong. Just prayer. How easy to romanticize the past, he thought again. Imagine what it would really be like, out on the open sea, in an open boat, driven before a tempest. It felt analogous to his own emotional state. And imagine if, alongside all that peril of weather and water, there was also that fear of unknown creatures of the deep lurking beneath. He could almost feel the gripping fear. He found himself entering into that nightmare state. It was like that very vivid terror that accompanies the fearful dreams of childhood: the monster hiding, lurking, prowling, ready to spring from the darkness at any moment and drag you down.

Then there was that sense of exile, of separation from all that was homely and comfortable. He felt torn between the two extremes of emotion that haunt the traveller and pilgrim on strange seas and foreign soil. There is the excitement, the exhilaration, the freedom and yet alongside, like the other side of the coin, the fear of the unknown, the sense of isolation from his peers and homeland, that setting off into the unknown alone, or if he is lucky, with maybe one other soul as a companion. A sense of belonging nowhere. For even if he should return to what was before called home, he would bring those new experiences, inextricably bound up with the new self, and those who had been left behind would not understand. In a way he thought, like soldiers returning from the unspeakable horrors of war to find home no longer a familiar place of peace and rest because they themselves were there, with their haunted memories.

That was also analogous to his own feelings, although of course soldiers are not to blame for having fought in war. He had made his own war, and it brought the opposite of honour; the victims were those closest to him. He no longer had a home, no longer deserved one. Not only because he had broken it but because he knew now that the problem was with himself. It was not "out there". *How can one escape oneself?* And the appalling isolation of it, of setting off from all that had previously been familiar, carrying the burden of his own consciousness, his own shame. Could he do it alone?

Rejection

"Come in! Bloody hell, Adam, since when have you ever knocked?"

Adam walked into the large, pleasant office of his colleague and friend Robert Du Prey. They had a long history together, and although Robert was technically his boss, they hardly marked that distinction, enjoying each other's company both professionally and privately, discussing ideas together just as readily as they had shared a pint and sometimes a girl. You could say their relationship had been one of a meeting of minds, pretty capable minds too.

"How are you, Adam?" Robert looked at him rather hard as he waved towards an easy chair set into the bay of a fine leaded window.

"I'm, well, things have been umm . . . difficult." Adam shifted his gaze uncomfortably.

Robert put a reassuring hand on his arm.

"I know, it's been bloody awful for you, with Cynthia and everything. I've been worried about you, that's partly why I've asked you to come over today. You haven't seemed yourself lately. I wanted you to know I'm here for you, if you need any support, you know."

"Thanks." Adam managed a weak smile.

"You also seem to have developed a taste for, how can I put it, strange company!"

Robert raised an eyebrow inquiringly, sardonically, as he spoke, scrutinizing Adam's face. And when he didn't reply: "Come on, you know who I mean! You've taken to hobnobbing with that wretched little creature from admin, the high and mighty one who thinks she might soil her halo if she were to come within a metre of us."

He laughed sourly. "If I didn't know you better, old man, I'd be seriously worried you were about to become her next victim, you know, target for evangelism!"

Adam went very red. "Robert," he began, "I know how I've been, how I've behaved, in the past, that night at the Christmas do . . . shit." He burrowed his head in his hands. "I feel sick when I think of how we, I, behaved to her that night."

"What the *hell* is wrong with you, Adam?" Robert's hitherto sympathetic, jovial voice took on a shade of anger and disbelief. "You aren't seriously trying to tell me that you've fallen for that pathetic, mousey girl? Come on, man, you're on the rebound, it does strange things to people, hell, I should know! You should have seen some of the people I woke up next to after Sally left!" He laughed thinly but was eyeing Adam now with suspicion and veiled dread.

"What you need is a night out, away from all of this shit. Let's get a few drinks inside us tonight and see if I don't find you a more suitable bedfellow to work your angst out on! Anyway," he laughed, "I don't like your chances of getting Saint Lucy into bed any time soon! Or is it the challenge, is that what it is? Can't see you getting much satisfaction either way," he taunted, "she's as frigid as a block of ice!"

Adam stood up abruptly. "I can't have you talk about her in that way, it's, it's not right. I can't explain it, Robert; you're right, I'm not myself, at least not the self I used to be, something happened to me." He broke off and looked into the hostile eyes of his friend. "Oh, I can't explain, not now. I don't expect you to understand, I don't even understand, but I am only just beginning to try to retrieve myself from under the rubble of, of my collapsed world."

"Like I said, it's not surprising, after what you've been through, but you just need to move on. Onwards and upwards, my friend!"

Again, the sympathetic voice, the friendly slap on the shoulder. "Meet me at six in the bar and we'll take it from there. Paint the town red, like the good old days?"

"I can't, Robert," Adam said hesitantly, "I must leave all that behind. I wish I could, if only I could, but I can't. I am more than happy to go for a pint with you. I'd love to. Your friendship means a lot to me, always has, but the rest . . . I can't."

"What do you mean, you *can't*? I knew it, she *has* got to you, hasn't she? Same thing again, strike while they're already down. Wait 'til I get my hands on the little bitch. She's gone too far this time!"

There was, under the anger, pain in his voice, loss even, for sins, betrayals of the spirit are always harder to forgive than mere sins of the flesh. Adam screwed up his eyes and put his hand to his head. "It's not what you're thinking, Robert. I sought her out. She's been nothing but professional. She's listened to me. Nothing more."

"Well, if you'd rather bare your soul to Saint Lucy than your oldest friend, then good luck to you, Adam, that's all I can say!" he said with deliberate contempt. "But, when you've come to your senses, let me know eh, and we'll go out for that drink. It's a shame really, you had the potential to go far, that professorship is coming up next term, I had hoped . . . oh well," he waved his hand evasively, "obviously mental rigour and the broadness of mind not to shy away from the cutting edge of things, ability to push the boundaries of the field are prerequisites. It wouldn't do to have someone with the squeamish sensibilities of an old maid now, would it? And I have been receiving some rather alarming reports of you, complaints even. I'm worried you're losing your touch, old man!"

"Robert, I am more than happy to have a pint with you, you know I am. We could have a late lunch together now if you like. I'd like to hear how things are with you."

"Would've loved to, old boy, maybe another time," he said coldly, "but must be pushing on now, rather busy you know. Shut the door on your way out, there's a good chap."

He was already looking down at the papers on his desk with a studied air of contemptuous indifference as Adam walked miserably from the room.

Foreign soil

They step out upon the shingle of a strange land,
And thanking the God of heaven for safe travel thus far
With upturned eyes, they bend their knees
Upon that foreign shore and feel the weight
Of burden and blessing well known
To strangers and pilgrims, aspects of emotion
Even akin to that of exiles, aliens and outcasts . . .

(Adam paused as he penned these words. He could readily identify with some of the emotions of which he wrote. His once familiar turf now felt like foreign soil and he an exile upon it, an outcast, and yet without the purpose and hope of those of whom he wrote. All burden and no blessing. He felt stranded in a strange no-man's land, unable to turn back, unsure of how to proceed, and yet none-the-less, driven forward towards an unknown shore. He sighed and, after a wistful glance out at the heavy, unrelenting sky, continued. Better to fill his mind with these other words than allow his own thought to overtake and consume him.)

. . . The privilege, peril and pain of their pursuit
Of perfect wisdom, beauty and truth
As servants of a higher heavenly kingdom. And there
In the gateway of Gaul, on the shoreline of Quentovic,
They leave the soft print of their knees upon the sand;
Like as to Saint Paul with the people of Tyre,
Who followed him and his friends outside the city wall,
Kneeling on the beach in trembling prayer.

Wary of what lay ahead and yet with faces set,
They wend their way towards the valley of the Rhone,
Through Paris, Sens and Autun; for to attempt
The awesome and snowy mountains of the Alps

By way of the fearsome Great St Bernard's Pass
Would be to invite danger of a pernicious sort
And tempt the good grace of God.

These great cities fill with awe
The unaccustomed eyes of Alwin as he gazes
Upon their glories and the seething masses of mankind.
A world apart it seems from his humble home,
Native Northumbria, that precious, purging
Wilderness of land and sea and sky;
Intoxicating and fearful in equal measure,
These sweeping beauties and the snares
Of man's achievements in ink and stone,
The passion and the peril of the Western mind
Paraded before his uninitiated eyes.
The criss-crossing of the many streets
As the countless paths a man may walk;
The hopeless tangle of human lives, entwined,
Sharing their learning, their laughter and their love,
Their yearning, their madness, their poison and their pain;
An interdependent mass of souls wound round and round
Like veins and arteries running to extremities,
And back to the beating heart. To tear
One from that teeming throng would cause
A fatal rupture in the whole, a body with a deadly wound.
So how then to live apart?
How simple to live and die within monastic walls,
Never tainted or enmeshed in this dear and dying world.
He has been spared this complex pain,
This bleeding beauty until now,
When all that familiar black and white
Has mingled into multitudinous shades of grey,
Or rather, many subtle shades of light and dark,
Beguiling heart and eyes.

As he regards these mysteries and these marvels,
Alwin muses upon the nature of man's life
In this mixed and mortal world; created
In the image of the divine and yet fatally flawed by sin,
Reflecting the Father of lights and yet children of the dust:
Sons of Adam, sons of God.
How do we balance these disparate states?
How hold them together in our minds?
Despairing of his own thoughts, he desires
Of his companion wise counsel to soothe his striving spirit.

Biscop smiles and nods. He too knows the struggle
Of an unquiet heart, straining to know and understand,
Craving to rest content as a weaned child
Upon the breast of God.

"There is much, my son, that we can know
From Holy Scripture and seek in the traditions
Of our faithful fathers who have gone before,
But also, much that we cannot in our fallen state fully grasp,
Or grasping, grapple with to our full content.
We have in us the breath of life, and all, from first to last,
The meanest beggar to the greatest king,
Mirror something of the majesty of the Maker,
Fashioned to bring Him glory, Father, Son and Spirit;
Living vessels for Him to fill, to overspill
With the outflowing of His vast and generous triune love
And yet polluted as it touches our totally depraved beings,
Tainted in every part and yet ennobled in every aspect also;
The tarnished beauty of the sons of dust,
Delight of our divine Master and yet, as rebels,
Objects of His righteous wrath, but reconciled,
We must remember, by His redeeming, reversing love,
Rescued by the bleeding hand that reaches down

To snatch us from our ruin and despair;
To bind with gold our broken bowl
That can hold neither wine nor water
For our dying soul; nor bread for life,
His body He breaks and offers free to starving mouths
And precious blood to parched and panting lips,
Partaking in our misery and pain,
Carrying our confusion and bewildering burdens,
He has walked the way before us,
Bearing our haunted human heart."

Kintsukuroi

Everything was unravelling: family, friends, his career, his mind. Everything was fractured and splintering.

Adam wandered unhappily along the corridor from Robert's study and out of the door into the cold afternoon. He walked and walked with no clear idea where he was heading. The lines of poetry he had been working on that morning were weaving in and out of his own thoughts. They brought both a strange comfort and yet further confusion. The sense of pain and confusion experienced by Alwin, or by his Middle English poet through Alwin, in this new environment, the complex mix of emotions and loss of the solid familiar, spoke straight to his own heart. Strangely, though separated by hundreds of years from them both, they all stood in the same tradition and understood instinctively that "*passion and peril of the Western mind*". What benefits, what blessings, and what squandering and abuse. What beauty, what splendour, what heartbreak. So many great monuments to human achievements and failures. So many crumbling Babels.

This confusion he could understand and empathize with. But he had no mentor to calm his own striving soul. He did not understand this double nature of man. Sons of God? He, Adam, a son of God? How could that ever be true of him, so soiled and broken? And *the* Son of God broken. How did that help? He did not understand. Yet how he longed to have that empathy of another with his plight, a companion not only to walk with him but to carry and help bear his own fractured heart.

To walk alongside the long-dead was not enough. He also needed the living. He felt isolated and alone; no longer belonging in his old world and yet without a foothold in the undiscovered country towards which he was being relentlessly hounded. A citizen of nowhere.

There were large groups of students walking around, laughing and enjoying the festive atmosphere. Lots of couples holding hands. He seemed to be the only person walking alone.

It was almost the end of term.

Christmas.

The thought made him shudder. And it would be even worse than usual this year. He had never enjoyed it, at least not since he was a young child, and perhaps just a little when his own children were very small, surprisingly but vicariously. Indeed, it is almost impossible not to, when their little faces light up with all the magic and beauty that the season seems to work in the very young. Of course, it doesn't last very long and after one or maybe two innocent years, they too are infected by the darkness and become the typical grasping little brats that we create in our own image, as we desperately try to recreate the beauty with our broken and ineffectual tools. But we do not have the magic in us and so simply revert to our usual fall-back, throwing more and more *stuff* at it, like a drug addict or alcoholic needing more and more of the poison to just get by.

It was on such gloomy thoughts, along with his recent interview with Robert, shot through with the confusing words from the poem, that he mused as he trudged along morosely. A sudden wave of self-awareness made him grimace despite himself—what a rank, mawkish sentimentalist he was at heart, full of self-pity, even when being determinedly cynical!

The air was bitingly cold, and it was already getting dark. *Bloody northern winters!* He angrily thrust his hands further into his pockets. A southerner born and bred, he had something of a love–hate relationship with his adopted home and could never get used to it beginning to get dark at half three. It was hardly worth bothering to return to his office but too early to go home.

Home. The four walls that kept the weather out.

He did not relish the thought of letting himself into the cold dark flat. Not yet. He would put it off to the last moment.

The traffic had built up and was steaming in the road like an endlessly coiling serpent. The lights were all on in the main library, hard and cold and clinical. On a whim he suddenly turned into the side road that led up to the Oriental Museum. He hadn't been in there for years, but he would go today. As a university employee he was entitled to go in for free. The lights shone beckoningly. It wouldn't close for at least an hour. It would be warm inside, there would be a coffee machine and even better there would be no hint of Christmas. The exotic artefacts might help create a momentary illusion of sun and mystery, so different from the one he now struggled with. For a few blessed moments he would turn his troubled Western eyes Eastward.

He went in and showed his pass at the desk. The lady at the desk glanced up distractedly from her work—or maybe it was a novel.

"We're closing at 5 mind, pet," was the only response he got.

"Right-ho."

It never ceased to amaze him how he, by his own reckoning, an attractive, intelligent, sophisticated man in his prime, could be routinely addressed as "pet", "flower", even "petal" in this place! And sometimes by women younger than himself. He moved away resignedly.

The coffee machine had a grubby "out of order" notice stuck on it lopsidedly. He sighed and walked through the small gift shop and cafe and began drifting aimlessly around the first floor, studiously ignoring an exhibition on "The Magi from the East", which irritated him inordinately. *Bloody hell, was nowhere free from the infection?*

He went down the stairs so as to avoid it altogether. The art here was delicate and detailed and alien. He found, as hard as he tried, it was not easy to connect with the passions and preoccupations of those distant artists. He felt so removed from them by space as well as time. Did they feel as he felt? Were they ever torn and battered by external and internal forces too great to control? It seemed unlikely judging by their disciplined and precise craftsmanship. And yet maybe this was the way to exert order over chaos. No great demonstrations of despair or desire but a conquering of them in the learning of quiet and diligent patience. A wisdom acquired through calmness and focus and exquisite mastery. Perfect simplicity? Was this the right way? The suppression of the passions, the renunciation of mind and flesh?

That idea did not bridge the gap but made him feel even more alienated. How could he ever even begin to master himself? He had given himself too much rope in the past. And now must he hang? He felt helpless and impotent.

He wanted to go and find Lucy but was also painfully aware of the nuisance he must be becoming to her. It was only a few days before that he'd pushed her too hard and as a result pushed her away. It had been awkward and tense between them ever since. She clearly did not want him hanging around all the time. And yet when he was with her, when his work legitimately brought him within her orbit, his yearning for something he could not articulate overwhelmed and tormented him. And when he wasn't, he longed for her inordinately and felt compelled to seek her out, inventing excuses just to see her, even in passing or out of the corner of his eye, all the time pursuing and being pursued by he knew not what. Was he mad? Maybe Robert was right, maybe he was simply a dysfunctional, screwed up middle-aged loser on the rebound. But then why was he so afraid? He felt like an obsessional stalker but at the same time stalked himself by some nameless dread.

But should he summon all his strength and determination to curb himself, at least attempt to rein in these devastating forces that were wreaking such havoc in his life; master himself like these oriental artists? He knew at once he could not. It was too late. Why do people always seem to believe that passion is the habitation of the young? In his own experience it had only grown with his years and become harder round the edges.

Suddenly his eye was caught by something glinting under the display lights. He moved closer to look. Before him was a ceramic vase in a deep blue, curiously lined with gold. The shining seam spread over the surface like the vein on a rock face or the spreading branches of a delicate tree against an azure sky. It seemed to stir a very early memory. As he gazed at it, he realized this was no simple design or pattern, but actually where the vase had been broken and mended, the mend becoming more conspicuous and precious than the original piece of work. This fascinated him. He read the card underneath:

Kintsukuroi or *Kintsugi*—

Literally "gold mend" or "gold joinery"—the Japanese art of mending broken pottery using lacquer resin laced with gold or silver. As well as practically providing a repair, *kintsukuroi* has a deeper philosophical significance. The mended flaws become part of the object's design, and some people believe the pottery to be even more beautiful having gone through the process of being broken and repaired. Through *kintsukuroi*, the cracks and seams are merely a symbol of an event that happened in the life of the object, rather than the cause of its destruction.

And then a quotation:

> Not only is there no attempt to hide the damage, but the repair is literally illuminated ... a kind of physical expression of the spirit of mushin ... Mushin is often literally translated as "no mind," but carries connotations of fully existing within the moment, of non-attachment, of equanimity amid changing conditions. ... The vicissitudes of existence over time, to which all humans are susceptible, could not be clearer than in the breaks, the knocks, and the shattering to which ceramic ware too is subject. This poignancy or aesthetic of existence has been known in Japan as mono no aware, a compassionate sensitivity, or perhaps identification with, [things] outside oneself.

"*To bind with gold our broken bowl ...* " came back to him as an echo from his own translation, itself a faint echo of half-remembered lines from a Christina Rossetti poem, and simultaneously collided with the lyrics of a haunting song, sprung from the recesses of his memory. He had listened to a lot of Leonard Cohen when he was young, and even now sporadically. The songs had always spoken to him in ways he could not articulate. As he stood there transfixed, the words from *Anthem* resounded through his mind, urging him to forget any idea of a perfect offering. Sometimes, he suddenly grasped, our ideas of perfection, the gods of our own accomplishments or acquisitions, are simply the masks or shields we construct to keep others out, to keep the truth out. It is only when our masks begin to crack that the light can get in. Nothing and no one can stand against the truth for ever. In the end everything else will crack.

Words and image fused. His mental scenery experienced a subtle shift in focus. Things out of kilter and dislocated suddenly reconnected. It was as if the hidden mechanism of the inner puzzle box had clicked into place, laying its secret sanctum within reach if he could only grasp the key and had the courage to peep inside.

Not all the bells were silenced. He repeated the words from the song slowly in his mind, as he gazed at the curiously beautiful object before him. The gold veins running through the broken ceramic were like dawn light spilling through the cracks of night; these new thoughts themselves like sudden beams seeping through his fractured soul. *It isn't until we ditch any illusion of our own self-sufficiency, and our carefully constructed egos begin to crack, that the light can get in . . .*

It felt like a little revelation. *They don't even try to conceal the breaks*, he mused, *they actually highlight them, so that something newly beautiful can come from broken beauty. The object is simultaneously the same thing, but not the same thing.* Could a vein of gold spread through his bruised and battered soul, filling the tears and holes and make him newly beautiful?

Maybe after all these distant artists did understand. The cracks were necessary. He had always tried to guard himself from any vulnerability. Never showing a gap to anyone, hardly acknowledging them himself, he had built an almost impenetrable ego. He had even almost believed in his own myth of himself, until driven to the limits of his world . . . then his strange epiphany and brutal awakening. He now felt a helpless heap of fragments but perhaps that was the beginning of healing, as he had sensed when bathed in the light of the window. Not the beginning of the end, even though that's what it felt like right now, but the beginning of the beginning, a realization not only of his hopelessly flawed state but of the cracks for the light to get in, the breaks to be filled with something precious.

How he longed for that light to pour in and overcome his darkness and drive it away and yet how simultaneously he feared it with a dread that was almost palpable.

Unconsciously he pulled his coat closer around himself. How could he endure that searing light to penetrate his dark places, so dark that even he could not face or own them? How could he bear for the rottenness and corruption, the cruelty and ugliness to be not only exposed but cleansed and beautified, put on display for all to see like golden scars, testifying to the skill of some divine artist or physician? The brokenness, yes, he was perhaps beginning to acknowledge, but the darkness? He was afraid, afraid of the light but more afraid of what the light might reveal, afraid of himself.

How he longed for Lucy, as a buffer both from that alien light and from that darkness that he must own. He knew, with that deep knowing beyond words, that if he could accept it, she possessed that compassionate otherness he yearned for. He felt he needed her as both shield and mirror. Perhaps through her he could tentatively approach the light as if by refraction; obliquely sidle up to the truth in her shadow.

*   *   *

He put on the Leonard Cohen track when he got home and sat in the window seat, looking out at the stars. The lyrics floated gently around him. His life was a cracked and broken bowl; he had nothing to bring, nothing to offer. He was an empty-handed refugee begging for love and forgiveness. The words drifted off into silence. To his surprise he found he was crying.

Numberless are we, all and each speak we, sounding in concert,
One on his own remains voiceless; black but we play upon white fields,
Though we converse upon high things, no sound beats on the ear drum;
Speak we the past and the now, foretell many things in the future.

Northumbrian riddle

Painting on silence

To preachers, prophets and poets,
Scribes, scholars and singers,
Words are the greatest gift of earthly existence;
As colour to the artist, sound to the musician,
Movement to the dancer, speed to the athlete,
So preachers and poets paint upon the pregnant silence,
Sounding the vast spaces with many voices,
"Bodying forth the forms of things unknown,
Turning them to shapes." So wordsmiths down the ages
Have wrestled in imagination and given
To "airy nothing a local habitation and a name" . . .

(Adam couldn't resist a rather loose translation here to incorporate Shakespeare's brilliant articulation, so perfectly pertinent.)

. . . Imaging in their little lives a fragment
Of the great Father and Creator of All,
Who in the beginning cracked the darkness
And spoke into the formless void,
Filling its absence with light, and sent forth
The teeming multitudes to spill across the nascent earth.
So black, but playing upon white fields,
The scribbling scribe captures in characters sacred truths,
Sharper than the two-edged sword,
Pouring them onto the virgin page, his ink the lifeblood,
His quivering quill quickening the blank emptiness,
Making it alive with animated, illuminated letters,
Jewels to delight the eyes and speak to ears and hearts.
Rightly has the blessed Boniface pronounced with the psalmist
That beautiful words are as honey or pure gold,
And to make manifest this mystery

To the poor pagans to whom he preached,
Desired he of the abbess of Thanet
A copy of the Epistles of Saint Peter,
A treasure trove of truth, written all in ink of gold,
To illustrate to those benighted souls
The illustrious value of their worth,
That even though illiterate, through the glowing splendour
They might glimpse gleanings of the Living Word;
That light and life to all the nations of this world,
The love of God and Truth incarnate,
Word of the Father wrapped in human flesh,
His story written from time eternal,
Inscribed in blood more beautiful than gold
Upon the foundation and fabric of being.

Such is the indescribable worth
Of these living gems of knowledge,
These letters, these building blocks of truth,
That though one on his own remains voiceless,
Yet when all and each speak, sounding in concert,
A heavenly harmony is heard, a music and a magic
To mirror the great dance of the sublime spheres;
Conversing upon high things,
Speaking of past and present
And foretelling even the fate of the future.
A conversation above all between God and his creation,
Between man and his Maker;
A manifestation of mysteries divine.

To obtain such treasures, such jewels of greatest price
What travails and travels would not the pious man endure?

And in search of such riches
Biscop and Alwin are earnestly employed,
That their monastery home may be enriched
By beauty, knowledge and truth.
That while the open book of stone and glass
May speak of glory bodied forth in matter,
So these treasure troves of precious words,
These tabernacles of characters divine,
Living dialogues incongruously contained by cow's hide,
These wondrous, magical books of illumination and delight
Might also speak, enlarging mind and soul.

In search of these treasuries then, they tread
The winding valley of the Rhone, where
In certain cities, purveyors of such goods may be found.
And with careful husbandry and a little haggling,
Many precious volumes are procured at acceptable prices
(Although who can put a price on beauty and truth?)
And these wondrous wares, and in some cases generous gifts,
Are vouchsafed to the care of trusted friends
Against their prayed-for return.

Words

Adam was working furiously, oblivious to all around him and the passing of time. He must get this translation finished. First of all, he must simply make more headway with his work. But secondly, he knew he was looking for answers. He felt certain the clues he needed were littered amongst these precious words from the past. He shared the excitement about the creative possibilities of the written word expressed by his poet. If only he had an interpreter. If only he could persuade Lucy to join him in his quest. She held the light he needed, he felt sure of it. If only he had not damaged the emerging relationship between them. *Why did he never learn?*

How many words now littered the earth though, an over-abundance, a tidal wave of information, not all useful; searching for truth was like seeking for a needle in a haystack. In some ways, he envied the men of the past. Written words then were rare and precious. Every manuscript a treasure trove. Yet words still held that amazing power and magic. They did hold truth. He was sure of it now, although he could not explain how. How to read and understand them? What a strange sensation for one of his profession. He was always interpreting words. But now it really mattered to him, he found he could not grasp them, make them his own.

He had reached the part where Alwin and Biscop, to their delight, have procured, amongst other precious texts, some volumes of Saint Augustine of Hippo. He knew little about this learned man but discovered that he also had shared the restless need to journey relentlessly towards finding peace and truth. And that his rest was only found, through all his torturous and circuitous paths, when he rested upon God. But what did that mean? He was increasingly out of his depth and also within him he felt bubbling up a sort of defiance. If God really cared so much about human beings, about him, why did he allow him to suffer like this? Why did he not help him, or at least provide him with a guide? It was unreasonable, unfair to expect him to figure things out for himself, to have to piece together scraps and fragments of truth. Why make it so difficult?

Augustine

Amongst the heavenly hoard acquired
Are great and wonderful works of learning:
De Arte Metrica, *De Schematibus et Tripos*, *De Orthographia*,
Isidore of Seville's famed *Etymologiae* and *De Natura Rerum*,
As well as various volumes of theological virtue
And philosophical discourse: the great Boethius' *Consolation*
And the famed *City of God* and *Confessions*
Of Saint Augustine, that ancient, honoured father
In the church of Christ across the world and all the West.
Alwin is intrigued and marvels beyond measure
At these most magnificent monuments
To the mind of man and grace of God,
And earnestly desires to discourse
Upon their merits with his mentor,
Who is even more eager to redeem the time.
And so they delve into the divine delights
Delivered up by this giant among men,
This father of the fathers to his heirs,
And talk of many things as they continue upon their path,
The miles slipping past to Alwin as his mind and heart
Are full of these wonderful words that come to him
Down the winding ways of history
And yet speak so fresh and full of promise,
His heart on fire with the love of wisdom,
Grateful to glean from the abundance of this wealth,
This gift of generous grace.

They speak of Augustine's great and central theme:
Man's journey towards rest in God;
That though carrying our mortality with us, the sign of sin,
Yet as sons of His creation

Something in us still longing to praise Him,
For He has made us for Himself,
And for all the distractions and desires of this world,
Its delights and diversions,
The human heart is restless
Until it finds its rest in Him.

Alwin speaks out of a heart full of excitement,
For here, he exclaims to his guide,
Are other glorious journeys and encounters,
Augustine himself expressing his own life story
As encounters with extraordinary books,
Even the pagan *Aeneid* providing pictures;
The Trojan hero Aeneas' wanderings after the fall of Troy,
And how he even came also to Carthage,
Before going finally on to reach his goal,
The founding of great Rome,
A model for Augustine's own life,
His *Confessions*, even his own *Aeneid*,
Recounting his spiritual wanderings,
Which would also take him from Carthage to Rome.
And as Augustine himself declares,
According to the wise,
"The world is a book
And those who do not travel
Read only one page."
But there are many ways of travelling
And not all are reckoned in miles.

To feel the physical and spiritual heir of such a man,
Though travelling from northerly Northumbria,
With a shared preeminent purpose as he perceives it,
And to be seeking the same city, fills Alwin with awe,
And Biscop is also encouraged as they discourse

On these divers things of divine delight
And present parallels of purpose,
But reminds his young novice also
Of the long and winding route
That even this great father had to walk,
As the Israelites in the wilderness,
Or even our first parents from paradise,
For his sinful youth is an ever-present theme,
And the seeming petty crime of stealing pears—
His own forbidden fruit—had first convicted
The boy Augustine that he was a fallen sinner,
Doing what was contrary to good,
Not through coveting the thing itself
But simply for the perverse pleasure of enjoying sin,
And perceived in himself, along with all mankind,
The tragedy of the human state in this fallen world:
That our sin uses God's good law not as righteous restraint,
But as an opportunity to show its natural desire
To rail and rebel against the Lord our Maker.

*   *   *

It was with increasing anger and frustration that Adam struggled on to the end of this section. He could take no delight in this, as Alwin appeared to have done. He finally flung down his pen in disgust. Why were boys stealing pears such a big deal? And anyway, even if it was, why dangle appealing dainties before people to try to catch them out? Why make them appealing and then hold them just out of reach or condemn those with the wit and bravery and strength to grasp them? Why should any fruit be forbidden? Who was this God anyway to decide where the boundaries and limits should lie? He shoved the sheaf of papers into the folder and slammed the drawer. As he did so the top sheets escaped from the bundle and floated to the floor. They could lie there. He was getting out of here. He put on his coat and headed home through the freezing rain.

Other fruits, other gardens

Damn it, he would call Robert. Why shouldn't he try to alleviate his suffering and have some respite?

The phone rang a few times and then the answerphone clicked in. He slammed down the receiver. Lighting a cigarette, he leant against the window frame and looked out upon the night. The transient lights of the city sparkled under the cold and constant light of the stars.

He jumped when the phone rang loudly beside him. Snatching it up he heard Robert's familiar voice. He sounded as though he had been drinking.

"Sorry I missed your call. Was in the bathroom. What? Fantastic! Knew you'd come round! Looking forward to it, no don't worry, not at all inconvenient . . . What? No, really I'm dying of boredom here, damn marking. Bloody first years get worse every year. Most of them can't even spell! Definitely, will make a welcome change! Meet you at the Golden Bowl in about an hour. Tell you what, I'll give Zoe a bell and see if she's free, and if she has any friends at a loose end. Don't worry old man, we'll get you sorted out!"

He ground out his cigarette in the ashtray, grabbed his coat and descended the stairs in a grim and deliberate way. He would happily sell his soul tonight for a few hours of oblivion and a warm bed, he told himself. Opening the street door he breathed in the crisp, glittering night air, full of possibilities.

As he headed down into town, he found himself, to his annoyance, having a fierce internal argument. His conscience, like a moth-eaten old coat, seemed to have been dragged out of the recesses of some dusty cupboard in his mind and dumped at the forefront. The unattractive, uncomfortable and frankly unfashionable item refused to be bundled back in out of embarrassment's way but kept sprawling out, spoiling his bid for freedom and relief. With a tremendous effort of will he shoved it in hard and slammed the door. But there was no lock or key so no complete assurance it would not spring out again at an awkward moment.

Never mind. He increased his pace and knowing he would be too early, took the scenic route. The trees were full of starlight and their beauty touched him in a strange and disquieting way. But then swirls of cloud began to scurry across the dark sky, obscuring the moon and stars, and large flakes of snow started to fall, gently, slowly at first, then more heavily and insistently. So soft and yet so cold. Before long everything, including himself, was dusted with a layer of white crystals.

He eventually arrived at the place of assignation. It was a historic building, tastefully decorated and serving ingenious cocktails to exactly his class. The amber lights flooded out of the windows, through the tumbling snow and onto the cobbles, invitingly. He could see his friend already seated at a window with a well-turned-out woman beside him and someone else opposite.

"Ah Adam!" Robert hailed him as he entered the bar, stamping the snow off his shoes. "What are you drinking? No, please, let me! But first, let me introduce you to Regan. Zoe of course you know."

Zoe gave him a supercilious nod and continued smoking elegantly through a black lacquer cigarette holder. It was a preposterous affectation that would have made anyone else look ridiculous. It made her look fabulous.

"Regan is a post-grad from across the pond, just up here for a few months to do some research—the culture of mining communities," Robert was saying. "Have I got that right?"

The auburn-haired girl turned intelligent brown eyes on him and smiled.

"Yes, almost right, Robert," she replied, in the distinctive drawl of the Deep South. She put out her hand, and Adam took it briefly. It was very cold. "Pleased to meet you, Adam! And just to clarify, it's Regan as in President, not as in King Lear—at least that's what I've been told!"

He laughed.

"That's a relief! So I don't need to keep a close eye on my eyeballs? Actually, how would one even do that?"

She laughed.

"I don't know what possessed my parents to give me such a hell-of-a-name, but I guess it always gives me an unusual conversation opener!"

Robert returned with some intriguingly colourful drinks, sporting little umbrellas, cherries on sticks and suggestive names. As he pushed her drink across, Adam's hand brushed hers again.

"You're freezing!" he exclaimed, turning his most charming smile on her.

"I am! This is a freezing country, particularly this part of it, and the heating doesn't really work anywhere! How are yours so warm?"

"Adam is a very warm-hearted gentleman," replied Robert with mock seriousness. "He'll be more than happy to share some of his warmth, I'm sure!"

He winked at Adam and Regan laughed.

"Well, when I'm in need of a hot water bottle, I'll let y'all know!"

"Please do!" He smiled.

Zoe blew a small cloud of smoke over her shoulder and turning, fixed him with her beautiful, mocking eyes.

"But I've heard he's already taken, and I should think hot water bottles and cocoa would just about sum it up!"

Adam had never liked Zoe. She was relentlessly disparaging about everything and everyone. Drop-dead gorgeous though. And didn't she know it. She knew exactly how to dress too. Adam surveyed her perfect complexion, shiny hair, long dark lashes and exactly the right amount of exposed skin with an expensive pendant hovering just in the right spot to draw the eye down.

"You mustn't tease him, Zoe darling," laughed Robert. "We are on a mission to save him from such hellish tedium!"

"I heard on the grapevine," she purred, with mock concern, in her refined home counties accent, "that our poor Adam is in danger of being caught by the office mouse! Isn't that the wrong way round?"

She smiled scornfully, putting the cigarette holder to her beautiful full lips. She oozed sophistication; clever too. First in her degree, had recently completed her PhD and now some advantageous moves within the department had put her in a strong position to develop a sparkling career. The arrangement worked well for both her and Robert, for now.

He had had a few weeks of flirtation with her himself a few years back, but she was an expert player and scrupulously pragmatic. She was only in the game for the highest bidder. Robert had won for now, but he doubted he would hold her long. He was only a big fish in a little pond.

Everything about Zoe was sharp and sparkling. Regan was much more natural looking and had a much nicer expression in her warm dark eyes. Less sexy though, in her cream jumper and straight beige cords, he thought, but soft and inviting. Something about her made him feel he would be just as happy hugging her as kissing her.

"Do y'all mean the girl with the cute accent?" she cut in.

"Well that's one way of putting it!" retorted Zoe. And Robert laughed.

"Yours is pretty cute too you know, but yes, that's the one. I'm sure she's true mining stock Regan, maybe you should interview her for your paper."

"You might dig out more than you've bargained for with her!" exclaimed Zoe. "You'll be dragged along to a bloody prayer meeting before you know what's happening."

This was intolerable. Adam flinched and glared at Zoe who just laughed and blew a cloud of smoke into his face. He knew he could either force a laugh too or walk out. The inconvenient old coat was threatening to burst out of the cupboard again. He hastily leant against the door in his mind and twisted his face into a smirk, although his eyes looked daggers at Zoe, daring her to proceed at her peril.

"Shall we change the subject, darling?" Robert put a languid arm around her bare shoulders. "I think we may have exhausted this one; there's not a lot to say to be honest, is there?"

Adam clenched his fists under the table. But above he merely shrugged. "Not a lot to say," he reiterated. "I've come out to see you all expressly for the purpose of stimulating company, so don't disappoint me!"

He felt like a cad. Inwardly his heart smote him for his betrayal.

Zoe, somewhat appeased by his climb down, smiled in a more friendly way.

"How's the translation going?"

"Well . . . " He thought of the papers scattered across his study floor. He didn't want to talk about this tonight. He needn't have worried.

"I'm working on a part which is mainly dialogue between Alwin and Biscop discussing Saint Augustine, as they have managed to get hold of a copy of his *Confessions* and *City of God* for their monastery, on their travels through the Rhone valley . . . "

"Sounds fascinating," cut in Zoe in a bored voice.

Cycles

In fact, it had been fascinating as well as frustrating, maddening, offensive. Adam had found that the course of Augustine's journeying resonated with him, unwelcome though that was. Although he tried to push it from his mind, he could not now un-know what he had known, un-hear words he had absorbed. He could readily identify with the idea of life-changing encounters with books. He knew the feeling, like no other, when for a moment, minds meet through black symbols on white pages. Those light-bulb moments yes, but also that other kind of meeting, the almost imperceptible shifting in the direction of thought, the gradual subtle seeping awareness of something significant—the gentle pattering of other people's words, passing through our eyes, falling onto our ears like rain, the sinking down into the depths and through the minerals and bedrock of our consciousness, the slow but incessant currents making new channels through our souls, the trickling or springing through the surface, the tiny streams, gathering momentum, racing down the mountainsides of our minds, the gushing rivers, the wide estuaries and then into the vast fullness of the sea, to be mingled again with other waters, other words, and then taken up again into the clouds of collective consciousness, to refresh, or poison, our fellow man. The cycle of truth or the cycle of lies. The cycle of life or the cycle of death.

Love in Carthage

But Love was secretly working her hidden bright designs
And slowly drawing Augustine towards grace,
Biscop demonstrates to his son in faith, And as Aeneas,
Was pursued by powerful affection in Carthage,
But unlike him, not found in the fleshly love of Dido,
But in another formidable, queenly book,
This time the Hortensius, the "love of wisdom",
And takes the admonition of Cicero
To seek and learn eternal wisdom
With all the longing of a lover's heart.
When retracing his winding road to rest he truly felt
These wondrous words began his search for Christ,
Who is indeed Wisdom incarnate, and began
His long and arduous search, as the ancient Magi
Following the afar off star of promise,
Though at that time he knew Him not.
And writes he therefore of pagan Cicero's words
A paradox: "This book changed my affections
And turned, oh Lord, my prayers to you."

And so Biscop concludes, from all noble themes
Truth may indeed be derived,
Even if only from fragments and broken beams of light.
For all mankind's creations come
From his own creation in the image of his Maker,
And none so base or dull as do not dimly
Reflect something of the divine.
So should we be surprised that these great
and gifted souls of antiquity, giants among men,
Even though still in pagan darkness walking,
Should be able to contrive such works of value

And glimpses of truth? So the man of wisdom
Would do well to gather the gleanings and gems
That have even by the wayside fallen—even as Saint Paul
Urges the Athenians when he quotes their ancient poets
And points them to their own altar to the "unknown God"—
And seek to piece together from such windfalls of wonder,
The great mosaic of truth, the divine pattern
Written into all the world, glowing yet more glorious still
When basking in the sunrise of the Word of God,
The revelation vouchsafed to man to dispel the darkness
And bestow the light of life.

However, he allows to Alwin, Augustine had
A hard and arduous journey ahead,
The harder still for having at the first
Spurned his mother's faith, for it had seemed to him,
In his youthful pride and folly, poor fare compared
To Cicero's rhetorical panache, naive and childish.
And so his search had turned instead to the sinister sect
Of the feared Manichees, strict dualists
Seeing even the body as evil, the soul alone as good,
Evil existing because matter exists,
The Creator censured for bringing into being
All that can be seen and touched, the soul remaining pure,
Untouched and untarnished by the body's sin, untainted
And aloof from fleshly lusts; verily an attractive doctrine,
Delightful to the young devotees of this creed!
But then tragedy struck to stop him in his stride
And give him pause; God's purging hand,
To prevent further plunging into error,
Snatched from life a beloved friend.
The great shock and grief causing Augustine to grasp
The impotent folly of seeking to find
In mere human friendship the fulfilment

Craved by our immortal heart; that void
That only our Maker can touch and fill; that space
That only the Spirit of God can sound and satisfy.

Touching the void

"Where the hell am I?"

He jerked awake in an unknown room, the early sun piercing his eyes.

The girl in the fleecy pyjamas beside him propped herself on one elbow and he looked up into her laughing brown eyes.

"Hey!"

"What happened?" he murmured as he flopped down again on the pillows beside her, hazy remembrance of a giddy taxi ride, followed by an intoxicating blur of heady drinks, soft lighting and soft limbs beginning to flood back, accompanied by a stabbing headache.

"Nothing!" She laughed. "You did no more or less than you promised! You were a most effective hot water bottle and saved me having the heater on overnight for the first time since I arrived here!"

He groaned. "What did I do? Or maybe even worse, what didn't I do?"

"Well, after a most gallant but ineffectual attempt to undress me, you passed out on the bed and have slept like a baby ever since!"

"Bloody hell! How embarrassing. I'm very sorry. I must be losing my touch!"

"Neither here nor there to me," she smiled, "suited me fine to be honest. I was tired; you were warm. Very convenient!"

"You must have a constitution of steel!" he exclaimed incredulously, looking at her with new admiration. "After all those cocktails and whatever that concoction was you bewitched me with back here last night, to remember as cool as a cucumber and wake as fresh as a daisy!"

"I guess I do!" she laughed ruefully. "More's the pity! Say, you want a coffee?"

"Like a parched man!"

She rolled out of bed and went off down the corridor to the kitchen.

He looked around. His jacket and shirt were hung carefully over a chair and his shoes were lined up neatly underneath. She must have taken them off for him when he was oblivious and then carefully covered him with the duvet.

He heard the distant strains of a radio, and then, after a few minutes, her approaching footsteps as she reappeared with two mugs, shedding their wonderfully aromatic fragrance.

"Nice and strong. And here's some paracetamol."

He took a deep draught and washed the tablets down.

"Thanks, you're a lifesaver! Why do Americans make coffee so much better than us Brits?"

"I guess for the same reason you Brits make tea better than us Americans!"

"I hardly know anything about you. Where did you grow up? When did you come over?"

"Not much to say really. Grew up in South Carolina, real Bible Belt country. My dad's a Baptist pastor. Have a load of siblings. Was homeschooled 'til right through high school. Was desperate to get away. I guess I love my family and they love me, but it was suffocating. Managed to land a place at Oxford to read English—got some sort of scholarship—lived amongst the dreaming spires for a few years and then found myself here doing some research for my PhD having strangely acquired a social conscience somewhere along the way."

"So you're a girl a long way from home?"

"A long way from home," she repeated, as if the idea was somehow a new one. "Yes, I guess I am!"

He offered her a cigarette. She shook her head.

"Do you mind if I smoke?"

"Sure, go ahead. It's not really allowed in here, but no one cares! I'll just open the window a crack. Not for me, thanks, never touch them, well hardly ever. Don't like the taste! Just a bit of recreational hash. Do you ever indulge?"

"A little, mainly as an undergrad. Can't say it did much for me!"

"Doesn't do much for me either," she laughed, "but I keep hoping! Anything is worth a try."

Her smile looked suddenly sad.

"You know, when I finally escaped home and arrived at university, I only really had two ambitions. One was to get absolutely blasted and the other was to lose my virginity, as quickly as possible. The first was surprisingly difficult to accomplish, the second unsurprisingly easy and done within the first week. Both disappointingly overrated. And now, the first becomes increasingly difficult to recreate, and of course the second is impossible."

She looked wistfully out of the window for a long while as the rising sun streamed through the wintry trees outside.

"And yet here we are," she said finally without turning her head.

"And yet here we are," he repeated. "Do you always talk like this to strangers?"

"I *only* talk like this to strangers! They are always kinder and generally more interesting."

He looked at her with curiosity.

"Well, I suppose strangers don't have to deal with the fall-out of our choices, do they?"

He flicked some ash into his empty cup.

"It's easy to be sympathetic as a one-off, and then move on."

"Always moving on is the only possible way to live. 'Never get attached' is my motto!" she pronounced with an air of studied glibness. "Emotional involvement is always a mistake. Attachments are like chains and the deeper the attachment the thicker the chain. Caring for people is dangerous, loving them is fatal. Love is the end—the end of the road."

His eyes fixed on the glowing end between his fingers. "Is that such a bad destination?" he asked quietly.

She glanced at him and replied with strangely suppressed emotion, "Yes, if you want to be free and don't want your heart torn to pieces."

He looked at her closed face and then back to the smouldering embers.

"I thought you just said you loved your family?"

"Of course! I don't have any choice, do I?"

She stabbed savagely at the mattress with her fingers.

"So you're running as fast as you can in the opposite direction?"

She continued staring at her hands.

"But don't forget," he observed more satirically than he intended, "the world is round, so you're likely to end up right back where you started!

Unless of course you prefer to envisage it as my seventh-century monks, like a great flat table with all the oceans pouring over the edges?"

"That certainly sounds preferable!" She forced a half-smile.

"And what if your 'chains'," he continued relentlessly, (*what made him always want to probe the raw places?*) "turn out to be the strands that hold everything together? What binds and orders the universe and stops everything spinning off into chaos?"

"Then the universe can go to hell, implode or explode for all I care!" she retorted, now provoked into some reluctant feeling. "Bring on the chaos! Better to be crushed under the rocks or blasted to smithereens and be free, than bound to that . . . that tyranny of existence!"

"But perhaps perpetual sentient existence is a burden we have no choice but to bear? I'm beginning to suspect that might be the case. (*And now I'm rubbing salt in the wound*, he thought, *but my own wounds too!*) What if we can't escape it, even if we were to blow ourselves and the universe up, or it were to collapse in on top of us under the weight of our feckless abuse? What if, having brought the universe down on our own heads, we after all don't even have the power to really die? That there's no way out? It's rather an appalling thought. But then so is non-existence. I can't decide which is worse!"

He raised his eyes to her face and gazed at her for a long time, contemplating. But she, lost in her own thoughts, wasn't really listening, seemed to be staring at some invisible point beyond perception, as if she had forgotten he was there.

For a long while neither of them spoke. The only sound was of a blue bottle, sprung out of hibernation, buzzing lazily in and out of the slanting dust-filled sunbeams and curling wisps of steam and smoke. Sitting on the edge of the bed she drank the dregs of her tepid coffee and Adam finished his cigarette in silence.

"You know," she resumed eventually, as if he hadn't spoken—lost in her own track of thought, "I used to be so rebellious and hostile to my parents' dogma. I felt so pinned down, like every thought had to be put into the right box. It felt like being buried alive because they were afraid I might glimpse the sun. I thought there must be some dangerous, delectable secret out there that everyone was trying to keep from me . . . But there wasn't. I've become much more tolerant over time, since I've checked out the alternatives." She laughed wryly, shaking herself out of her sombre reverie. "Hell! I sound like Solomon in Ecclesiastes!"

"*Vanity of vanities* . . . but without the thousand wives!" quipped Adam.

"Indeed! I'm not quite that liberal minded! And I may have a constitution of steel, but even I couldn't manage more than a handful at once!"

He raised an eyebrow. She merely shrugged. He shot her a quick penetrating look but couldn't decide if she was just winding him up or not.

She reached across and took the cigarette from between his fingers and putting it to her lips took a long draught. She blew it out with a disgusted look on her face and a snort.

"No! Just as foul as I remembered!" she said with a short laugh and handed it back. "I thought it was worth another try, but obviously not!"

He smiled and took a slow draught himself.

After a pause she carried on, "I joined the Socialist Workers' Party when I was at Oxford, you know. I had just devoured things like *Les Misérables*, and it was thrilling to find a leaflet in my pigeonhole one day addressed to 'Dear Comrade' and inviting me to a meeting in the college bar. But when I got there, it was just a load of louts swilling beer. I never went back. But I guess I still feel more should be done. I guess that's why I'm looking at old mining communities in the Northeast. They've been betrayed over and over again, by the Right, by the Left, by everyone. The poverty and hardship in some of the villages round here, the lost pride and way of life, just a few miles from all this opulence, makes you want to weep."

"Your social conscience!" he said sardonically. "Interesting for someone who doesn't want to care! And if you were going to care, why should you care about that? Wouldn't civil rights or something be more up your street? Seems rather an obscure little tragedy for you to fix on!"

"Maybe other people's problems are more interesting and maybe not so close to home. But you can't talk when it comes to obscure! Translating unearthed medieval documents about seventh-century monks! Seems spectacularly unsuited to you! Anyway, I don't know, but it seems one has to care about something, to just keep going, right? Even if we don't want to. We need to manufacture some purpose. Complete indifference to everything seems a luxury too far for the human mind. I guess we're hardwired that way."

There were a couple of obvious sequiturs to this, but he refrained from pointing them out. Instead he observed, "So you're an Existentialist then?"

She smiled.

"I'm a nothing . . . or an everything if you prefer! I am all things to all men!"

She held out her arms in mock drama.

He smiled and then breathing out the last of his cigarette meditatively he ground the end into the mug.

"They still had the same fundamental issues, back in the seventh century, you know," he said, "and in the fifteenth for that matter. Nothing really changes. They weren't all saints either. And speaking of consciences, I've been having great trouble with mine recently. It keeps leaping out and ambushing me when I would much rather it behaved like a proper Victorian child—not seen and not heard!"

She smiled thinly. "If you shove it back one way it'll just pop out somewhere else! I should know. Don't try to silence it, it's the inner voice. You need to learn to listen and be true to yourself."

He lit another cigarette and leant back against the headboard, exhaling slowly and surveying her as she sat on the end of the bed, hugging her knees.

"And are *you*?"

She merely shrugged and looked at him strangely for a moment or two, then said in a flat voice, "I just know that without it you're lost, completely lost, without a compass."

This was surprising after her other disclosures but certainly resonated. He knew that feeling too well; a vessel driven before storms with neither pilot nor compass . . . well, until the lodestar of Lucy and the strange spiritual awakening had broken through.

It was almost as if the disquieting American could read his thoughts. She suddenly said, "This girl from admin, the one with the cute accent, you really like her, don't you?"

He was surprised and not really sure how to answer because he didn't know himself.

"I'm not sure it's like that," he replied after a moment. "To be honest, it's more like an insane obsession . . . I hadn't really thought about her in that way. She's more like a spiritual visitation that's broken into my life. A point of light."

"I like that," she said slowly. "That sounds authentic. The body is nothing is it? It's the spirit that's important and must remain free and untouched."

This struck another chord. The poetic threads of Augustine's sojourn with the Manichees and their alluring Gnosticism were weaving in and out of his mind, lines rising sudden and unbidden like tips of foam and then swallowed again by the swelling deeps. *Was the body, physical matter, really nothing, evil even?*

She was continuing, "I'd like to get to know her. She sounds interesting and maybe she would help me out with my research too? But don't tell the exquisite Zoe!"

"You don't like her either?"

She shook her head.

"But Robert's been very good to me . . . "

I bet he has! thought Adam.

"And," she continued, "although I can imagine she could make life rather unpleasant if you got on the wrong side of her, she's unlikely to be a problem while I'm no threat to her and useful. As she's smarter and prettier than me, I'm unlikely to be much of a threat and I may prove useful!"

"Useful?"

"Uh huh, they prepped me, of course, on your situation before I met you. I'm sorry about your wife and kids by the way . . . "

Adam waved his hand and she continued, "But Robert is perturbed by your interest in, what's her name, Lucy, and would prefer you were distracted! If he's happy, he's easier to manage and so she's happy."

"What infernal cheek! I do apologize. Shame on them for treating you like this."

She laughed merrily and shot him a sharp look, penetrating to the heart of his own hypocrisy.

He couldn't hold her gaze and shifted uneasily.

"It's really of no account. In fact it amuses me! Say, shall I be your cover so you can carry on investigating this obsession with your spiritual soulmate unmolested while they think I've managed to put you off the scent in a much more conventional manner? Be kind of fun!"

He laughed. "Would serve them right! But not much fun for you."

"Oh, it's as good as anything else! I'm pretty lonely here you know, so if you're at a loose end you know where I am. You can fuck me, smoke a joint with me, drink with me, eat sushi with me, cry on my shoulder or just talk! Whatever you like, or all together. I'm pretty indifferent and it makes no difference. None of it matters. And it all helps pass the time."

Her brown eyes were looking into his, disarmingly open, guileless and kind, but weary with a soft melancholy. Despite himself he was shocked by her unapologetic vulgarity and calm vulnerability. He felt unaccountably sad. *She's a nice girl*, he thought to himself, *generous in her own way*. He put his arm around her and drew her close. She leant her head on his shoulder, her rich auburn hair pouring in a smooth cascade down his arm.

"Or perhaps," he said gently as they stared straight ahead, "it helps us avoid facing the abyss?"

"Oh no," she replied, turning and looking him directly in the eyes, "it's embracing the abyss!"

Cynic though he was, he felt himself shrinking, recoiling from her casual nihilism, even with its sugar coating. It would be like returning to a longed-for home and finding it burnt to the ground and all the people you loved dead. Alwin floated across the wild seas of his mind, adrift on his precarious wooden boat. Imagine if there was no safe haven, ever. He shuddered. Perhaps it was just his innate romanticism, his taste for melodrama, his need for a progressive narrative, but he sensed it was also something else. He could not, would not embrace the void. For all its promise of unaccountable moral freedom it was really the embracing of death. It would be a denial of reality and being, just emptiness, flatness, nothing. It was what lay at the polar extreme of his fear of the divine—and it was worse.

He disentangled himself gently and took her hand.

"You are brave, and kind. *And* pretty! Much braver and kinder than me. And you're worth a thousand Zoes! I wish I could help you, but to be honest I'm out of my depth and don't even know how to help myself. I think you are as lost as I am, and I have no map."

"I thought I was the one who was meant to be helping you!" she retorted indignantly. "Walking uncharted territory, exploring my own identity, my truth, is not the same as being lost!"

"Isn't it?" he replied quietly, looking at her.

"And anyway, what makes you think I *want* to be found?"

There was a hard edge to her voice.

"Doesn't everyone?"

She didn't reply.

"You know where I am too," he said after a pause, releasing her hand, "if you want to talk, or the boiler breaks down and you're in need of a hot water bottle!"

They both laughed and she said, suddenly brightening up, "Say, there is something you can do for me after all! Would you take me out for breakfast? I'm famished!"

*　　*　　*

Walking along the river path towards the city, with the winter sun reflecting pale and silvery on the gently flowing water made Adam's senses revolt even further from his fair companion's stark philosophy. And what on earth was all that conscience and spirit stuff about? The long, brisk walk had helped clear his head a little. The shining ripples were like her own inconsistencies, sparkling in spite, almost in defiance, of the murky depths and the immutable bedrock below: her substance in the teeth of her words. How could this all be meaningless? The beauty, her beauty even, was too great, too poignant, too good.

They sat in the window of a small cafe eating croissants and drinking more coffee. Regan was surveying Adam mischievously.

"I hope my American vulgarity didn't offend your English sensibility earlier? From what I've heard I don't think it can have offended your morality!"

For once he was at a loss for words.

"But '*Let us call things by their proper names*'," she continued in a teasing voice, "'*it makes matters simpler . . .* ' Now, Prof, where's that from?"

"Sadly I am not a professor," he said drily, "nor at this rate am I ever likely to become one. Ok, give me a moment . . . Wilde? *The Importance of Being Earnest*?"

"Half right! *An Ideal Husband.*"

"Well, that's definitely not me!"

"Yes, so I gather! Although isn't that kind of the point?"

"But it's interesting, the idea of *proper names*," he continued, partly to shift the emphasis of the conversation. "Do things have proper names? Are some names more true than others? I suppose it's part of the perennial question: would a rose by any other name smell as sweet?"

"Well, there is no point dressing things up with Romanticism simply because we're squeamish about words, particularly when we're not squeamish about the accompanying actions," she retorted.

It was a fair point. These were the kind of conversations he enjoyed, although in this case it was perhaps a little close to the bone for comfort. He just wished his head didn't ache quite so much and he could spar more effectively. Evading her direct challenge he continued, "Does the physical rose, and our sensory appreciation of it, and indeed the concept of it, inform the word? Or is it the other way round?"

"If neither really mean anything, does it matter?" she fired back, stirring more sugar into the remnants of her coffee.

"But hang on, didn't you just say we should call things by their 'proper names'? How can anything have a proper name if nothing means anything?"

She laughed and said teasingly, "I can't believe calling a spade a spade is the same as calling, or not calling, a rose a rose!"

"Why on earth not?"

"Because one sounds just so much nicer!"

She was enjoying winding him up and playing with his overblown sense of serious self-importance.

"Aren't you rather inconsistent?" He laughed.

"Of course! Why shouldn't I be if nothing means anything? I'll just say and do whatever I like and whatever amuses me!" She laughed merrily. "And isn't that a woman's prerogative anyway?"

"Of course! I'd forgotten that!"

Adam, smiling, nodded his head in an admission of friendly defeat, looked at his watch and sighed. He was enjoying the banter, although it was beginning to have the slightly nauseating, but still addictive, effect of too much icing and not enough cake. He could have happily sat talking nonsense with her all morning, although he suspected he would have regretted it afterwards, and anyway, he must try to do some work. He had become more and more unproductive even with his translation and it was increasingly beginning to show.

"We'll have to continue this another time, sadly! I really must get to work."

"Ok! I might stay here for a bit and catch up on some reading. See you later and thanks for breakfast."

As he opened the door onto the street, he noticed a familiar figure hurrying past on the pavement outside. It was Lucy, as usual running slightly late with somewhat dishevelled hair and one shoelace undone. He grinned.

"Morning!" he called with an unconcealed touch of amusement and sarcasm in his voice. "You're in a rush! Meant to be somewhere?"

She jumped. Her mind had been miles away.

"Oh! Hi, Adam!" She looked up, flustered, and noticing Regan sitting in the window watching, turned a little red. "Um yes, sorry, running a bit late this morning, but will be there in a couple of minutes. The bus was late . . . "

"When isn't it?" he teased her. "Come on in here for a moment!"

He held the door open and after a moment's pause she was obliged to push past him into the warm interior.

He shut the door again and returned to the table he had just left.

"Sit down!" he said in a peremptory voice. "Two such lovely ladies should know each other properly. Lucy, this is Regan. Regan, Lucy."

"Hey!" Regan held out her hand and smiled in her easy manner. "Good to meet you, Lucy, been hearing all about you!"

He could see Lucy's mortified face out of the corner of his eye. Never mind, he thought to himself grimly, it would do her no harm.

"Hello," she stammered shyly.

"Robert mentioned last night that you might be able to help me with some of the research I'm doing? Would you mind awfully much if we met up sometime and I asked you some questions?"

Lucy looked mystified.

"Me? What kind of questions?"

"Oh, just about your upbringing, what it was like growing up round here, the culture surrounding the pit workers—your dad was a miner, right?"

"Oh, yes, yes, he was. Yeah, that's fine I don't mind answering questions if you think it will be any help. Don't really know very much, but I'll do my best. Let me know when would suit you. I really should go now though, because I'm really late for work and . . . "

She shot Adam a quick look. He was leaning back on his chair, surveying the pair of them with an amused, sardonic expression.

Ignoring her discomfiture he replied, "Don't rush on my account! Talk now if you like. I'm your boss, so I believe I can give you leave to be even later than usual! Another coffee, Regan? Have you had any breakfast this morning, Lucy? You look a little pinched!"

She flushed. "Um, no actually, I didn't have time . . . " she trailed off.

He laughed and went up to the counter, soon returning with a couple more steaming mugs and a bacon bun. "I don't like to see young ladies deprived of their breakfasts, whether they've earned them or not! Do you want any more, Regan?"

She demurred.

"Well, there you are! Now ladies, I must be off, but you take your time. No, really Lucy, it's fine. Indispensable though you are, I'm sure I can manage without you for an hour or so!" She looked reproachfully at him. "And Regan, it's been an . . . unforgettable experience meeting you, most enjoyable. Thank you for your hospitality. We must do it again. I'll pass on your best to Robert. I'm sure he'll be delighted to receive your report!"

They shared a momentary flash of private amusement, and Lucy, noticing, looked uncomfortable and embarrassed. Oh well, he was feeling a little irritated and thwarted by her at the moment. It might do her good!

Grinning to himself he took his leave, glancing back over his shoulder a few paces on. The fair head and the auburn head were bent towards each other over the table. One shy and awkward, the other at ease and solicitous. Despite the night's exploits Regan looked perversely more rested and refreshed than Lucy who was looking noticeably strained and tired. And she certainly looked a lot fresher than he did—he had caught an unflattering reflection of himself in the plate glass of the cafe window.

What a girl he thought in admiration. Regan was slight but with the constitution of an ox, in mind and body. She seemed to have almost succeeded in placing herself beyond harm—and help—a kind of desperate tranquillity achieved in the face of life's storms and disillusionments, but without yielding to bitterness or resentment. So open and yet so closed. Could it endure? What would old age look like once the piquancy of youth was spent? Anyhow, he knew instinctively it was too barren a wilderness for him to tread.

What would Lucy make of her? Did he detect a hint of primness in her face, jealousy even? He grinned. Oh well, she could jump to her own conclusions. Regan would soon make her feel comfortable. She had a wonderful gift for that. Two girls from two such different worlds. And yet perhaps with more in common than one would expect. *I wonder if they will figure that out?* he thought.

He knew it was unfair of him to throw Lucy in like that, particularly as she was so unsure of herself in this kind of context, but he hadn't been able to resist the temptation. He loved seeing worlds collide and watching the fallout. It would be interesting to see how the experiment went. He smiled again to himself, but then he frowned. He knew there would be a reckoning sooner or later and he also knew, if he was honest, he would struggle to keep himself from Regan's door seeking comfort before the end. And it didn't take a fool to point out that pleasure will be paid, one way or another.

The cup of wrath

He held out for a couple of weeks but eventually found himself, as he knew he would, with a bunch of flowers and a bottle of wine at Regan's door. It would help the subterfuge they were practising on Robert, he told himself lamely. He had had an empty and frustrating time, attempting to really throw himself back into his lecturing properly, but with limited success. He had found himself unwilling and, he told himself, lacking the inspiration, to return to his manuscript. He was lonely and adrift. She had said she was lonely. They could eat together, he could order a takeaway perhaps, they could have a drink . . . It was a cold night. Nothing wrong with that.

Regan had a large, draughty room on the ground floor of Shincliffe Hall, a converted country house owned by the university, providing accommodation for, mainly international, post-graduate students. It was a beautiful spot, a mile or so out of the city, surrounded by beech woods and farmland, right next to the river, where sometimes, if you were lucky, you might even see otters. It was a bit of a walk, though, and not particularly appealing in the dark, so Adam had driven. He could always get a taxi home if necessary, he told himself, although if he was honest, he wasn't really intending to leave that night.

The bright, full moon hung like a great, empty dish in the sky, cold and impassive, and the frosty stars peeped through the skeleton fingers of the bare trees that enmeshed them. Somehow they had made him feel exposed and uncomfortable as he had walked from his car to the building. He been glad to get inside, into the faded grandeur lit by the harsh fluorescent tube lighting; that strange juxtaposition so customary in British university buildings. He had wandered along the shabby corridors, trying to remember where her room was. *Ah yes, it was past the shared bathroom and through the common room with the cracked window.*

A few students had been in there, huddled round the old TV on typically threadbare armchairs, while the eerie strains of the *Twin Peaks* theme wailed around them. The melancholy sound had followed him up the corridor, gradually growing fainter, until a heavy fire door of chipped gloss paint and wired safety glass had sprung shut and abruptly cut it off. He had sauntered, with an attempt at nonchalance, up the next dingy corridor, feebly lit by an annoying flickering florescent tube, until he recognised the door. It had her name, written with a flourish, and a very sentimental picture of a kitten stuck on the front.

There he had hesitated, grasping the flowers and bottle tightly, feeling unaccountably uneasy, and then, with irritated decisiveness, had knocked firmly.

He was taken aback when Robert himself answered. *What the hell was he doing here?*

"Oh, hi, Adam . . . " He shifted his feet uncomfortably.

"Who's there?" Regan called cheerfully from behind him.

"Uh, it's just Adam."

Robert's voice sounded strained and oddly high with a kind of forced casualness.

Adam was flummoxed and didn't know whether to go in or not. A delicious smell of home cooking wafted out from the nearby communal kitchen.

Then Regan came to the door in an apron, oven gloves in hand. She was looking very pretty. Her cheeks were flushed, her eyes sparkling with welcome.

"Hey Adam!" she beamed, "So good to see you! Come on in. You're just in time for dinner. I was just going to check on it."

He moved aside uncertainly to let her out and then walked hesitantly into the room, having to brush past Robert to do so.

"I'll just check the casserole then come back to pour some drinks," she called over her shoulder.

The two men stood awkwardly in the sparsely furnished room, not meeting each other's gaze.

Regan seemed entirely unperturbed, reappearing shortly with three glasses, laying cutlery for three on the small, scratched table, making the odd comment now and again in a cheerful voice.

"How are you, Adam?" ventured Robert eventually.

"I'm ok, thanks. How are you?" He looked up and met his eyes suddenly. "And how is Zoe?"

Robert shifted his gaze and mumbled, "Oh, she's fine. Just away for a few days . . . "

Regan smiled at them both and invited them to sit down. She had brought in a delicious looking dish from the kitchen and laid it on a mat in the middle of the table, bustling round in a most homely manner. Adam found he was still wearing his coat and holding the bottle of wine and bouquet of lilies. The air was heavy and oppressive with their scent. He laid them down on the bed and put the bottle on the table.

"Aw, thanks, Adam, that's perfect! Such beautiful flowers, what a divine smell! And the wine will go just right with the food. It's almost as if you knew."

"I'll just visit the bathroom, Regan, before we eat, if that's ok," said Robert and disappeared purposefully down the corridor.

He seems to know his way around very well! thought Adam and then said so out loud.

"He does!" replied Regan, with an air of puzzlement. "Why shouldn't he?"

"Oh well, only because he's already with someone else and I suppose I expected to find you alone . . . "

"And why should you expect that?"

He realized there was absolutely no reason at all. In fact quite the opposite. She had been brutally honest with him before. None of it meant a thing. None of it mattered. And yet he felt a furious wave of anger boiling up inside himself. Anger towards her, anger towards Robert, anger towards himself.

Strange. Why was this bothering him? It never had before. Why was he bothered about her? It would have seemed the perfect arrangement before everything had been turned upside down, almost too good to be true. An entirely open relationship, with no strings attached. A purely physical transaction with no emotional inconvenience. But now it was driven home to him what it meant when only the body was on offer, that fragile shell, and despite his own body's need, his soul quailed. Alongside his thwarted

111

desire and pride and his unexpected anger, he felt a ridiculous, almost fatherly impulse to protect her. From what? Or perhaps, rather, a desire to shake her until he had awakened that close-cloistered soul, or drawn it back from its remote ascetic pillar.

What was he thinking? She had no need of him. This sister of mercy was beyond anything he or Robert could do, for good or ill, in a league apart, her arms and heart so warm, her soul so aloof and unreachable, in a self-imposed exile beyond an impassable arctic wasteland.

An image of her as a two-faced Janus rose like a spectre in his mind— one countenance, brutal and unflinching, looking squarely inwards towards herself, straight into the eye of the dark abyss; the other of generosity and warmth and kindness gazing outwards into the world, keen to alleviate suffering, to soften the sting. A kind of martyr to the cosmic emptiness. And yet the generosity suddenly felt perverse and obscene, like the nauseating sweetness of the lilies. It was like everything and nothing, life and death, being offered in the same draught. He would not drink this cup.

He put his arm around her and gave her a quick kiss on the cheek. She stared at him.

"I'm sorry, I have to leave . . . " he muttered in a strangled voice. "Say goodbye to Robert for me."

He turned quickly and strode off down the corridor and eventually out through the main door into the cold night air. He breathed in its freshness in great gulps of relief. He would never go back.

Privation

And so, rejecting the Manichees and refuting
Their great master, the famed Faustus,
Augustine moves at last to Rome,
And finds a little light to lead him on the way
In the monism of the Neoplatonists
And their divine triad: the One, Mind and Soul,
The most real of beings, the most non-bodily
(for still he struggles with the flesh)
And most good, from whom all being emanates;
And at the far end of this thread,
Where light and goodness and being expire
And are utterly spent, lies its extremity, its antithesis,
And there is left but darkness, nothingness, evil;
An utter lack of being and good;
A great absence of all that makes for life.

Thus evil can be rightly said to be
The absence of being, a lack and deficiency,
With no true existence of itself but rather
A yawning hole, a great void, spoiling what is,
But with no independent substance of its own;
A great and terrible nothingness,
A scar, a tear, a blemish in the fabric of reality,
A black hole that would seek to suck our spirit
And the human marrow from our bones, wither life,
Extinguish light, and empty words of meaning.

*   *   *

As he translated these lines feverishly in the cold and dark of that ruined
evening, Adam felt he was at last beginning to grasp something of the

darkness that lay at the extremity of creativity and goodness. He had driven straight from Shincliffe Hall to his office with determination and resolve. *It's not yet the end of her story; it's not yet the end of mine*, he had consoled himself as he had sped through the sharp night. Collecting together his papers and arranging them in the right order he turned back to the troublesome manuscript. Through the merest glimmer that was beginning to rise in his own life he was paradoxically more aware, more able to begin to fathom and face the darkness, the void, the absence of all goodness. There could, however, surely, be no darkness without light? He feared both darkness and light. But the fear of the light was a better fear, a primal fear. He couldn't really explain it, but he knew it in his heart. Everything in him recoiled from the horror of that empty darkness and compelled him desperately to override his natural reluctance and to reach out towards the thread of light.

The rising

And then, according to God's gracious providence,
Augustine, full of these new thoughts is introduced
To the eminent Ambrose, the admired bishop of Milan,
Who, along with many ancient men, is also attracted
To this movement of mind, despite its pagan premise,
This perception that seems to speak sensibly
Of a reality "not of this world".
Ambrose thus believed some biblical stories
Should be seen symbolically, and offered Augustine
The possibility of more sophisticated application,
Alluring allegory, infinitely more refined, it seemed to him,
Than the naive doctrines of his native North Africa,
Giving his childhood Christianity
A new appeal in Augustine's eyes, reconciling
His affinity with the Neoplatonic, appearing compatible
With Plotinus' philosophy. And so, armed
Paradoxically with the artillery of the pagan world,
He is at last persuaded of the intellectual superiority
And sanctity of the saving doctrines of Christ,
For only there can be found the wonderful truths
Of incarnation and atonement; the identifying empathy
Of God with man and the cleansing
For his infirmities and salvation from sin.

And so, as Cicero had first directed Augustine's eyes
Toward the divine—like as to Romulus and Remus
Raised by Lupa, the tender she-wolf—the pagan Neoplatonists
Even nourished and nurtured their foster son
In his growing knowledge of the one true Word of God.

As reason reaches its limits, revelation and faith must flourish
To enable that final step across the unknown frontier.
Biscop's voice rises as he reaches
The climax of his great narrative
And Alwin is equally eager to hear its end.

Thus Augustine's long and unlikely journey,
From Cicero, to Mani, to Plotinus—
Concludes the good bishop triumphantly—
Converges finally on Christ and the book of books;
From moral incontinence to the climax of conversion;
Not a rejection of the physical but an embracing
Of all the fullness of reality,
Body and soul, matter and mind.
And his own journey to peace and life—
As a mirror image writ-small of the great story
Of paradise lost and regained, redeemed
By the second, perfect Adam—would end as it began,
And where all mankind begins and ends,
Beneath a tree in a garden; the forbidden fruit
Of the knowledge of the evil and the good
Supplanted by the sweet and wholesome
Word of Truth. And Tolle lege, "take and read",
Whispered to his despairing soul as he lamented
His desperate state and captivity to sin,
The Spirit of God hovering over the deeps of his heart,
Imploring him, offering the food that is life indeed,
The Word made flesh; bread of heaven to the human race
And the blood that is the richest wine.
As he received this life-giving draught of grace,
The darkness of doubt was dispelled at last
And the sun of righteousness rose in his heart
With healing in His wings.

*   *   *

Adam had worked frenetically through the long night and into the pale watercolour dawn of the following day. He found himself envying Augustine's sudden and brilliant sunrise, unmistakable, free from doubt. But he had had a hell of a journey to get there, he had to admit. Not months but years of soul-sorrow and seeking.

He did sense his own feet may well now be approaching that well-trod path too, that narrow and winding way that so many, and yet paradoxically so few, tread and have trod through the winding roads of history. He had always wanted to forge his own path, be the captain of his own soul and destiny. What absurd presumption. What dangerous folly. He could at least see that now. That way lay nothing but emptiness and despair.

But how could he be sure this was the right path? The light was still so dim. He could hardly see to place one foot in front of another. But perhaps there on his horizon was just the merest hint of a paler band of grey? Maybe the thinnest line of dawn was just beginning to rise in the east?

Magi

"Will you have lunch with me?" he asked tentatively as Lucy put down a large file on his desk. He must try again. "There's something I wanted to show you in the Oriental Museum. I stumbled across it the other day. It's made me think. There's a cafe in there, not much, just sandwiches and stuff, but hopefully they've mended the coffee machine by now!"

Lucy looked at him with momentary indecision.

"Why not!" she suddenly smiled.

It could hardly do any harm and it would be good to try to clear the air between them. She had felt uncomfortable around him after their argument the other day, her strangely haunting dream and the embarrassing breakfast encounter.

"Actually, there's an exhibition in there I wanted to see. I saw it advertised in the university newsletter; it's about the Wise Men."

Adam attempted to twist his grimace into a convincing smile. He was doomed to see the wretched thing.

"Great! Let's head over now then, shall we? It's already 12.30."

They sauntered along in the pale winter light, through the pervasive whiteness, or rather lack of colour. It was as if the universe had taken a long breath in, sucking out all the marrow and goodness from the world and everything was hovering on the brink, waiting for the eventual exhalation of new life. The trees were completely bare and, in the shadows, where the sun never reached, there was still frost clinging to the edges of each blade of grass.

Their breath hung in the air in silver clouds like their awkwardness.

"What are you doing for Christmas?" asked Adam eventually, chiefly for something to say.

"Oh, I'll be at home as usual with the whole tribe," laughed Lucy nervously. "I don't know how we all fit into mam and dad's house, but we manage it somehow!"

"How many of you are there?" he enquired, finding himself, to his surprise, genuinely interested. His awkwardness was ebbing away, and she felt her own evaporating too. He was easy to talk to.

"Well, I'm the eldest, then there's our Tom, Jess, Rachel and lastly Daniel; quite a crowd, particularly with Tom's wife Jane and kids in tow too and various other halves. What about you?"

Immediately the last words had left her mouth she could have bitten her tongue. How insensitive in the light of his current situation. Her awkwardness and confusion engulfed her again.

"I'm sorry," she muttered, "I should have been more sensitive."

"Don't worry about it," he replied wearily, "it's not your fault. I asked you first. And to answer your question, I don't really know. I'll get by somehow. I'm certainly not going to go in for those ghastly emotive arguments about who gets the kids which days and hours. Cynthia can have what she wants. She always gets it anyway."

He knew immediately that this was neither fair nor true, which made him perversely feel more bitter towards her and more irritated with the world in general. He kicked a discarded Coke can out of his path. Making a big effort he wrenched himself out of his juvenile pit of self-pity and turned towards her again.

"But tell me more about what you get up to. Sounds exhausting!"

She smiled uncertainly.

"Well, we meet up at the chapel for the service first and then after that we all go back to mam and dad's and help get the lunch sorted, which seems to take an age, and then have dinner, and then clear up, which also takes an age, and then have to rush the last bit of washing up to watch the Queen's Speech while we're having a cuppa, and then quickly have a walk round the block because it's getting dark, and it all takes a complete age and my poor niece and nephew are getting increasingly desperate to get to the present opening! Then finally we sit round the tree and they get to start. It's all part of the fun really, the tradition, but I remember how when I was little, I always felt we'd never get to the presents!"

He found he was unconsciously smiling at her. A real smile. There was something in her face and soft lyrical accent that reminded him of how his children had looked and sounded during those first Christmases, when it was still pure.

His smile revived her, like sunshine after a grey and cloudy dawn. They turned down the side street and towards the museum.

The coffee machine had not been mended. It irked but did not surprise Adam that Lucy insisted on paying for her own limp sandwiches and dry scones. Afterwards they moved across to the exhibition that she had wanted to see, and he had not.

Adam found it surprisingly interesting, despite himself. The theory that these shadowy mysterious figures might have been Zoroastrians was compelling and appealed to his imagination, helping to dispel the primary school nativity play image of three kings with paper crowns (which could apparently be blamed on the later Roman tradition). Instead, it was suggested, they were likely to have been astronomers, philosophers and priests. Some traditions had it that they were from Arabia, Persia and India respectively, although of course, as the information boards pointed out, the number of persons is not actually specified in the Gospel, only the number of gifts. The theory that they may have originated from the same area in Mesopotamia as the Old Testament prophet Balaam also fascinated him, which might explain how they supposedly knew of the ancient prophecy:

> I see him, but not now;
> I behold him, but not near.
> A star will come out of Jacob;
> a sceptre will rise out of Israel.

But then the effect was somewhat spoiled by the usual visual of the silhouetted, turbaned figures on camels against a desert scene and far in the distance the little town of Bethlehem and the great star hovering overhead, leading them on.

This Christmas card effect was too much for Adam. He couldn't help snorting, and turning to Lucy he asked incredulously, "You don't really believe in all this stuff?"

She looked back defiantly.

"Of course! It's all or nothing."

She had pondered on this question many times over the years as she had watched her cherished dreams one by one crumbling to dust. But still she clung to the "all", returning to it after every futile dead-end detour, sad, weary but thankful, like a petulant toddler, relieved to at last return to the parental embrace. The "nothing" was quite literally unthinkable, and certainly unliveable.

"Nothing else makes sense of what I see in the world and in myself. Nothing else fits with the stark realities. And anyway," with a sudden smile, "it's a wonderful story: the ultimate journey and quest. I love stories of quest and adventure and discovery, don't you? And these adventurers discovered the most important, beautiful treasure of all."

"So now we move to baby worship!" he scoffed, although also with a smile.

He did love the great sagas and epic journeys of antiquity and the medieval quest literature, and was secretly pleased at her admission. He was enjoying the journeying aspect of Alwin and Biscop's journey, and those parts felt more accessible to his mind and imagination than the long, sometimes hopelessly alien theological discussions on the nature of art and idolatry, truth, beauty and love. He had always been drawn to accounts of quests, even if not, until now, pilgrimage. Reading *Sir Gawain and the Green Knight* was one of the few things that made Christmas time tolerable. It was his own private tradition. He would always make time over the holiday period, ideally when Cynthia and the kids were out of the house shopping, to sit down with the original text in front of a blazing log fire, with a large glass of single malt, and read it from beginning to end, losing himself for a few hours in the wintry landscape of the old Northern world. In his imagination he traversed the great swathes of bleak, icy plain and ivy- and holly-festooned forests, while under a snowy moon the ambiguous lady waited in her splendid castle. And at the end, the fearsome challenge of the Green Knight in his eerie enchanted chapel at the crossroads between realities, and the remnants of integrity clawed back from ruin.

His mind was pulled back abruptly to those other travellers from the East or, as the original text poetically put it, *"from the rising . . . "*

"Not baby worship, God worship!" she was saying with a laugh. "Although at this point, God also happens to be a baby."

And then seriously, "Although he was born to die, not to stay a cute baby in the manger. There is no Christmas without Easter, and no Easter without Christmas. The myrrh was laid by the manger along with the frankincense and gold."

"I suppose he had a long journey to travel too, but of a spiritual more than a geographical kind, from cradle, or manger, to cross and grave," Adam murmured.

"The longest and hardest journey ever travelled by a human being," replied Lucy quietly. "And the last stage, up to Jerusalem and the betrayal and trial and crucifixion, the most lonely, bitter journey in the world."

Adam was quiet for a moment. Loneliness. Betrayal. He knew about that. He had never considered the human feelings of Christ before in this way. The idea of trying to empathize with the divine seemed a strange one. It was usually his condescending empathy with us, in assuming flesh, that was emphasized in any Christmas service he had ever attended.

He looked again at the image, the ever-travelling Magi, fixed in our minds as a symbol of the human quest for truth and wisdom and meaning.

"I think perhaps we are both restless spirits too, you and I," he said softly, turning to face her. "We both desire to know more and more. But somehow, I don't know, you seem to know where you are going, like the Magi, with a star to guide. I feel so lost. I always believed that the journey was more important than the destination. I am no longer sure, no longer sure about anything other than that I need a star too. You seem to me like a star that has risen in my life, when the rest of my world went dark. I don't want to pressure you, I'm sorry I'm being such a nuisance to you, I just can't help myself wanting to seek you out, to be near you. It helps me feel a little less alone in this appalling, dreary world. Can you put up with me being around sometimes?"

She smiled tentatively, unsure how to respond, then noncommittally, "I'm sure some of the time will be fine!" And then quickly, "Come on, show me the thing you mentioned before, you know, the thing that you said made you think."

He led her down the stairs and pointed to the beautiful, broken ceramics. When it came to it, he felt suddenly shy trying to explain the feelings that had before passed through him as swiftly and unerringly as an arrow from an expert archer. His sensations were also, unusually for him, quite difficult to articulate coherently now.

Her mind was still coloured by the Magi's journey, and she was looking at the exotic objects against that backdrop. Did she sense the essence of what he was trying to communicate?

"Gold, frankincense and myrrh," she was murmuring. "All human flesh is like clay, even his, to be smashed and fractured. But the resurrection, the new creation, makes it even more glorious than before it was broken; the glorified wounds of king and priest and sacrifice . . . "

"Come on, Kintsukuroi! This isn't even Christian; this is Japanese '*wabi-sabi*, an embracing of the flawed or imperfect, derived from Buddhism', can't you read the card?" he snapped irritably.

"All truth is God's truth," she replied evenly, looking him steadily in the eye, "so why should we be surprised to find strands of it everywhere?" Then with defiance, "I'm not afraid of you!"

But for all that there was fear. Fear of what? She hardly knew.

"Well, you said you were the other day, and maybe you should be!" Adam replied drily, but what he was thinking was, *No, but I'm afraid of you. I'm afraid of myself. Perhaps I'm afraid of truth . . .*

She had such confidence, such conviction. Her priorities and preoccupations were so different and the ways she saw things, the connections she made, what she found to be significant. He knew he was primarily concerned with himself; she was speaking of another. His journeying turned always inward; her eyes were focused without, towards that elusive point of light in the dark sky. She was preoccupied with the eternal, he with the finite. He felt frustrated. Why this constant rush to the transcendent? Jesus didn't need her sympathy! He had the rest of the world. Could He not spare him one single human soul? Must he always have a rival for her attention? Had she even understood him? Had he understood her? Or were they two minds speaking different languages and missing each other in the dark? Was it even possible to understand another being, or even oneself? What after all was man, this little handful of dust?

Even so, he must keep trying. He had no choice, he felt compelled to travel onwards. Onwards and onwards with no respite and no rest. But at that moment he felt he would rather follow her relentlessly through this new darkness than follow anyone else through the old, ordinary light of day.

The book of memory and dreams

What are we but a composite of memories and dreams
Embodied in dust? As age and youth combine
And walk and talk a while upon the road together,
We witness a picture of man
And his pilgrimage through this passing life;
Biscop, old and full of wisdom born of years,
With many more steps behind than before,
Alwin, young and full of hopes and fears,
With many miles left still to tread,
And yet for a time their ways converge,
And their purposes and pursuits are one.

They continue their companionable conversation
On great Augustine's Confessions, moving
From his conversion into this monumental theme:
The very nature and identity of man.
Augustine, Biscop explains, envisages the inner being
As analogous to the Trinity itself,
An internal triad of memory, intellect and will:
Memory the very root of being,
Compared to God the Father;
Intellect, the seat of logic and reason,
To God the Son, the great Logos;
Will, source of desires and affections,
To the Holy Spirit.
And if mankind is made in the image of his Maker,
Although this is a mighty marvel, might not, he muses,
This meditation on the nature of man enables us to grasp
Something of both the nobility of our own nature
And the mystery of the divine
But also cause our hearts to mourn the more

At our great and tragic fall from grace?

And yet though like in these many marvellous ways,
So are we also unlike our great and heavenly Maker
For it is our lot to be bound in time,
While He inhabits eternity.
Our memories are but the fragile bindings
Of our little lives upon this earth,
Our small accruements of experience
And perhaps some scant wisdom,
With a hazy beginning and, to us, an unknown end;
His is a repository of all knowing and all truth,
Of all that is, was and ever will be,
Without beginning or end,
Authoring or ending of days: infinite, eternal;
We the finite things of dust,
He the source and perfection
Of all light, being and grace, the genesis of good.
And thus, He that inhabits eternity
Brings time itself into being,
The little stories of our lives progressing
As we travel through His abundant creation,
Exuberant organic explosion,
Begotten of His eternal love;
His out-flowing of all existent things,
And all that He makes He pronounces very good,
The epitome and essence of excellence.
Man in his folly and pride may seek
To call good evil and evil good,
Infected as he is in every part of his person
By persistent, pernicious sin,
But God alone can create substance from nothing
And pronounce it very good,
Bringing forth abundant matter from the formless void.

Our small creations are but the workings of our human hands
With such material as He permits and provides,
And meaningful only as measured against His perfection.

The garden of the Lord

It was ceasing to surprise Adam that whatever questions arose in his own unquiet heart should also be simultaneously raised by Alwin, or his poet. As he sat at the library desk in the soft lamplight during the next dreary afternoon, he reflected on his new, strange existence. One foot in the vivid past, one in this terrifying new present, the strands of story were becoming ever more closely bound, quickening one another, sparking like two live wires. It now seemed the ordinary pattern of things. Something to be expected and anticipated. *Was this strange? Was there something wrong in his head?*

Perhaps it was not so very strange after all, when one considered properly . . . It was hardly surprising that he should be influenced by what he read, following the line of reasoning and revelation, and then recreating it in his own words. Encounters with extraordinary writings could change lives, that much he had already conceded to Augustine. And if so, those words must have real meaning, real transformational power.

Even when not translating, hadn't he always found that being immersed in a book, another's creation, had pervasively seeped into his own mind and coloured his own perceptions, finding sometimes that he was even thinking in the author's words and figures of speech? It was a common experience, he supposed, for all who love to read and be transported in their imagination into the real or imagined world of another and see things through their eyes. People writing of their own lives, as they perceive them, is always powerful, but perhaps fiction is the most powerful way of all to communicate with another person, he reflected, for paradoxically it enables the reader to see what that person perceives to be the very core of reality. It is always a kind of allegory or picture. We are invited by the writer to enter into their creation, their story, and so in a way, even into their mind. It is in the stories we tell, the images we use, that we say the most about ourselves, as individuals and societies.

Was it the same with God? he wondered. We walk in His garden and experience the work of His hands in all the beauty around us, encounter other divine image-bearers, other human beings, who in turn create their own stories and works of art, discoveries and inventions, out of the raw materials He has provided. For a moment Adam had an absurd picture in his mind of small children in a nursery school making things from brightly coloured playdough. But of course, it was so much bigger and more glorious, if Augustine and Alwin and Biscop and Lucy were right. If it was actually true, it was mind-blowing. But it was also terrifying. Terrifying to think of all of those inert potent raw materials, all of those brilliant nascent human minds waiting, simmering in the shadows, ready to erupt into fantastic being when the gestation was complete and the time was ripe. All that latent creative and destructive power hovering in the wings of history. What wonders of beauty might yet be made manifest? But, if human beings could create the atom bomb, what other powers and horrors were yet to be unleashed? Just because we can create does not mean that we will create what is good. *How easily*, he thought gloomily, *we can turn creativity into destruction.* He could see that in his own life. *If left to ourselves, how skilled we are at creating our own little hells.*

Beatitude

For it is from the fullness and abundance of His goodness,
Not His need, nor its right, that God's whole creation subsists.
And not only did He simply make, but He also made it good
By causing His wondrous works to turn
Towards Himself, their Maker,
That His own brightness may be cast upon them
And they might be bathed in blessed light.
For to be, is not the same as to be beautiful,
Nor to live, the same as living wisely.
So, for the human spirit likewise, we must cling to Him
And live ever closer to the fountain of life.
Once we were all darkness because we had turned away
And hid our faces from Him, our holy light,
And in the remnants of gloom we groan and labour
Until we are redeemed by the glorious Living Word.
Only He can never change,
Because He alone is absolute simplicity,
For whom to live is to live in blessed happiness,
For He is His own beatitude.

*   *   *

Simplicity
Light
Beatitude

Adam lingered long as he formed these wonderful but unfathomable words. They brimmed with a mysterious hope.

Could they really converge on a person, on a personal God who could know and be known? If so, how wonderful and how terrifying.

Christmas

He couldn't tell what had finally wakened him, dragged him unwillingly from the respite of oblivion. Was it the acid light sliding in under the curtains, the insidious smell of coffee creeping through the chinks in the polished boards from the flat below or had there been a noise? He listened intently for a moment; eyes closed. Yes, strains of that bright, ruthless music beloved of early morning radio presenters, were piercing through the floorboards with particularly repellent festive jocundity, along with the more pleasant coffee aroma—but was that also the sound of footsteps quietly retreating? He flung back the sheet, snatching around for a pair of shorts which he dragged on as he groped towards the door, cursing the empty whisky bottle that had impeded his path and stubbed his toe. Yes, that was the quiet click of the street door closing. He glanced around and saw at once, lying on the mat by his door, an envelope. He stooped down to pick it up and retreated back inside his flat.

Flinging himself back onto the bed, propped up on one elbow he opened the envelope. It was a Christmas card, with a scene of three exotic figures crossing a desert and the caption "*Follow the Star*". He smiled despite himself. She really knew how to wind him up! Throwing the envelope on the floor he opened it. Inside was written simply:

Adam, thinking of you today. Lucy.

He felt grateful she had not said she was praying for him, for him all alone on this day of days, grateful for her sensitivity and not rubbing his nose in it. But he knew that's what she really meant all the same, and knew she would be praying. It was a strange feeling, but he found he didn't mind; in fact it was strangely comforting. And it was immensely comforting that she cared.

He felt an odd pricking sensation in his eyes. Leaning back he lit a cigarette and slowly exhaled into the still air. Through his half-shut eyes he could see the beams of light penetrating and illuminating the wisps of smoke as they curled upwards towards the window. Somewhere, very far away, he heard bells ringing.

Sabinus

And so their winding steps bring them at length
Through Lyons, Vienne, Orange, Avignon, Arles;
All names to thrill the heart of Alwin,
So exotic and new to his Northern eyes and novice heart.
Carefully procured and amassed against their returning,
An increasing trove of treasures has been accrued.
Amongst them a magnificent gem,
Pressed into his palm by an ancient monk, who whispered,
That as it had been assigned to his care by a great King,
He now felt led to entrust it anew to Alwin,
To enrich his virtuous purposes and picture precious truths.
But also other jewels, rich wonders in words and paint,
Are gathered in; and yet more precious still,
Promises of skill and craftsmanship,
Many gifted, generous souls willing to leave home and hearth
And journey with the brothers back to wild Northumbria
When the time for their return should come;
To make and mould, bend and build, chip and carve
And create in the crucible the brilliance of that liquid light,
To fashion the glorious glass
Alwin has been commissioned to oversee.
To bring to fulfilment that gracious vision
Entrusted to him by Biscop, he has sought out
And entreated the services of one Sabinus,
A gifted glazier, who will also bring again
The skills of Gaul to new blossoming Britannia
And so, Alwin hopes, prove a double blessing
To their great endeavour. A master of his art
And good governor of men, he appears to Alwin,
And he feels strangely drawn to this man of craft,
For he discerns in eyes and countenance a depth

Wrought through trials and suffering, as well as joys,
And senses the grace of God has moved in heart and life
In a multitude of mysterious ways,
His face alive with the aura of one who has achieved,
Through love and hardship, a deep and lasting peace,
And wrestled through the waters of despair
To reach at last the welcome haven;
One who has been refined in the crucible of life,
Emerging, as his glass from the furnace,
Through fire, more beautiful and pure,
The shadows softened, the rough places smoothed,
The light radiant, the beam bathing
All those who draw near in beauty and beatitude,
For all his rough artisan's exterior,
A true son of the heavenly king,
A servant not simply to his craft, but to his calling,
An ambassador of the divine realm, bringing embassies
Of hope, peace and mercy to mankind, employing
His God-given gifting to speak grace, truth and healing
Into a broken world, which upon him has also broken,
Stealing his earthly loves as its treacherous tide retreats.
But he, bringing forth from the battering waves
His hard-won treasures, wrested from the wreck,
Holds them aloft in triumph, beauty recast
From the shattered fragments of light, made manifest
In broken rainbow shards, carefully crafted and bound
With love and lead, reconstructed piece by piece
Into a glowing mosaic of grace, taken and skilfully
Rewoven in glorious patterns of paradise and peace,
A dim picture of the golden thread that binds
All reborn life into the glorious body of our Lord,
A faint reflection of a new, a whole re-creation
Of perfect fullness and resurrection life.

New Year

A new stage of the journey for Alwin and Biscop, a new year for himself. Adam sat in his office in the cold, empty faculty building, pen in hand and mind far away. How to picture this new character Sabinus? What language would he have spoken? What would be the tenor of his voice?

No one else was here. They were with their families. It was still the holidays. But he found it helped to keep working. It helped to have a routine and sense of progression, particularly now that he had refound his thread and inspiration was flowing.

The eighteenth-century clock ticked quietly on the shelf next to his desk, chiming mournfully to mark the passing of another hour. A tenth wedding anniversary gift from Cynthia. It had not been a happy day. The extravagant celebration had gone ok, but then they had argued, in the luxury of their expensive hotel room. Inevitably, after many wounds inflicted on both sides, it had ended with her crying.

A new year. The year of our Lord nineteen-ninety-seven. Time. A time for casting off the old and embracing the new. A time for resolutions—*New year, new you!*—the trite adverts proclaimed from the rooftops. As if a new brand of shampoo or perfume, a new gadget or even a new lifestyle could really make a difference to the fundamental problems facing humankind, facing himself. No one could really believe that, could they? Then why always the same tired old meaningless message?

But even so, there were the beginnings, the slightest dawning of hope within his breast, the thread of light running along his horizon beyond the dark ocean of doubt. Was it just another phantom light, luring him to his doom? But these stirrings of a new life really did feel different. If only it was true! If only he could really believe it and grasp it and make it his own.

It felt too hard to set off alone, onwards into that grey dawn, that gloaming that was hardly brighter than twilight. *The darkest hour is just before dawn*, he comforted himself. Had he reached the darkest hour? He had been in dark places before and not even known it, and he had escaped other dark and cruel places by the skin of his teeth; even the cruel places he had fashioned himself. Were there still precipices to be walked over the abyss? To know and to look down is perhaps worse than not knowing at all. The misery of self-awareness and of facing the dark unknown across which the light beckons requires a great steeling of courage. In himself he did not feel he had the strength, the resilience. He feared his foot would slip and then down, down, beyond hope and redemption. He felt so weak, thin and somehow one-dimensional, trying to navigate this new, three-dimensional world, for which he was so ill-equipped. His humanity, through lack of use, felt shrunk to merely practical faculties and appetites. How could he become a fuller, proper human being again? Could he still remember earlier, better impulses, seared by years of neglect? If he was truly a divine image-bearer, how to begin to flesh out again that calling, to become what he should always have been, was made to be? For the first time in his adult life, he found he was praying. *If you are really there, save me from myself. Forgive me. Teach me to live. Help me to love.*

Dead white men

"So you like the company of dead white men, do you?"

Adam, wandering, unnoticed and uninvited, into her office one lunchtime, plucked the book from Lucy's hand as she sat reading while eating her sandwiches, and glanced at the cover. She gave a little gasp, having been engrossed.

"You are bucking the trend then!"

"Well sometimes they are preferable to the company of live ones!" she retorted, with some irritation attempting to snatch it back. "And for your information I have no interest in whether they are white or black, male or female, or even alive or dead for that matter, if they have something to say and know how to say it. Give me back my book!"

"Good answer! So, you are quite a reader?"

He grinned at her and held it provocatively just out of reach as he flicked through the dog-eared pages.

"*Brideshead Revisited*! I remember reading this first when I was an undergrad. Loved it."

He looked more thoughtful. "So full of passion and poignancy . . . "

Their eyes met for a moment, and she looked away, embarrassed.

"And then there was that wonderful TV series in the eighties," he continued. "Did you ever see it? I can still remember the theme tune!"

"No, we didn't have a telly then, and I'd have been a bit young!"

He laughed.

"Oh yes, of course!"

"And anyway, I don't know if mam and dad would have liked it."

He eyed her with interest. Her family held a strange fascination for him. He found them hard to imagine.

"No, perhaps not. Do *you* like it—the book I mean?"

She pondered a little.

"I like the characters. They are so complex and interesting. I find the world they live in hard to envisage, but it's kind of intriguing, appealing. It feels sort of sad and beautiful at the same time. I can't really explain it—a bit like autumn, if you know what I mean? But what I really like is how God is just a natural part of the story. The spiritual reality is just part and parcel of the whole thing. He's just there in all the mess and heartache. That's unusual I think, well unusual in a fairly modern book."

"Yes," he mused, "yes, you're right! That's very interesting. I don't think I'd really thought about it before, but you're right. I wonder why that is. When did God, or even the concept of a 'higher power', as a true protagonist, or at least as a back-stage member of the cast, drop out of our literature? And why? He's there centre-square in all of my medieval stuff, even when there are quite ungodly goings-on!"

"I suppose because most people stopped believing in Him," she replied quietly. "I think the First World War probably had a lot to do with it. And of course, you can understand why, but the seeds go deeper and further back, I'm sure."

"You're right, though," he replied with interest, "the twentieth century hasn't been a good time for God in literature. It's not been a good century for mankind either for that matter. Perhaps that's why I have tended to avoid the Moderns. Too raw." *Although evasion is futile*, he thought to himself, *for even the ancient words are hunting me.* What he said out loud was, "Undoubtedly the First World War was the most appalling human catastrophe of the millennium; everything, everything unravelled and fell apart. I mean, if one were to think about it too much it would be completely devastating, paralysing. It would drive one mad. And perhaps it has to some extent, perhaps it's driven a century of literature that's become ever more inward looking and neurotic, at least a lot of it has—with some notable exceptions of course—but perhaps the more people look inside themselves for answers the less they notice the big picture (if there is one) and then perhaps they stop asking the really big questions. And I suppose God is a natural casualty. And yet in many ways *Brideshead* is exactly that, full of that introspective madness and the banality of war, but somehow it's different too—through it all, there is always that small, inextinguishable flame, flickering in the darkness, even though it's not clear what it signifies. There's a rare honesty about the human mess, but without absolutely losing hope."

137

He settled himself down in the chair opposite her, put the book down on the table, losing her place in the process, stretched out his legs and lit a cigarette.

"Oh, you don't mind me smoking, do you?"

It was clearly a rhetorical question.

"It's a bit late now if I do, isn't it!" she replied indignantly. "Well, I am going to at least open the window, however cold it is."

He took a meditative draught and slowly blew the smoke out, not really paying attention to what she had said, too busy pondering this interesting question.

She looked at him in exasperation, sighed and put her half-eaten sandwich back in her lunchbox. It *was* an interesting conversation.

" . . . a strange combination of despair, self-sufficiency, narcissism . . . " he was continuing, with a frown on his face.

" . . . I mean in a lot of twentieth century stuff, often very thought-provoking though, insightful in a way. But mostly very inward looking."

He looked across the littered desk at her, with a ghost of a smile.

"So what do you think? What's your theory?"

"Oh! I don't think I have a theory!" She felt rather put on the spot. She had been expecting to have a quiet half hour of escape to herself, not having to suddenly come up with a theory of twentieth-century literature! "I don't know enough about it all. Mainly I have just read the classic nineteenth-century novels, but I decided to give *Brideshead* a go, and it's interesting and quite different. But mainly I suppose I've read more poetry. And I did notice God 'dropping out of literature' as you put it, in some nineteenth-century poetry."

He raised his eyebrows, and said, slightly more sardonically than he intended, "An expert on poetry too! You are a bit of a dark horse, aren't you!"

"Of course I'm not an expert!" she snapped rather savagely. "But I like it, like reading, why shouldn't I? Why else do you think I've ended up working here?" There was a hard edge in her voice. "It's hardly for the wonderful pay!"

She looked as if she was going to say something else and then stopped herself. Her face went a slightly darker shade of pink and he couldn't tell if she was tearful or angry or both. It rather perplexed him, and he carried on more gently.

"What poetry do you like? What are you reading at the moment?"

She looked at him with a touch of resentment but carried on, gradually warming to her subject despite herself.

"Well, of course I love Shakespeare and Milton, did them at school. And I recently discovered Spenser. It's hard going, but I am enjoying it. I love the beautiful sound of Shelley and Keats and that lot. Not always sure about *what* they say, mind, but I love the, the musical way they say it and the images it creates in my mind. I love Christina Rossetti, feel I can really, kind of connect with her . . . "

She stopped abruptly and coloured, feeling suddenly shy and exposed.

"Go on!" He ground out his cigarette on the metal leg of her desk and threw it into the bin.

She glowered at him, but he didn't seem to notice.

"Why *do* you smoke?" she asked with sudden irritation. "Don't you know it's really bad for you? And for other people?"

"Eh?" He looked at her vaguely. "Oh, I rather suppose it's not as bad for me, or other people for that matter, as many of the other things I do . . . Anyway, back to poetry. What was the last poem you read?"

Somewhat grudgingly she carried on. She felt as if she was being both disregarded and interrogated, and both made her feel small.

"Well, I read *Dover Beach*, you know, by Matthew Arnold the other day in my anthology, and it made me feel so . . . sad. He talks of bringing "*the eternal note of sadness in*" and he really does, right back then, before the world wars and everything, almost like he was foreseeing something, more than that, almost as if he was willing it, that disillusionment, kind of perverse, and kind of superior, but almost . . . almost self-indulgent, determined to be bleak, like a teenager determined not to believe in their happy childhood—thinking they are too grown up to see goodness!"

"Not everyone has had a happy childhood!" he interjected. "But I think I know what you mean—you're using it as an analogy for Western society? And really, one could argue that the trend can be traced from even further back. Look at the so-called 'Enlightenment' when people became too clever to believe—what did that actually lead to in reality but bloodshed and brutality and disenchantment?" *The irony of it!* he thought. *I used to think myself such an Enlightenment man and look where it has led me—down a dark alley with a knife in my back!*

He smiled rather sourly to himself. She glanced at him inquiringly. "Perhaps what we see in the twentieth century," he continued, after a pause, "is the inevitable harvest of the eighteenth. I mean, when one thinks about it, God does seem to be beginning to drop out with Enlightenment rationality, as if He is no longer needed, as people have figured things out so nicely for themselves now, thank you very much, with their neat and tidy philosophies and sciences and systems. The brave new world of materialism and rationalism, education and sanitation, unfettered by superstition, was going to make everything wonderful. Didn't quite work out like that though, did it? Then those idealistic nineteenth-century Marxists, and the real-world horrors of Communism, and Fascism for that matter, sprang up in opposition, that ravaged the twentieth century, along with the wars and devastations. Seeds sown in false optimism, reaped in despair. Perhaps those eighteenth-century worthies in their powdered wigs should have paid more attention to Hamlet's comment to Horatio before opening Pandora's box! I believe I teased you with that quotation too, when we talked first about the window. Too many things in this world, I'm discovering, that don't fit neatly into tidy doctrines or dogmas. Too many gaps and mysteries . . . And then there is human nature to contend with. We don't fit neatly into boxes either, do we?" He brushed some ash from his trousers onto the floor. "But, to return to your point—I agree. It seems to me that literature often *does* prefigure or foreshadow history, possibly even directing its course to some extent. Or, to put it another way, I think that trends of thought are often first seen in fiction before they become fact. In so many ways I believe fiction, great fiction, or let's simply call it Art, is more powerful than fact, and even in a sense seems to have the capacity to create its own truth. I have been thinking about this a lot lately. Perhaps it is because good art always touches on the deep things of our humanity. I mean, think about it; the England of Shakespeare's Histories has never really existed—except in our minds. 'This Sceptred Isle'! But we love it just the same. And it has actually, to some extent, made us who we are; perhaps genuinely ennobled some as a result, made them better people even. We become the stories we tell. We can't help it. But of course it can work both ways—for good and bad."

She frowned, interested, and frustrated that her own thinking often felt so woolly. Words created strong feelings in her and half-formed images and ideas that she felt she was trying to grasp hold of, to explain and understand. But they were often elusive. She tried to grapple with this newly articulated idea.

"Yes, maybe. So it's really important that we tell the right story . . . "

"If we can work out what it is!" he interjected.

"Well, this poem doesn't seem a good place to start for that! I suppose I feel, in this poem I mean, there is a kind of . . . a kind of rebelling against peace and meaning. The story it tells is of lost faith, as if it's as inevitable as growing up. Almost an embracing of the idea of despair as if it's the same as maturity, which maybe actually generates a real sense of despair. Oh, it is an awful poem, devastating, but still kind of beautiful. Why is that? Maybe because it's partly true? It kind of strikes a chord but is also jarring. A bit like a beautiful chord of music but sort of . . . a bit off key."

"Both resonant and dissonant you mean? Yes, maybe it is."

> *The Sea of Faith*
> *Was once, too, at the full, and round earth's shore*
> *Lay like the folds of a bright girdle furled.*
> *But now I only hear*
> *Its melancholy, long, withdrawing roar,*
> *Retreating, to the breath*
> *Of the night-wind, down the vast edges drear*
> *And naked shingles of the world.*

He quoted from memory, looking at her intently, in a way that made her look away.

Ah, love, let us be true
To one another! for the world, which seems
To lie before us like a land of dreams,
So various, so beautiful, so new,
Hath really neither joy, nor love, nor light,
Nor certitude, nor peace, nor help for pain . . .

"But I don't believe it!" she said, interrupting with sudden vehemence.

He looked at her in surprise. "Oh?"

"Well, I mean the first bit is true in a way. The 'sea of faith' has retreated. That's what we're saying, isn't it? But whose fault is that?"

"I don't know."

"It's people, isn't it, who either believe, or do not believe? God's existence is not dependent on *our* faith. Truth, reality I mean, it remains the same, whether we choose to believe in it or not."

"Does it? Some would say not."

"Well, they are wrong! I know they are wrong, and that last bit of the poem is wrong! It's . . . it's a lie—a clever, beautiful sounding lie."

He was looking at her in fascination. He didn't usually have conversations like this about literature, where the other person was fully emotionally invested and involved. It was refreshing and somehow endearing. It was as if she herself had somehow, in a world of jaded cynicism, retained the childlike sense that everything really mattered.

"How do you know?"

"In here!" She involuntarily put her hand to her heart. "And in my head! It doesn't fit with the . . . the reality I see around me every day, of what the world is, what people are really like."

"People can be real arseholes and the world can be pretty shit. You of all people should know that!"

She shot him a frown.

"Yes! But the point is, they aren't always, all the time! And the world is so beautiful, as well as so full of pain. That's what makes the poem so . . . so one-sided! It makes even its own beauty really maddening and . . . and perverse. Things are never simple black and white! That's a lazy way of looking at things. It's always so much more complicated. People do awful things, evil, wicked things, but they do amazing things, wonderful things too, sometimes even the same people, even when it really costs them to do it, sometimes even their lives! That doesn't make sense if things are as bleak and meaningless and hopeless as he tries to make out."

"You know, you might enjoy Graham Greene," he said, lighting another cigarette meditatively. "Well, maybe not enjoy, find interesting. He is another more modern one who has God as a kind of unseen protagonist in much of his work. Talking now has reminded me of him—he only died a few years ago. I read an interesting piece on him in the papers at the time—and it's unexpected, because you think you're reading a gritty, modernist thriller. It's certainly not anachronistic or sentimental. In a way his stuff is pretty bleak too, but there's always more, another level, so you're left feeling it's not ultimately meaningless, although it's not always clear what that meaning is, at least it wasn't to me."

He knocked a bit of ash into an empty mug.

"I hate to have to say it, but, in most cases, thinking about it—with the notable exception of Lewis of course—it seems the Catholics have done a better job of keeping God alive in literature and art than you Protestants!"

He smiled at her, and she looked thoughtful.

"I think perhaps," she said slowly, "that when it comes to art we are more worried about images, and even with words, particularly when it's creative, more worried about getting things wrong, compromising or fudging, not knowing where the lines should be drawn, so it's safer to say nothing, or not tell other people what we might want to say."

"To say nothing and do nothing," he replied quietly, "could be considered a kind of withdrawal, a retreat. And perhaps our culture would be in a better place if people were braver."

She looked at Adam with increasing interest despite herself. It was good to have a conversation like this. Usually, the only place this kind of conversation occurred was inside her own head, with access to very limited knowledge and information.

"If your people have something to say," he carried on, and his voice became ever so slightly supercilious, "which I presume you believe you do, why don't you say it? I don't mean just sermonizing to each other in your poky little gospel halls, but out there, in the world, in culture, in art and literature. It's what filters down, you know! What eventually forms attitudes and opinions in society. Your forebears didn't have a problem with getting out there. Think of Milton. When did you lose your confidence?"

She looked at him in disbelief.

"You haven't got a clue, have you?"

Her voice rose in indignation and frustration.

"You think it's as easy and simple as that! We don't all have your big voice and education and . . . and entitlement!"

She scowled at him through his cloud of smoke and although somewhat taken aback at this outburst, he couldn't help smiling at her a little. She looked so fierce.

"But you're probably right." She suddenly deflated. "I don't know enough about it. I expect there is some cowardice and narrow-mindedness. Can't always blame everyone else for not doing things. So easy to make excuses."

She looked down at her feet. She couldn't tell if he was really taking her seriously or just playing with her. He took another draught from his cigarette, contemplating her. He minded the silence less than she did.

"I will try to borrow a Graham Greene book from the library," she said eventually. "Sounds interesting."

"He is interesting on relationships and human nature too," Adam carried on, after a pause. "Thinking of what you said before, I'm sure he says somewhere, '*human nature is not black and white but black and grey*'."

And then words from his own translation ran through his mind. Alwin's awareness of "*all that familiar black and white*", when he came up against a bit of experience, mingling into "*multitudinous shades of grey or rather many subtle shades of light and dark*". He was coming at it from the other way round, from the simple light of a monastic sanctuary into the complex shades of real life, whereas Greene seemed to grudgingly accept the light, because without it the intensity of the darkness made no sense, but he ended up with a similar conclusion.

He hadn't said much to Lucy about his translation. He said nothing now. For reasons he hadn't fully articulated to himself he had a sense that he didn't want to prejudice things, to know that any contrivance came, as it were, from the outside. So he just carried on.

"It all connects with his religious vision, so to speak. And he's particularly interesting because he also talks a lot about writing itself. In at least one of his books the main character is a writer, and he talks about it in his autobiography. His ideas about the creative process are very closely connected with his ideas about God, from what I remember—very interesting now I think of it again—although I've never been able to write, write my own stuff, I mean. I wish I could . . . "

He trailed off. She stole a glance at his face, which had a momentary far-away and humbler look.

"He, Greene, I mean," Adam pulled himself back, "he talks about the empathy involved in the creative process, both as writer and reader, being essential for our humanity. I think he somehow connected that with God's great empathy and identification with us. I read it a long time ago; I may have misremembered, so don't quote me, but I think he also demonstrates in one of his books, the title evades me, that the ability to create empathy between people can keep them from committing atrocities—although of course it doesn't always—but I seem to remember there is this situation where someone is going to murder someone else, I even can't remember why! Anyway, he finds he can't do it because she has spoken so much to him and told him about herself to the extent that she 'comes alive' to him, and he can no longer keep her in a separate category from himself. I may have got this wrong, but, I think, Greene has a theory that crimes committed against other people result fundamentally from a 'failure of the imagination'. But I'm not convinced, myself. Knowing how someone is going to feel, being able to connect to that feeling, that gives you power over them. The best torturer would also be the most empathetic. A kind of twisted empathy is a terrifying thing, to inflict and to endure."

He stopped and a dark look came over his face. She glanced at him and felt an involuntary shudder. *What had he felt? What cruelty was he capable of inflicting?* But then, she had to remind herself, he was, like her, a human being. If she recoiled, wasn't it in part because, if she was honest, there was that note of recognition, ironically of empathy, theoretical maybe, potential, but still real. And hadn't she just said herself that the paradox of mankind, his evident capacity for both great good and terrible evil, was one of the reasons she rejected the bleak doctrine of complete despair and clung to her faith? There were not "good" people and "bad" people. There were just people. All children of God, all children of men, all fallen, all refugees from Eden, all in desperate need of redemption; however great or small their crimes against God, humanity, the world and themselves.

She found she was getting really fascinated. As her self-consciousness became less acute, her confidence grew.

"But I suppose that's where his theory connects with his ideas about God," she said eagerly, "because if you see other people as made, created, in God's image, and yourself in that way too, then you are connected through that ultimate creativity, and how you treat each other really matters. You are dealing with the image of God after all! Perhaps that's what holds most of us back from the worst possibilities of our natures—even if it's subconscious. Maybe deep down we know that He will hold us accountable. And, it says in the Bible, '*For everyone to whom much is given, from him much will be required . . .*' Perhaps the worst evils are committed by those with either too little or too much imagination, or at least a twisting of it, or a crushing and silencing. And perhaps the more capacity we have for empathy the more capable we are of giving and receiving great love or feeling and inflicting extreme pain. That's a terrible awareness, responsibility . . . "

Her eyes were bright with interest and fear.

Everything seems so alive to her, he thought. He had never before felt so connected to the mind of another.

"Truth often seems so complicated, doesn't it?" she carried on eagerly. "And yet really, it's also beautifully simple. The opposite of lies—lies are much more likely to be easy black and white, so much less work, so appealing in a way, but also actually not simple really, not in a good way, but in a kind of dead-end, torturous way, that takes you nowhere."

"Reductionist you mean?" he replied with almost as much eagerness.

"Yes! And so, kind of shut in on themselves, torn between two impossible points, impossible to bring together."

He laughed.

"Yes! Very binary! I like that. You *are* bucking the trend, aren't you? How countercultural! So lies are condemned to existing in an impossible binary world, turning ever inward, tearing themselves apart in constant and inevitable warfare until they destroy themselves—the '*darkling plain*' where '*ignorant armies clash by night*'. And yet truth, truth is fully diverse, and yet exists in perfect harmony, perfect simplicity."

He laughed again, but she didn't understand why he found it amusing or what trend she was bucking. To her it all seemed rather self-evident.

"And I suppose then," he carried on, "you would say that when we create, we will get nearer to the truth by looking outwards, rather than looking inwards?"

"Well," she said with a slight frown of puzzlement, "I don't see how we can know anything about ourselves, or anything else unless we do! Otherwise, it's like we're completely alone in a black pit. How can we know anything if we can't or won't see anything else?"

"Perhaps we can't know anything?"

"But that's nonsense! No one really lives like that; I mean, as if that's true."

"No, not many," he conceded, "although perhaps some people don't really care either way."

"Well, I feel sorry for them then!"

"How do we help people to care?"

"Well . . . it seems as if imagination is really important to human beings—I mean, it must help if people can be inspired to really imagine—to look out from themselves and their own lives; to imagine the feelings and lives of others."

"Absolutely! I have a theory that without art we cannot be fully human—whatever that means. Art isn't a luxury but a necessity if we are to be fully rounded human beings. It shrivels humanity to take these things away and makes people less able to be empathetic, humane, sympathetic, compassionate . . . "

He paused, and looked suddenly defeated, weary—inexpressibly weary—and sad. The kind of sadness, almost sickness, bordering on despair, that makes you wonder what that person has seen or done.

"But it's not enough. Art, literature, poetry even, not enough on its own, not enough . . . Of all people, I know that."

She looked at him and felt surprised by tears pricking her own eyes.

"But maybe it's a good start?" she said gently.

She felt she wanted to reach out to him, to comfort him, even though he was so annoying, so arrogant so much of the time. She didn't know why he was suddenly so moved or why that strangely moved her, but she felt in that moment an inexplicable connection with him. The pain in his face hurt her too in some subtle way she could not put her finger on. And it wasn't just general empathy or common humanity. She carried on hurriedly.

"Even the very act of creating, or responding to someone else's creation, maybe even this brings us a little closer to what will really help us? We are made in the image of God! When we create, we are doing one of the things we are made to do and that's why it feels like it's doing us good. That's why it feels fulfilling when we create and fulfilling to appreciate what other people have created. At least, that's what I believe. And it's amazing isn't it, when you really think about it" (and she had thought about it a lot, in the long, dull and lonely hours in her dreary office) "that when we, I mean human beings . . . "

She corrected herself quickly, dropping her eyes. There were still things she did not wish to share, did not want him to know. And yet this was a subject which evoked a real passion in her and she struggled to conceal her ardour.

"It's amazing that when we imagine—a thing or a person—in a way we bring something into being that wasn't there before! And when we speak or write that thought down, we make it . . . make it live in the world. And then, then other people can know it too, and so then it is alive in their minds as well. Like Mr Darcy! Everyone knows him and half of them are in love with him, particularly since the series on the telly! And he will never get any older, or die. I think that is amazing! And it's because we are made in God's image ourselves that we can do that. Isn't it a great, a wonderful gift He has given us! And we should use it to speak truth, to bring more truth and goodness and love into people's lives. It seems very wrong, very wicked, to use that gift against Him, to use it to twist truth, to give lies a body and an independent life in the world. Although . . . "

She paused and shot a quick glance at him.

"Although really, I suppose it's not always very easy for us to separate things out. I mean, I suppose there'll always be a mixture of truth and error in what we think and write, what we read. We can't always tell where the lines are, and things can get so mixed up, even when we're really trying hard to be truthful and actually, even when we're not. A lie is only ever a twisting of truth, it can't exist in its own right, I mean as something completely original and . . . and other, because we only have what God has given us to work with. So when we try to be true, there'll be a little bit of error mixed in, but it works the other way round as well, and when we lie, we can't help there being a little bit of truth mixed in it too, because we have to work with what *is*, what exists . . . Oh, I wish I could explain it better! I suppose only God can speak and write pure truth, but the good thing is, because He has made words, they can at least speak for themselves up to a point. I mean, there's only so far we can twist them, otherwise they completely break and . . . and we have to use the tools He's given us, we don't have any others. It's all we have to describe what we feel, what we see. So however much we try to tear them away from reality, and however much we damage them, we actually only have them, words I mean, to use against themselves, and so they'll always pull us back, even when we don't want them to. We can try to work against them, but we can't escape them."

She tailed off sheepishly. She was confusing herself in her inability to fully articulate her thoughts and ideas, and she also had the uncomfortable feeling that she was giving away too much. She hoped he wouldn't ask her any more questions just now.

He, though, was staring at her in a kind of blank wonder. Here she was, passionately, unconsciously, echoing sentiments in her untutored way, so similar to his learned Middle English poet and yet with even more insight, going even further. Perhaps after all she really could stand in the tradition he had been goading her people for neglecting. There was a long pause, in which the smoke curled in strange shapes through the dancing sunbeams. She fidgeted nervously with her pen. And then he finally spoke , in a quiet voice, quoting the Shakespeare lines that he had so recently adapted to his own translation:

> *And as imagination bodies forth*
> *The forms of things unknown, the poet's pen*
> *Turns them to shapes and gives to airy nothing*
> *A local habitation and a name.*

The ways of love

As he turned, Alwin's gaze was grasped
By a ray of radiance, a gleam of warm and living gold,
More beautiful in his sudden stricken sight
Than all the wealth of wonders he had witnessed
Arrayed before his eyes in those many days
Of magnificence and marvels. There she stood,
Her shining hair come loose beneath her veil,
Reflecting back the setting sun, her eyes flashed
Green and full of grace under pale lashes
As she lifted their light to his. For the merest moment
The world in all its manic motion ceased to move,
And rooted to the ground, nothing existed
But their mutual melting gaze.

He felt the fatal flame sear him suddenly to his soul,
Felt the irresistible pull of those piercing eyes
Reeling him in on an invisible line or
As a compass' steel needle, compelled
To strain towards the north.
The crowds closed between them like a curtain,
The needle spun, the golden strand was snapped
And she was gone, as swiftly as she'd come,
Borne away on the tide of life,
On the tide of another life.
He felt, as it were, a moment of perception
Into a parallel existence, the possibilities,
The life that might have been.
An insufferable sense of loss swept
Over his stricken soul as he staggered, straining
Towards the place where last she'd stood.
If only space mattered, and not time,

Their beings would now be mutually mingled.
He gasped like a drowning man
For one more glimpse of that glory,
One more breath of life-giving air,
Just one more, it would be enough!
A dew drop of eternity snatched from time,
A dazzling diamond displaying divine light,
The veil momentarily pierced before dark curtains closed,
Returning familiar night to his dim eyes.

A kind, rough hand squeezed his arm,
Good Sabinus steering him away towards a squalid square.
"Easy, brother!" as he fought against the friendly grasp,
His gaze all the time turned towards
The place where last she'd stood, the space
From whence time had sped her far away,
Where the veil had fallen,
And she had vanished from view.

"Where did the girl go?" he struggled, "you surely saw?"
"Bless me!" Sabinus started with a laugh,
"A girl, you say, a solitary soul in a stampede like this?"
"She seemed like an angel from heaven,
A shining one!" he stammered.
His companion laughed his loud and merry laugh,
Slapping the stunned youth on the back.
"Well then, you'd best leave her to heaven's care,
For I'll warrant she's no good for thee!"
But noticing now the pained look in the novice's eyes
He answered more gently, "Come and take some ale, my lad,
You need maybe to calm and settle yourself,
And now I come to think, I'm mighty dry myself."

And with a firm and friendly arm he manoeuvred
The miserable Alwin towards a makeshift bench,
Instructing him to wait and rest until he returned,
Which soon he did with two frothing flagons,
"To drown fierce sorrows and cheer the heart."
He found Alwin, his head in his hands, weeping woefully.
"Nay lad," he cajoled, "do not wail and give vent
In this public place like a weak woman!
But bear yourself like the man you are,
For I know now, though novice, you are truly man indeed,
For in one moment, I think, you have looked
On love, or the possibility of love, and loss."

"I have brought shame on myself, my noble house
And my Lord," mumbled the boy miserably.
"I am a disgrace to my calling. I have yielded,
I suppose, to the flesh and the devil and fallen
At the first block of stumbling, as surely
As a foolish and unbroken foal."

"Do not speak of the devil for what has he
To do with beauty and love?" exclaimed Sabinus,
As wealthy in experience as Alwin in youth.
"You said yourself she appeared
As an angel from heaven, yes?
Well then, I believe, nay I know,
Beauty and love always lead us nearer to God
For they surely, as all good things and true,
Proceed from Him, the sole source of all grace.
Drink deep son," the kindly man softly urged,
"And I will tell you a tale." And thus he spoke:

There was once a young man who was wild and godless,
Who brawled and drank his way through his days,
Hardly sober enough to do an honest hour's hard graft
Or earn enough to keep body and soul entwined,
And what he got went mostly on mead or ale,
Which brought more malady than mirth.

It had not always been thus. His mother
Was a pure, pious woman, although poor.
His father had been struck down
With sweating sickness when he was young
And life was hard and fate felt cruel.
But the sacred charity of the brothers at Saint Stephen's
Sustained and succoured them in their sore need.
Mother and son therefore loved
And revered the holy brothers in their turn,
And as the boy grew his greatest desire
Was to enter that noble house
And devote his life to divine service.
Thus when the time was ripe he applied to the abbot
And was summoned to see that saintly man.
However, for reasons he could not then comprehend,
His suit was rejected, his vocation not recognized,
His pleas silenced. And so
In his sorrow and bitterness of soul,
He spurned what formally he had so loved,
And vowed he would not have a God
Who would not have him, and slowly
His heart within him turned to stone.
But for the sake of his mother, he buried
This root of gall deep within his shattered soul,
Lest learning of it her grief
Would be beyond endurance,
For her life had been one long string of searing loss

And she clung to faith and son
As her last and only treasures; to own
That each had rejected the other would
Have utterly overwhelmed and broken her.

But then the plague that swept through the lands
In the year of our Lord six hundred and sixty-four,
Bore her frail spirit far beyond this vale of tears.
This was the final blow for the wretched youth
Whose rage and wrath towards a God
Who brought him only rejection and loss,
Although called loving and righteous,
Spilled out at last, and the bitter root nurtured
In the dark depths of his desperate soul broke free.
Discarding all pretence of piety and pity,
He gave himself over to every manner
Of vicious and destructive vices,
Imagining himself to be at last free
From the fetters of a miser God and Father,
Determined to drain every last drop of pleasure
From indulging in each and every lust,
He shook his fist in the face of his Maker,
Full of passion and fury.

At first he did not fully perceive
That his pleasures and pernicious lusts
Would become terrible, tenacious taskmasters.
What he had mistakenly felt was freedom,
Was in fact slavery, deadly and cruel.
In woeful bondage to the gods of drink,
Violence and the whorehouse,
He became a miserable, penniless wretch,
Rather to be hissed at and shunned in his shame
Than pitied. Eventually, when he could no more

Earn the bread to keep himself alive,
He succumbed to a serious sickness
And lay down in the gutter to die,
Cursing in his hardened heart the God
Who had given him this hated breath
Simply to mock and torment him
And drive him to despair and death.
The darkness overtook him
And he knew no more.

When he opened his eyes, all was light
And luminous brightness. Changed,
He was lying in a clean bed in an airy room
With dawn rays pouring through the casement.
He felt embraced by the light and welcomed
Back to life, as if a hand was reaching out to him,
Hoping, imploring him to come.
The surroundings seemed strangely familiar
And beloved. Where was he? His weakened mind
Could not fathom the mystery until a breath of air,
A door opened upon a benign face and a brother
Of the monastery entered, bringing some broth.
Finally the pieces of the puzzle fell into place.
While lying in his deathly stupor
He had been discovered and carried directly hence
By the good brothers of that saintly house
That had before so sustained him and his mother
And had riven and ravaged his heart
When his vocation was rejected.

Under their diligent daily healing of body and soul
He duly recovered and prospered.
And when come to full strength, he was with care,
Apprenticed to skilled craftsmen, gifted glaziers,

And learned the gilded magic of their glorious art,
Transforming sand into solid light,
And staining it all the colours of the spectrum.

His newfound craft became a cathartic healing
Source of great delight and charm to him.
And as he gazed upon the beauty
That his human hands could make,
The more he began to meditate on God the Creator,
And thought him how He must delight
In His Creation and how He must mourn
The marring of what He has made;
The destruction and spoiling of His dear delight
And the work of His divine hands.
He knew then that he had marred
The good creation of God in himself
And had been brought back from the brink
And restored by those he had rejected
Because he had felt they rejected him.
And as he thought on these things
And on the steadfast love and care of those brothers,
He knew in his heart that their love
Was but the agency of a greater love,
And he began, little by little to understand,
Something, in his humble human way,
Of the heart of God.

Around this time he met a maid, the daughter
Of his master who had taught him his trade.
And she was more fair in his eyes than even
The beauty of his craft, more elegant and excellent,
She was gentle and pious and wise.
He felt he could never be worthy of her
But wished it with all his heart and yet

By God's good grace she looked upon this marred youth
With generous eyes, showing him favour,
And in the fullness of time, and with the consent
Of her father, she became his bride.
The bliss of this union brought together not just
The bodies and souls of these two children of God,
But also consummated the new creative thoughts
That had been springing up like sweet streams
In the soul of the renewed young man.
And as they welled up within him, God
Was finally revealing his vocation and his work,
And it was to love, simply love.
Just as it was the vocation of the holy brothers
Whom he had formerly longed to join, also to love.
("And," he said as an aside, "do not mistake me,
Because something is simple it does not mean it is easy.")
But his love was to course through a different
Earthly channel, that was all.
And what a consummate calling, so perfectly suited
To his particular needs and peculiar make-up.
His wife taught him to love in ways
Beyond his wildest, worthiest dreams
And bore him, in due time,
The blessed fruits of love in beautiful babes.

After the nuptials he spoke again with the abbot
Who had all those years before rejected
His application to take orders:
"My son," said he, "I think you now see why
I could not receive you as a brother of this sacred house?
I could discern your extraordinary zeal and your earnest desire
But I perceived you needed an earthly anchor to learn
The love of God. For He has woven marriage
Into the web of His good creation to reflect

The mysterious union betwixt Christ and the church:
'Therefore a man shall leave his father and his mother
And cleave to his wife, and they shall become one flesh.'
And whether through holy matrimony or bridled celibacy,
We must follow the path of light to love,
For God is Love."

Alwin was looking at him with undivided attention,
His ale undrunk, his heart undone.
"Master Sabinus, I believe you speak of yourself!"
"Aye lad," breathed the older man softly, "and I wish
You could have beheld my beautiful Liliola.
But it is three years this harvest that
I laid her in the hard and thorny ground."

His eyes carried that curious faraway look of one
Who has gazed upon the distant horizon.
He wiped them with the coarse back
Of a craftsman's hand, revealing the short nails
And razor thin scars around the ragged fingertips
That betrayed his trade, and symbolized his trials.

Alwin awkwardly rested his own untried hand
On Sabinus' shaking shoulder.

"It's alright lad, she was a jewel lent me
A little while to lighten my path and now
She's been taken home, with our sweet babes too.
They will not come to me again,
But by God's good grace I shall go to them . . .
But I told you this tale to try to help you see,
All true love is really the love of God.
We are called to love in different ways,
Down different paths, that is all.

I wished to be as you now are when I was young,
And although a worthy wish, it was wrong for me.
You, it seems, are doubting the life
You have undertaken and have seen
And felt, as if in a flash of fierce yearning,
The other alluring, untried and unknown paths
You might have followed to Love.
Well, these are weighty matters and for you alone
To weigh in your heart before God,
But understand, all loves involve affliction
And aching loss in this fallen world.
To embrace one vocation you must repudiate
And refuse the other, or be rejected by it,
And all is marred by that last enemy, death.
It is not, I fear, 'til heaven and new-created earth
That we will have all in all, full love without loss."

Terror of love

Adam sat a long time pondering these words. Unaware of time passing the room grew dark around him.

Love.

What did he know of love? Of what did it consist? He had had so much opportunity and yet he had always squandered it, had somehow shied away, let it slip away, never prepared to make that final commitment, to let go of himself. Was he simply too selfish?

Now pleasure, he reflected, simple, self-serving pleasure anyway, was a very different matter. It cost less, at least initially, but also yielded less, and in fact each time, he was beginning to see, cost the soul more and yielded mind and body less and less in return. A negative carry investment but relentlessly, cruelly addictive all the same. In the early stages it was even possible to mistake it for love, but the long-term trajectory told a different story.

But love? Real love?

Was he afraid of it? Had he been afraid to give or receive love, to open himself up to it, to make himself vulnerable? Perhaps the acknowledgement of human love is also the acknowledgement of mortality. We cannot control it or what it will do to us. We are completely at its mercy. We cannot hang on to it, but it hangs on to us with its tenacious, unshakable claws embedded in our hearts. And in the end, even what we have managed to cling onto, is torn away by that last enemy, death. And he thought to himself that love was a terrible, dangerous, exhausting thing. But what was life without it? To live fully, it seemed, was to love, but the price for love was pain. The more love, the more pain. That was the deal. Was it worth it?

But as soon as he had posited the question, he knew it was now purely hypothetical. There was no choice. And there was no guarantee either that he would experience the joy of love, but he would certainly experience the pain. He could no longer be indifferent, even if he wished it. He was compelled to care. He braced himself internally for the unstoppable onslaught, like a small vessel at the foot of a colossal, crumbling dam.

The subtle creep of spring

Very slowly, almost imperceptibly, the days began to lengthen. The darkness before dawn shrank further back into the night and the darkness of twilight retreated a little more each evening. As Adam worked away in the library, he noticed the afternoon sun striking the cathedral towers just a little further round and higher up each day, like the fingers on a giant sundial. He gazed out upon the ancient stones that the strengthening sun was transforming into mellow gold. The birds could sense the turning of the season too and, instinctively believing in its promise, were beginning to gather twigs and moss to build their nests round its protective buttresses and in the nooks and crannies of the carved stones. The life and light that had seemed to desert the earth and himself was on the move once more. The perennial miracle of spring, persistently edging forwards, had not abandoned him after all. There was still time. He felt the relentless grace of creation inexorably sweeping him towards brighter days and fairer shores. If he could just believe. He could sense the rippling currents, but something in him still clung futilely to the fraying weeds of winter and the old familiar darkness. Before him lay that great ocean of doubt and fear, at times menacingly overcast and foreboding. The undiscovered and unknown. Could he really let go and trust himself to that overwhelming, advancing tide? He knew that once he did there would be no turning back. Did he even have a choice?

Elegy

"Your sister! You want to bring your bloody sister along too? What do you think I'm going to do to you that you need a chaperone?"

"I don't need a chaperone, because it's not a date!" she laughed. "I just thought it would be nice, though actually perhaps it is wise with you around! Safety in numbers!"

In reality she had most definitely not wanted to be alone with him.

He grinned at her.

"Ok! In that case I'll bring my kids—sounds like a family-friendly affair, so why not!"

"It would be great to meet them properly," smiled Lucy.

"Good. That's settled then, meet you at the boathouse at eleven on Friday. No point in having to get up at the crack of dawn in the holidays."

It was a start, he smiled to himself as he walked home. Christmas had been survived, New Year endured, albeit with the help of a considerable amount of solitary alcohol, and there was still the best part of a year before he'd have to do it again. The light had finally returned to the northern hemisphere and an early Easter was approaching. Best of all Lucy had finally chosen to spend a day of her own with him.

They had often snatched lunch together in recent weeks, in her cramped office or his more opulent one, but cautiously, for fear of the scorn of colleagues and awkward questions. Sometimes they had spoken again of poetry, sometimes of theology and sometimes just of their own small lives. She had told him a little more about her brothers and sisters and her parents. Her mam had been ill again. Her younger sister Rachel had got engaged. He spoke of the days he had seen his children. He confessed to feeling at a loss as to how to entertain them, of feeling a distance between them and himself that he did not know how to span. She was kind and sympathetic, although straight talking too. She refused to flatter him or pander to his vanity, folly or self-pity. She seemed unusually impervious to his well-worn charms. He had never encountered such resistance in a woman alongside such easy friendliness at the same time. His previous

163

distrust and dislike of her had turned on its head, like his life, and seemed strange and alien to him now. He now found her charming, fresh, and no longer just a place of desperate refuge from the storm. He found himself longing to be part of that unsullied world she seemed to inhabit. Her reticence piqued him and her openness drew him. She was authentic. She wasn't pretending. How unusual that was. How strangely unusual to find a human being somehow comfortable in their own unremarkable skin in this weary, impossible world.

Good Friday. Adam woke up with a sense of lively anticipation that he hadn't felt since childhood, at the beginning of the summer holidays or on Christmas Eve. He almost laughed at his own unclouded eagerness to spend the day, a cold day at that, rowing on the river, picnicking with a couple of kids, a secretary and her sister. A few months back he would have scorned the idea as unbearably tedious and dull. Oh well, if this was a mid-life crisis, bring it on, he thought to himself as he got ready and set off to fetch his children.

They had stayed with their mother in the elegant townhouse on South Street that had been their family home, while he had moved into a flat they also owned. It wasn't so bad. It was right at the top of a large Georgian house on Western Hill, quite near the station and the impressive viaduct. It had been converted at some point into four pleasant apartments and his attic floor had a view of both the cathedral and the castle. When he looked out of the dormer windows at night, he could see those twin monuments to God and Man lit up ethereally, seeming to float in the sky at about the same height as his attic window, with the expanse of the city lying in the valley between them. Of course they stood firmly on the top of the hill on the peninsula, with the river circling them far beneath, but particularly at night they looked as if they had slipped their earthly anchors and were soaring upwards to meet the stars overhead.

The children were already standing outside on the narrow, cobbled street waiting for him when he arrived. As he pulled up, he was suddenly struck by how grown-up they seemed. They teetered on the brink between childhood and adulthood. They were beautiful. In their prime. His son, tall and handsome but still with the freshness and hope of boyhood on his cheeks and in his tousled fair hair. His daughter with the same beautiful thick dark hair as her mother, elegant, slight but full of life and vibrancy. She looked a little defiant but at the same time unsure of herself. Her eyes were like deep dark pools under long dark lashes, still trying to work the world out, still not sure if she should reach out or shut it out.

He felt an overwhelming desire to protect them, shield them from the inevitable pain and disappointment and despair. He felt powerless. They would be corrupted, consumed and would corrupt and consume in their turn and all would come to emptiness and dust and ashes. "*What a piece of work is man . . . ,*" he thought bitterly to himself. And yet, and yet . . . perhaps there really was hope after all. Perhaps the ray of light in the darkness was real. He almost daren't let himself believe, particularly there, in that split second of awareness of his children, all they meant to him; in that implacable agony of parental love and fear. How could he bear it, how could he bear it on their behalf, if it was just another illusion? He felt desperate to get to Lucy, to feel reassured by her substance.

The moment passed, as mercifully these moments do. He opened the door and jumped out. He kissed his daughter and gave his son a quick rough hug. "Where's your mother? How is she?" he asked awkwardly. One had to try. The children looked uncomfortable.

"She's umm, still in bed. We didn't want to wake her, so we just got ready and thought we'd wait out here," muttered Sebastian, his head down and his cheeks flaming. Margo snorted and rolled her eyes.

Determined not to show any emotion Adam clenched his teeth behind closely pressed lips and fumbled unnecessarily with the car keys. He mastered himself with a twist of internal struggle.

"Ok, in you get," he said with forced cheerfulness.

They parked nearby, at the end of Pimlico, and decided to walk the scenic route, strolling slowly across Prebends' Bridge in the clear morning light, pausing briefly to gaze over the stone parapet of one of the raised enclaves at the shifting reflections in the water below. They cut through the echoing tunnel into the College, down the cobbled Bailey, each stone rounded and smoothed by centuries of feet, to the marketplace and then down the steep steps towards Brown's Boathouse. The river was sparkling joyfully, gurgling along, as if laughing at some private joke. His children, though, were quiet and seemed distant and uncomfortable. Adam tried making conversation with them but mostly found himself answered in monosyllables. He was realizing more and more, with each painful visit, how little he had ever talked to them, really talked. How little he really knew them, their hopes, their fears . . . He almost felt in the presence of strangers. He started to feel awkward and self-conscious himself. This was terrible. They were his own children for heaven's sake, and he couldn't think of a thing to say beyond the usual bland, vacuous phrases reserved for acquaintances.

Lucy and her sister Jess were waiting for them by the boathouse. It looked as though they were going to be the first customers of the day, possibly of the year. The old man was still dragging the rowing boats into the water while he chatted to the two girls. Adam noted with a pang how much more easily they were conversing with a stranger than he was with his own flesh and blood. He lifted a hand in greeting, very grateful to have the empty intensity of his family group diluted.

They were both friendly and did their best to put the two children at ease, although Sebastian and Margo still hung back shyly, sullenly. This wasn't how they had wished to spend their holiday, their life. Parents! Why did they have to make everything so difficult? Why were they so selfish and so crass? They knew very well if they behaved in the same way they'd have been censored on every possible count. The hypocrisy. And now they were supposed to act as if nothing had happened and humour their pitiful father and pretend to enjoy this ridiculous trip with his boring colleagues. No doubt he had his own agenda going on here somehow, they knew him too well. *Which one was it? Or both?* Neither of them looked his usual type though, both fairly ordinary, thought Margo, looking a little more closely from under her long lashes. In fact they were very different from any of the other women they had grown used to hovering on the fringes of their lives. Despite herself she found her interest rising.

They climbed into a boat with "Suzanne" painted across the back in flaking turquoise and gold paint.

Suzanne . . . The words of the song floated through his mind. She would carry them, tea and oranges and all, down the honeyed river, mirror to the morning sun, while all living things strained towards the light, leaning out, yearning for love. If you knew where to look you could see it everywhere, amongst the debris and the snowdrops. Could even he, even he, hardened and half-crazy as he was, be touched?

He was shaken out of his reverie by the old boat man who handed them a couple of oars and with a cheery, "See yous later!" pushed them off. Adam took the oars and steered them into midstream. The willows hung low, the tips of their branches brushing the surface of the silky water. The river reflected back the pale blue sky and they almost looked as if they were flying.

The children both took turns with the oars, chatting increasingly easily with Lucy and Jess and gradually they began to loosen up, like plants slowly unfurling their tendrils. Adam watched, grateful, himself beginning to relax. Lucy deliberately splashed him when it was her turn to row, which of course set the children off.

"I'll get you for that!" he laughed trying to wrench the oar from her hands.

Soon they were all laughing and messing around.

"It's not a good idea to get too wet; it's pretty cold!" shrieked Jess. "Let's at least have our lunch before we all get soaked!"

They tied the boat to a tree and climbed up the bank. It was a bit of a scramble, particularly with the picnic bag. Muddy and breathless they flung themselves on the grass laughing.

It was too cold to sit for long, so they made short work of the sandwiches and cake Lucy had packed and Adam produced a bottle of champagne and real glass flutes.

"Very sophisticated!" grinned Lucy. "I could get used to this!"

He raised his glass to her.

"'You can wash a lot down with a glass of champagne.'" Then a little sourly, "I should know."

A flask of hot tea followed, supplied by Jess, and then they found themselves chasing round on the bank, partly to keep warm and partly in continuation of the play fight begun on the boat.

Margo and Sebastian became increasingly relaxed and Adam felt the sweetness of this childlike scene pierce him strangely. What relief to feel emotion beyond anger, loss, jealousy and burning desire. Simple laughter, kindness, happiness, had been strangers to him for so long. The odd lack of intensity and yet gentle peace felt like joyful ripples breaking over him, as they broke over the quivering surface of the water beneath them.

They walked for a while, Margo now chatting easily with Lucy and Jess some way ahead and Sebastian at his side telling him about his music, the girl he liked at school but didn't dare to talk to and so on; all the ordinary things. He found in his turn he was talking quite naturally to his son. What a wonderfully beautiful thing it was. The channel felt open. The words became communication and not simply arrows fired at random, never reaching their mark. They were loaded now with meaning, with relationship. They were no longer simply empty social forms, the husks of love.

After a while Sebastian looked slyly at his father.

"I like them, dad! Which one is it then?"

Adam felt himself blushing like a schoolboy.

"They're just friends," he muttered, "well, in fact I don't even really know Jess, only met her for the first time today. I work with Lucy, you know, in the department . . . "

Sebastian grinned. "She's canny!" he said quietly. "I like her!"

Adam felt a warmth swelling inside him. He squeezed his son's arm.

The exquisite happiness of the scene, the extraordinary ordinariness was like a tonic to the rawness of his soul. For so long he had been driven by those two ruthless task masters of pain and desire, the stick and carrot of human experience, or this distortion of humanity. To just *be*, to just engage with other people with no consciousness of what he wanted from them, blighted by no agenda. He realized how much he had been craving this, the need intensifying in his mind since reflecting on the words of Sabinus—translating but not really relating. His tale to Alwin had caused him to consider the multifaceted nature of love in a new and different way. He had allowed his own potential loves to be corrupted and disintegrate into mere status symbols or desires; lusts that demanded an ever-greater sacrifice of his soul every time; gods that demanded blood and were slowly bleeding his humanity dry. He knew instinctively, here and now, amidst the gentle scene of generous being, and sharing in that being, that this was what he was made for, what human beings are made for: for relationship, for communion, for love. Not just desire but *love* in all its many facets, however much pain that might bring, however great the cost. To deny it was to deny life, to exist only in the shadows.

Back in the boat they glided slowly down the river until the tower of the cathedral came into view. They were quiet now, tired but happy, and the earlier awkwardness had completely melted away. Margo sat with her head resting against her father's shoulder while Sebastian rowed smoothly. Jess leant over the side letting her hand trail through the silver water, leaving a tiny wake behind her. Lucy gazed dreamily at the shimmering river and the trees slipping by, with a faraway look in her shining blue eyes, the dying afternoon sun lighting her hair with pale fire.

There was truly something almost heartbreaking about the beauty of that afternoon—the light sparkling on the water as they drifted along, the crisp frosty leaves on the banks, the tiny new green buds on the trees and the quiet happiness of the human creatures amongst it. Everywhere felt as if ready to burst with new life amidst the debris and ruin of the old year.

He felt a vague and unfamiliar sense of that new love well up inside him, for his fellow creatures and for the world around him, in all its tainted beauty.

Perhaps all glimpses of real beauty break our hearts, he mused, *for by its very nature, in our human experience, it is ephemeral. The beauty and the happiness cannot be caught and held but slip through our consciousness as surely as the water is slipping through Jess's fingers.* He also realized, in a flash of understanding, that his rare experiences of contentment always contained within them, at their core, the taint of fear and yearning, for even in this moment of almost complete happiness Adam realized he did not want that beautiful day to end but yet was already longing for more.

In the bleakness of the dying year we long for the snowdrops, the promise of spring. And yet, he thought wistfully, how we long for snow and cosy winter nights during the damp greyness of autumn. And when it's hot and itching and full of biting insects we welcome the autumnal tang as much as the blackberries and golden leaves. But then we feel the sadness of the swallows departing and yearn for their return and the endless dreamy northern summer nights, when it never truly gets dark, and the sun-tipped barley sways in the breeze and the fragrance of elderflower hangs heavy on the air.

Why can we never seize and hold the moment? he thought. Why this urgent rush to possess what we don't yet have, this failure to enjoy the now? Is this mortality—the curse of time? This living in a state of perpetual loss, having lost the past without gaining the future; always striving forwards to what we can never grasp, unable to inhabit the present, mourning what is lost; for what are we then but merely a collection of memories and dreams? *But perhaps, just perhaps,* he suddenly thought, *eternity is the opposite . . .*

He had never given the concept of eternity much thought before this strange new life had broken in, except disparagingly in the most vague, hypothetical and external religious sense, and then it sounded at best tedious and static, and at worst unspeakably bleak, "deserts of vast eternity . . . ", but now it sprang alive to him in the potency of this new insight. What if really it was the antidote to the poisonous serpent Time, that outrageous thief of human love and life? What if it was actually a state of enjoying simultaneously all that is good and beautiful but with no loss, and what is even more precious, no fear of loss. For without that hope, how tragic, how utterly futile the human condition is, he thought. He looked up at Lucy and saw she was looking directly back at him. For one brief moment their mutual gaze locked in wordless understanding, and he saw eternity in her eyes.

The lighthouse of Ostia

The gracious goal is now in sight, the destination
Of their desire and daring journey's end,
All things converging on their pious purpose
And sanctified searching. From Arles they take again
To the waters and embark upon a ship
To carry them across the Tyrrhenian Sea,
To the port of Ostia and gateway to great Rome,
This warm and sunny southern sea a far cry
From the channel crossing earlier endured,
And with balmy breezes playing on his face,
Alwin stands at the prow gazing
At the coastline coming slowly into sight,
The great portentous lighthouse standing proud,
A marvellous beacon and shepherd of the ships
That pass safely through the dark watches of the night
By the grace of its guardian beam,
Warning of the treacherous rocks and reefs
Lying hidden beneath that glassy sea,
Ready to claim the unaware and unprepared
And drag them down to deep watery dungeons.

So many trials and dangers in this fallen world
To be navigated and negotiated, Alwin muses:
Some great and obvious towering teeth of evil black,
Some snares on the surface seeming safe and sane,
And yet lurking beneath still waters where sunlight plays,
The hidden menace lying full fathom down.
Without the guiding beam of God's good grace
And the revelation of his Holy Word,
How we too, the flimsy ships sailing the perilous
Sea of life, would be so easily wrecked and ruined,

Cast adrift from true and safe waters, lured
Into the many snares of Satan, that ferocious lion
That paces back and forth across land and sea
Looking for whom he may devour, and catches
Some in the dark and cruel places of the world
But others in their seeming good intentions
Insidiously designed to trap their deceived souls.
How we must, he reflects, keep our eyes raised
To that lofty light of life, to not be tempted
To the right or left but to follow faithfully
The fair path trod before us by our Lord.
To enter his sheepfold of safety we must heed
His voice and guard our hearts that we may enter
His garden of grace, using only the door that is Himself,
For He, as He Himself proclaims, alone
Is Way and Truth and Life
And no one comes unto the Father but by Him:
The great shepherd, the great gardener,
The great artist, the great architect,
The great light, the great lover,
The great author and finisher of faith.
He draws us by our personal paths
And through our different desires, turning them,
If we will, as Augustine writes,
Towards his perfect light, that being bathed
In beauty divine, they may be redeemed
And restored to become what they
Were always made to be, gifts
With which to glorify our Lord, the giver
And receiver of all goodness, grace and love,
Returning them to us beautified,
Worthy and glorified, sanctified
For service in that holy realm,
Cleansing us as gift and image-bearers to be

A perfect, beautiful bride for our heavenly king.

Alwin's heart is full of these reflections,
And it greatly pleases Biscop to hear
His novice expound upon these heavenly truths,
To witness his worthy growth in grace and wisdom
As the months have passed; his strengthening
In mind and soul from emerging spring,
Through seductive summer, the mellow beauty
Of autumn and the testing trial of winter,
And back again to spring renewed.

And now, anchoring in that haven, safely steered
By the beacon of trustworthy, saving light,
The holy city of Rome, only a day's journey hence
Beckons the weary but happy travellers.

Animae dimidium meae?

"I'll drive you home," Adam said, as they stood together in the twilight after they had returned the boat and had a meal together in the riverside pub. He did not want the day to end, was putting off the inevitable moment.

"Oh, there's no need . . . " Lucy cast around for a reason to deter them, knowing her flat was in a bit of a state and suspecting that she would have to invite them in to appear polite.

"It's fine!" Adam said cheerily. "The car's just parked at the end of the bridge. And I can drop Jess back wherever she needs to get to as well."

"Ok," Lucy agreed reluctantly, "thanks." It would seem rude to refuse and it would save the bus fare. She wished she had tidied up a bit before coming out. Somehow too she felt a sense of unease about admitting Adam into her personal private space.

They walked across the bridge chatting and watching the moon slowly rise in the dusky sky overhead, turning the water beneath to quicksilver. When they reached the car, Adam eyed his children.

"Do you two want us to walk you home first as it's just round the corner or do you want to come for the ride?" He looked at his watch. "It's only just gone 8."

Sebastian and Margo glanced at each other. "We'll come for the ride," replied Margo quickly. It was definitely a less awkward option than returning home too early in the evening and surprising their mother.

When they pulled up outside the flat, Lucy hoped they wouldn't take her up on the offer of coffee. Of course they did. Under the guise of getting the kettle on, she dashed up ahead of the others as they removed their muddy shoes and coats in the communal hall downstairs.

She flicked the switch as she looked around desperately, grabbing a few piles of washing and shoving them into her bedroom.

Tidying up was not her strong point and generally consisted of stuffing everything into cupboards and when it overflowed, into corners, everything jumbled together, jammed behind the thin partition walls of respectability, like her mind.

While she was in the process of gathering a pile of stuff from the sofa, the others burst through the door.

"I'm sorry," she panted slightly with her frantic activity, "it's a bit of a mess! I wasn't expecting visitors. It doesn't always look like this!"

"No!" retorted Jess. "It's normally a lot worse! You've come on a good day!"

She dodged a cushion thrown at her head by her sister.

Adam laughed. "Don't worry at all; it wasn't really fair of us to invite ourselves over. It's got a nice feel anyway. I'm glad you didn't have time to clear up. This is much more real. I never feel comfortable in houses where everything is perfect; it puts me on edge."

He thought momentarily of his own family home that Cynthia had kept so spotless, tasteful and empty. A shadow passed almost unnoticed over his face, but Lucy was watching him out of the corner of her eye.

"Nice of you to say so anyway, even if you're just being polite!" she smiled uncertainly.

"When am I ever polite?" laughed Adam. "I meant it. It feels lived-in, no," he laughed again, "that came out wrong! I mean, it feels alive. Give me mess and life anytime, always preferable to stultifying order, reality neatly tidied away, coldness ... death ... " His smile had faded and his eyes had taken on again that bitterness she had seen before when he had first come to talk to her in her office.

There was an awkward pause.

"Please sit down, if you can find a space!" Lucy gestured with a small nervous laugh.

"Would you prefer tea or coffee?"

"Don't suppose you've got anything stronger?" With an effort he broke through the cloud.

"Only hot chocolate!"

"Oh well, I'll make do with a cup of tea, I suppose!"

The others duly put in their orders, squeezing into the chairs and sofa and beginning to chat again.

Lucy nervously watched Adam as she began to make the drinks. He restlessly wandered around the tiny flat, forgetting it was rather rude to do this uninvited. None of the doors would properly close so he could see into each small, cluttered space. He noted with approval the number and variety of books, both on the shelves and everywhere else.

She was always reading at least five books at once and these were scattered around in various states of disarray: one open on top of the loo, another upside down next to the bed, a well-loved Bible, by the looks of it on the bedside table, a creased paperback half under the bed, in danger of being lost for ever in the dusty recesses. By the kettle sat yet another dog-eared volume with the corners of many pages turned down, Adam noticed as he drifted back towards her. He began to flick through it absent-mindedly, intrigued to see lots of sections emphatically underscored with a blunt red pencil, scribbled marginal notes and in some places inexplicable series of question marks. He turned it over to see the title: Augustine's *Confessions*. A strange feeling gripped his heart. This was remarkable, extraordinary. Or perhaps not. Why was he still surprised by these unlooked-for connections? Coincidence was perhaps just another way of describing divine contrivance, or Providence, if you wanted to be theological. Was it not really the most natural thing in the world after all that life, reality, be so closely knit together, back and forth, in and out of souls, a conversation across time, echoes even from eternity, the divine voice whispering through the words of others, those words taken up, made their own by yet others, a chain of wisdom and revelation down through the ages, connecting minds and knitting souls, a great, intertwined web of being? It seemed so now for all his former blindness. And how amazing to think that those words written by Augustine all those many long ages ago had been speaking still to Alwin 300 years later, and a thousand years later still to his unnamed poet; and were even now, at the end of another millennium, continuing to speak to Lucy and himself. Those ancient words still had the power to speak truth and bring light after 1,500 years, and would go on doing so long after he, Adam, had passed away. People pass but words remain. And it struck him once more—the incredible power and gift of words, both to bestow and to receive. Words cannot be stolen by death. They defy, even collapse, the tyranny of Time. They exist in the present in a way that we cannot, yet are rooted in the past and reach forward into the future. Their light cannot be extinguished by the darkness. But for all that, he still felt like someone groping in the dark with only the flickering flame of a small candle to guide him. There was so much light that, as yet, he could not see.

He glanced round the room. The coffee table was also littered with books, poetry this time by the looks of it, mixed up with bills needing attention, loose scraps of paper covered in intriguing scribble and the various kinds of post that arrives every day but no one knows what to do with—the kind that defies categorization, even if one was organized enough to have a filing system.

Adam smiled to himself. Somehow the mess, if that was the right word, didn't feel oppressive at all but creative, evidence of an active and multi-faceted mind, an interesting peep into the backstage of someone who generally managed to keep up an appearance of bland and acceptable efficiency during the public show. He was glad to discover the hard evidence for his growing private and instinctive sense that there was so much more to this woman than met the eye. He was glad she also loved words and how dull, he mused to himself, how dull the person with no clutter shoved into the corners of their homes or minds! How little to discover and unfold.

He looked quizzically from the arresting book to her face, a slight frown of concentration playing round her eyes as she poured milk into the chipped cups.

Her mind.

Her mind that Adam so desired to sift, to find refuge in, to inhabit. He wanted to understand what fired her.

In truth her mind was as cluttered and eclectic as her flat. She loved stories, people, ideas, things. All sorts of bits and pieces of information, meaningful and trivial, joyously seized and treasured. She was like a magpie, with shiny things piled higgledy-piggledy, the gilt alongside the precious in glorious chaos, never ceasing to be interested in everything and everyone, her mind a teeming mass of half-baked ideas.

"It is a shame our Lucy never got to go to uni."

Jess, observing him looking through the book, had come up behind him without him noticing, speaking softly while Lucy was busy handing cups to Sebastian and Margo.

"Lucy's the bright star of the family. But our mam was poorly. She needed to stay at home, with being the eldest and some of us quite a bit younger. Dad had to be able to work."

Another pang for Adam. How easy he had had everything. What a mess he'd made of it. That was real mess, and there was no way of simply tidying it up.

Her mind . . . he pondered as he gazed at her, intensely, almost greedily, as she stood there bustling with mugs in her small living room, her hair messy, her cheeks flushed and her clothes muddied from the day's exertion. He wanted that mind.

And yet the moment these thoughts crystallized, he knew immediately that it wasn't enough. She was a woman. He was a man. "*Nature to her bias drew* . . . " Words from the deep, deeper than he could fathom. Human passions must run in the channels etched by nature on the face of reality. He could not create new ways of being, of existing, in relation to himself or others. He, like all humankind, must follow the pattern. And hadn't it all been, after all, so physical, that strange epiphany? He felt instinctively in that moment that the mind is not enough, it is too thin a wrapping for the soul.

He felt her palpably taking shape around the shadowy recesses of her compelling consciousness, the lines at first sketchy and then fuller and fuller. How strange it was for him to be growing in awareness of her this way round. How opposite to his usual experiences with women, where if he was honest, the mind had hardly mattered. And she, no longer the terrifying vision in medieval brilliance, with its uncompromising refusal of perspective in two dimensions, no longer even the existential refuge of recent weeks, but a softer, fully human shape with subtler lights and shades was gradually taking its place in front of a distant horizon. There she stood before him, revealed, appearing to his hungry soul glorious in all dimensions. He knew then he needed the grounding of her body too, to know that completeness. He knew it with a sudden desperate certainty, the colour of his whole awareness stained with his need, like blood mixing through water until the two are indistinguishable. He felt saturated with his longing, his longing for that full union with the compassionate other, to escape the unbearable confinement, the terrible isolation of his own being.

His need strained painfully towards her across the small room, twisting in his gut and overwhelming him like the surging of a great and sudden wave, thrown up from the depths. His passion, that driving force that had wreaked so much destruction, must have a physical grounding. *Perhaps these feelings were inevitable in the end, the way of all flesh?* But it felt so much more than that. She had been sent to him, he had no doubt, like an angel from heaven, first the dark angel of terror and death, now of light and radiance and hope. He knew with utter conviction that he needed her, needed her wholeness; a safe haven where he could anchor his own strivings, the beam of light to draw him safely home through the storm. God alone knew on what perilous reef he would be wrecked left to the restless and untamed surging of his own soul, forced relentlessly onwards, alone and adrift, beyond hope and reason, "*a condemned ship without masts, dancing, dancing, on a monstrous, shoreless sea*".

Those terrifying lines of Baudelaire that had always haunted him struck him now with new force:

> *Et mon âme dansait, dansait, vieille gabarre*
> *Sans mâts, sur une mer monstrueuse et sans bords!*

Monica

With eager steps they climb safely ashore
Into the crumbling grandeur of this once great port,
Now forlornly fallen from its former glory.
But still it holds a great promise for our pilgrims
And a place in their hearts, a holy site,
For it is known to be the final resting place
Of pious Monica, mother of great Augustine,
Who has afforded them, and so many,
Such blessings of wisdom and devotion shared.
It was she, who through her ardent prayerful striving,
Finally saw after seventeen summers of resistance,
The fruit of her weeping in the saving of her son,
And the fulfilment of the words of the blessed bishop,
From whom she had besought comfort,
That "the child of those tears shall never perish"
And received the reward of knowing,
Before she flew from this earthly realm,
That he was safe in the fold of the heavenly flock.

They read with heads bowed the epitaph
Conceived by Anicius Auchenius Bassus
And inscribed on stone in indelible letters
To inspire all who pass by:

"Here the most virtuous mother of a young man set her ashes
A second light to your merits, Augustine.
As a priest, serving the heavenly laws of peace
You teach the people entrusted to you with your character.
A glory greater than the praise of your
     accomplishments crowns you both
—Mother of the Virtues, more fortunate because of her offspring."

Alwin and his aged mentor are moved to tears
As they remember the unflinching mother-love
Of Monica towards a seeming prodigal son
And ponder on the picture it provides of the patient parent,
Our own Heavenly Father, who perceiving us still afar off,
Casts off His outer robe and runs to greet us,
Welcoming us home, embracing us
In forgiving, gracious, eternal arms that encircle us
And the whole universe in incarnate Love.

They recall the ninth book of Augustine's Confessions
And they recount the blessed dialogue between mother and son,
So precious for devotional delights, recorded
Soon before her soul departed this realm of tears,
In which both drew richly from the deep wells of salvation,
And took great comfort in their conversation
That led them to conclude that no bodily pleasure,
However great it be and whatever earthly light
Might shed lustre upon it, was worthy of comparison
To the happiness of the life of the true saints.
And as the flame of love flared stronger in them
Giving their souls flight and raising them
Higher towards the eternal God, their thoughts
Ranged over the compass of material things,
Over their various degrees, up to the heavens themselves
From which the sun and moon and stars
Shine down their guardian beams upon the earth.
Higher still they soar, basking all the while
In wonder at all the Lord has made,
Until they come, at length, to their own souls, and pass
Beyond them to that place of everlasting plenty
Where the Shepherd of Israel for ever feeds his flock
With the food of truth. There life is, that Wisdom
By which all these wondrous things that we can know

Are made, all things that ever have been
And all that is yet to be.
But that Wisdom is not formed,
It is as it has always been, and as it will for ever be,
Or rather as it simply is, because eternity
Is not past or future, but is always present.

And as they spoke of the eternal Wisdom, longing
And straining for it with all the strength of mortal will,
For one fleeting instant felt they reached out and touched it,
Felt it even in their fallen, finite hearts. Then with a sigh,
Leaving their spiritual harvest bound to it,
Returned to the sound of their own speech,
Where each word has a beginning and an ending,
Far different from your Word, your Wisdom, our Lord,
You who abide in Yourself for ever, yet never grow old,
And yield life to all things.

So sanctified mother and son spoke together.
And suppose also, they said, that the tumult of man's flesh
Were to cease, and that all that his thoughts can conceive,
Of earth, water and air,
Should no longer converse with him,
Suppose that the heavens and even his own soul was silent,
No longer conscious of itself but passing beyond,
Suppose that his shadowy dreams
And the visions of his imagination spoke no more,
And every tongue and every sign
And all that is transient grew silent and still,
For all these things have the same message to tell,
If only we will hear it. And their message is this:
We did not make ourselves, but He
Who abides for ever marvellously made us.

Suppose, they said, that after giving us this message
And bidding us listen to Him who made them,
They fell silent, and He alone should speak to us,
Not through them, but in His own voice,
So that we should hear Him speaking,
Not by any tongue of flesh, or mouth of man,
Or made manifest by angel's voice,
Not in the terrible sound of thunder
Or in some thin-veiled parable,
But in His own beloved voice,
The voice of the one whom we love
In all these various created things.
Suppose we heard Him Himself,
With none of these things between ourselves and Him—
Just as in that briefest moment mother and son
Had reached out in thought and touched
The eternal Wisdom which abides over all things—
Suppose that this state were to continue
And all other sights of things inferior
Were to be removed, so that this single vision
Entranced and absorbed the one who beheld it
And enveloped and encircled him in inward joys
So that for him, life was eternally the same
As that illuminated moment
For which understanding he had so much longed,
Would not this be what we are to understand by the words:
Come and share the joy of your Lord?
And would not that be the blessed home of all beatitude,
The convergence and expansion of all beauty and all truth?

Knowledge of the evil and of the good

"Damn, I've left my keys behind!"

They must have slipped out of his pocket while he was sitting on the little sofa. He hadn't got round to adding the flat keys to his car keyring—perhaps was subconsciously avoiding that small act of finality and defeat. He had just dropped Jess and his children back to their respective homes. Should he go back and get them? It was quite late now. But how tempting. Of course he wanted to go back and now he had the perfect excuse—she didn't need to know about the spares kept by the neighbour.

He had his folder of work resting on the dashboard. He had shoved it there on his way home last night and had forgotten to take it out of the car. He paused, his eyes resting on it. He knew exactly what was written on those topmost sheets of paper. He knew of the great lighthouse, warning of imminent ruin, of the beseeching tears of the pious mother, that faithful parent, the long-awaited return of the prodigal son, the glimpse of that purest, fullest and most blessed life. The shabby foolscap, reflecting the lurid sodium orange of the streetlights, had become, momentarily, an ominous beacon.

He looked away, put the key in the ignition and sat there with the engine running. He didn't have to go in. He could just see if she was still up . . . and he did need his keys back—they did have his key for the department building attached too. He turned the car around and drove back, managing to park quite close. He hesitated in front of the numerous bells. What if she had already gone to bed? He looked up and could see the light still on in her window and a faint silhouette moving behind the frosted glass. He put his finger on her bell and pressed gently. After waiting a few minutes with no response, he tentatively tried the handle of the outer street door. It was not locked. She must have forgotten. He quietly let himself into the communal porch and crept up the stairs to her flat door.

He tapped gently and held his breath for a moment. No response. He tapped again and whispered, "Lucy! Lucy, are you there? I'm sorry, I've left my keys behind!"

Lucy, in fact, had been in the shower and was only now emerging, her wet hair hanging loose around her face. She heard the tapping and then Adam's voice. Her heart leapt in a most uncomfortable way, part shock, part fear, part something else. She stood there paralysed, rooted to the ground.

She heard his voice again, slightly louder, more urgent.

"Lucy!"

As he called her name, she felt something twist inside her, halfway between dread and desire. Still she didn't move. She didn't want to open the door. She was afraid and she couldn't gather her scattered senses. She heard him finally turn in the corridor outside and then his footsteps quietly retreating.

No!

She suddenly knew she could not bear for him to go. Not again, not like that terrible dream. Must she keep reliving the nightmare? Flinging on her dressing gown she ran to the door, her warm, damp hand slipping on the handle. Finally she had it open and she rushed from the door to the landing at the top of the stairs just in time to see him open the outer door.

"Adam!" she called, unable to quite keep the desperation out of her voice, "Adam, I'm here!"

He turned, an even darker shadow against the dark night. She by contrast was illuminated by the light streaming out from the open door behind her.

Shutting the door again he made his way carefully back up, climbing that kindled stair to where she was waiting in her white robe, her smooth milky skin, slightly flushed, her hair pouring like haloed honey over her shoulders. How beautiful she is, he mused to himself, overwhelmed. Nothing fake, just pure beauty, like a gold embellished icon, emitting radiance.

He steadied himself on the banister. He must be careful. He must not let himself get carried away or frighten her.

"I'm sorry," he whispered, "I've left my keys behind. I hope I didn't disturb you?"

Lucy thought to herself that she found him most unaccountably disturbing but all she said, with an effort at normality, was, "No, not at all, I've just got out of the shower."

She wished at once she hadn't quite said that as it seemed to conjure inappropriately intimate images and she blushed. *What was wrong with her? Why couldn't she be normal?* She unconsciously pulled her dressing gown more securely around herself and again summoned her scattered wits. "Can you remember where you left them?"

"I'm afraid not," he said smiling, although this wasn't entirely true.

"Perhaps you'd better come in and take a look," she said, before thinking what she was saying. Then in panic her mind began to spin. *What was she doing? This was wrong! Where was it all going to end?* She didn't trust him. She was afraid of him. And she had a strange sense that by letting him in she was crossing some invisible rubicon, for better or for worse. But there had been no time to think, no time, and it was done, in a fraction of a heartbeat, and there was no going back.

"Thanks."

He paused for the briefest moment, a lame internal token gesture of resistance, and then brushed past her through the door. She quickly shut it behind him. Better to have left it open she realized, too late. She was trapped. She hoped no one from the other flats had witnessed the odd little scene just played out on the landing, or inhaled the air, heavy with unspoken meaning.

He walked over to the sofa where he thought he'd probably left the obliging keys, his conscience smiting him just a very little.

I shouldn't have let him in! What am I doing? Am I mad? She hadn't wanted to be rude or spoil the day they'd had, and now it was too late. Part of her was in free-fall panic, desperate for him to just take his keys and get out; get out of her space, get out of her head, get out of her life. But another part, a darker, more complicated part, wanted him to stay; in that moment desired to cling to his presence above all things. Her chaotic mind and heart strove within her, and before she knew it consciously, she'd lost the battle, like a moth before a flame, compelling her to make the insane and absurd invitation:

"Can I get you another drink while you're here?"

The words were out of her mouth before she had consciously assented to them. She knew somewhere deep down that she had crossed a line, but in that moment she didn't care. She was accelerating down a slope of increasing gradient, unable to stop or slow down, slipping towards the heaving depths that she could not, would not comprehend.

He sensed her uncertainty, distress even. He looked at her with indecision. He did not want to spoil things either or push his luck. He knew the decent thing to do would be to take his keys and go, immediately. She was like a snared animal. He could taste her wild fear but also something else. Something subtle but overwhelmingly strong. Even he, a connoisseur of women, could not yet quite place it. He should leave, but he was piqued, and he had had years of practice in crushing his threadbare conscience.

"Well, as long as you're sure? I don't want to keep you up."

How strange words are. How many different uses we put them to. How often they are used to conceal rather than illuminate, a wide gulf stretching between what we say and what we mean; the acceptable mundane formulas we have agreed for communicating with or confusing one another, huge vessels of meaning indicated by a small wave of a flag, both parties playing a game of deception that even so oils the wheels of human communion. And how terrifying in our darkened state if we were compelled to expose our minds and hearts before one another and receive the unmediated truth from them in return. Words can become for us the hastily grasped fig leaves sewn together to cover our shame, or the skins granted us to hide our naked souls from the unbearable purging light.

She stared at him, managing to gather her few remaining wits to say something vaguely rational and snatch back a bit of integrity.

"Don't worry, I don't think I could sleep yet anyway! I'll put the kettle on and then get some clothes on."

Well, it was true. The worst thing of all would be to lie alone in bed, sleeplessly, endlessly replaying the whole absurd scenario, wondering what might have unfolded if she had turned to the left or to the right, had had a little more courage, a little more strength . . . and not ever knowing, or ever being able to know the outcome. And anyway, it was already too late, the path was set.

She went over to put the kettle on for the second time that evening. For the second time he stood and watched her silently, sifting her in his mind. She was so young and vulnerable. He could do anything, absolutely anything with her if he wanted. He held all the power; he had all the experience. He was an expert. She wouldn't have a hope of resisting him if he really determined on having her. Robert was wrong. He could sense the kindled fire in her. He could have her now, right now if he wanted, on the cold, dusty floor. She was fragile tonight, disoriented and strangely stirred. He knew the scent of weakness. She was a rare fruit, ripe for the plucking, a deeply sensual being, although not yet fully self-aware. She would succumb; voluntarily, actively—and against her conscious will. Whatever she believed, whatever afterwards might ensue, in this moment he could break her, break her resistance, with the lightest of touches. She would be putty in his hands, a quivering, desperate shipwreck of desire. He could crush her and like a bee leave a mortal sting behind to work its poison, and while she writhed in her own exquisite hell, walk away, dying just a little more himself inside.

He felt insanely cheated and disillusioned. She was in the end just an ordinary woman, with the potential to fall, a flawed idol after all. And he despised her.

These thoughts all flashed across his mind in a moment, and he instantly felt appalled at himself. What kind of predatory monster was he? He felt like a heretic who has wrongfully strayed into some sacred place.

A sudden rush of tenderness, that seemed to pour in from outside of himself, engulfed and swallowed all his contempt and took possession of his heart. He found himself vowing silently that from this moment onwards any strength or knowledge he had would always be used to protect her, from himself if necessary, and preserve that pure beauty at all costs from any taint. He would lay himself, his imperfect offering, on the altar for her, even if he was consumed and destroyed in the process. In that moment he finally understood what it meant to love. And he found he loved her. Anything, everything to do with her must always be about giving, not taking, if he had anything left worth giving. And how weary he was of taking, always taking, consuming and spitting out the husks, but never being any more satisfied. This was not why he had pursued her. And anyway, the self-defeating folly of it. It would be like snapping the golden thread of his lifeline, smashing his own sanctuary, desecrating his own temple. And for what? For a few moments of vicious pleasure of the same kind he'd had so many times before and walked away from each time a little more achingly empty and alone.

How could he, even for a split second, despise her? He despised himself. How could he, of all people, censure her for being flesh and blood too? Had she ever presented herself as anything more? It was he who had foolishly set her on some imagined pedestal and then cruelly desired to drag her down and grind her into the dust.

He forced his eyes away and sat down on the little sofa while he waited, deliberately distracting himself by examining the intriguing scraps of paper covered in scribble that he had half noticed before. He recognized her distinctive, slightly childish hand.

She came over with two mugs of tea, spilling them slightly as she walked. She had forgotten to even ask him what he wanted.

"You write?" he enquired with unmasked interest and delight. He was genuinely distracted. His other great passion.

"Well, sort of I suppose," she replied, flustered and embarrassed to have been found out in this way and by him of all people.

"Can I look?"

"Oh, well, I suppose so, if you want to. I have no idea if it's any good . . ."

She gabbled on nervously, somewhat incoherently. "But I feel sort of compelled, almost despite myself sometimes, to try to just get out what is inside, a kind of purging, I suppose, to get some peace. And what is the point of all this stuff floating around in my head if I can't communicate it to anyone, even assuming it's worth communicating? I sometimes feel I will go mad for all the ideas and feelings and desires bursting out of my mind! I feel like I'm full of chaos that needs order imposed upon it. I try to get some relief by writing poetry. I don't know if it's any good as poetry, but in a sense that's not the main point of it. I just have to try to get things out of my system, work them through, try to make some sort of sense of them . . . you know what I mean? You are educated and clever. I wish I had had a better education. It was good in some ways, don't get me wrong. I'm grateful for the opportunities I had and some of the teachers were great . . . but there is so much I don't know and want to know but I don't even really know how or where to start."

She stopped to draw breath.

He was looking at her once again in blank wonder, in amazement, fired by her energy and passion, hungrily drinking it in. He had spent so long in the shadows of academic toxicity and posturing.

She did surpass all his intuitions about her, after all, the instinct that had been growing increasingly since the conversation in her office that cold lunchtime. It was just that the reality was far greater and more subtle than his fiction of her. Why must she be either crudely painted Madonna or fallen Magdalene? Why this foolish dichotomy? He was staggered by the realization of his own vast prudishness and hypocrisy. He who had thought himself so modern, so liberal, so liberated found himself to be riddled with unconscious prejudices enough to shame any Victorian caricature, each chauvinistic view more deeply embedded than the last. Had he even ever truly *seen* a woman before, even his own wife, or had he only looked, voyeuristically? What a terrible husband he had been to her, she who had borne him his beautiful children and borne with him for so long. He found himself suddenly hoping with all his heart that her new man would see her more clearly and cherish her as he should have done. He had learned so much about himself over the last few months, more than he had done in the lifetime before and it was devastating. And now, he was the one trying to force a gilt halo onto Lucy's human head. Why should she not have her own fears and desires, her own struggles and needs?

Was she too not merely flesh and blood?

Perhaps not merely.

For somehow, beneath it all he still felt an unseen hand, mysteriously, terribly had driven him to where he now sat, amazed and humbled by his own folly and her reality, a higher hand that had stayed his own when faced with the almost overwhelming temptation to desecrate and destroy and cast himself adrift from grace. Miraculously, even supernaturally, he had been empowered to master himself and choose the better path.

He picked up a crumpled page from the table and spread it out and read the scribbled lines. She vaguely and ineffectually protested.

Eventually he looked up. "Did you really write this?"

"Yes," she whispered, squirming with embarrassment. To have him, anyone, read her secret writing made her soul feel naked, like winter skin suddenly exposed to the burning summer sun, the layers of protection ripped away.

"You weren't meant to see that! Particularly you of all people weren't meant to see it when you actually know about poetry and literature and all! I know I have something to say, I just wish . . . just wish I could learn to say it better. Like with this one . . . Oh, I just couldn't get it right, to get the words to have the right sound, give the right meaning. You know how satisfying it is when they just seem to fall into the right, the perfect pattern, like the perfect chords in a piece of music? I've always wished I could write music, play music. It seems to be able to speak straight to the heart, to touch the soul, without even needing words."

"But your words are wonderful!" he said, staring at her in astonishment without any trace of flattery or disingenuity. "Extraordinary. You have a real talent, a gift. Yes, I'm clever, I'm educated, I can write well about other people's writing, translate them even, but this, this is different, this is inspired. You have created this, not just basked in someone else's glory. And this is when you say it hasn't really worked! You must keep writing. What's in there is definitely worth getting out. You cannot keep all that treasure locked away; you must share it with us lesser mortals!"

"Don't tease me!" she said, almost angrily. "I need to know if what you're saying is really true. It matters to me. It's too hard to lay myself out, expose myself if it's not really true."

He took both her hands in his and looked directly into her eyes, frankly and honestly and finally as an equal, in mind, body and spirit; not as a goddess or a hapless femme fatale, a minion or a seer, or an object existing simply for his own convenience, gratification or even salvation, but as another truly compassionate, comparable human being. Not *merely* anything but a wonder of perfectly designed, miraculously formed compatibility. In fact nothing more or less than herself, her true self, and not just a projection of his own fantasy. Was this not enough? Even if she gave herself to him, he would never own her. Consent. On how many subtle levels we must wish to share and yield to give ourselves fully, freely and unreservedly to another human being. And are we even ourselves to give?

"It *is* true! It's beautiful and it's true, just like you."

She felt as though a maddening fire was streaming through his hands into hers, coursing through her whole body. She couldn't bear it. She felt she might be sick, or faint, or even die. The blood was pounding in her head. She was trembling all over. Her body did not feel strong enough to contain such feelings. She felt she was fighting for her life, her existence. The stakes were high. It was a battle on the field of spiritual reality. She did not know that he had already fought on her behalf, and won. She just felt she must try, however hopelessly, to stop this at all costs. She must deflect him and strike straight to the heart.

"So you believe Keats is right?" she gasped, tearing her eyes from his and wrenching away her hands.

"Eh?" He was momentarily thrown. It gave her space to gather herself.

"You know, when he says that '*Beauty is Truth and Truth Beauty*'?"

He instinctively felt a little threatened, being challenged on his own turf and the surprising way she'd turned the words round on him. But although it was unexpected, he perceived the strange genuineness of the question. She was not trying to catch him out, trying to be clever or even simply changing the subject. She really wanted to know what he thought, as if her life depended on his answer. It was a question, after all, that went right to the heart of the matter. Her utter directness disarmed him though, broke the ecstatic intensity of the moment and feeling emotionally thwarted he mechanically reverted to form. He just couldn't seem to help himself. Old habits die hard, both the superficial ones and the deep hidden streams that direct the courses of our lives.

"Well, I don't know. I've always gone in for beauty more than truth myself!" He grinned.

Then looking at her pained face he pulled himself together and forced his mind in a different, less familiar, direction. Alwin, he felt sure, would have known the answer. He owed it to her, to himself, to be serious, more serious than ever before.

"I suppose I thought it was rather a sentimental view," he said after a moment's pause. "But," he gazed at her thoughtfully, "there's nothing sentimental about you or what you've written. Perhaps there is something in it after all. You make me feel there must be something in it."

He looked at her quizzically. "And what about you? What do you think?"

She furrowed her brow and began falteringly, "I don't think they are umm, what's the word . . . synonymous, and no, I don't think he was probably right in the way he meant it. I mean, I don't think it's *all* we need to know, but I do believe perhaps," she spoke slowly, "that *true* Truth is always beautiful and *real* beauty is always truthful, if you know what I mean? Things can appear to be beautiful and appealing, but they only stay that way, are only beautiful all the way through, if they are also true."

She was in part catechizing herself, trying to stay herself against the maddening temptation to throw herself over the cliff edge of her desire, to yield to the tide of her longing.

"Yes, yes, you may well be right," he agreed eagerly. "At any rate you seem to embody the principle in yourself." He smiled, but this time it was entirely spontaneous.

She reddened and looked away. She didn't know how to feel, what all this meant. Unconsciously she was gripping the sides of the sofa as if she was afraid of falling, her knuckles white, her head giddy. She believed he was at least half-sincere, at least in the moment. But how could she know it was true all the way through and in the cold light of day? And did she want it anyway? How could it even be right? He moved her strangely. Half of her wanted his admiration, felt excited by his approval even, and was intoxicated by his physical presence, the other half felt troubled and distrustful. He stirred new feelings in her that intensely disturbed her but also had awoken a deep sense of yearning.

"And what about broken beauty?" he suddenly said, moving round to face her again. "Is that True? Like the Japanese bowl?"

He needed an answer to this—this question that had also haunted parts of Alwin's narrative.

"Well . . ." she pondered, emboldened by his affirmation of her and his genuine engagement, ideas crystallizing as she clothed them with words and gave them voice, the emotion spilling out of her eagerly, "I think . . . I think broken beauty is perhaps the most beautiful and truthful of all. It must be because even God's greatest glory is in the broken beauty of his Son. He made us in His image and then when we smashed it, He smashed himself too, broke His very heart . . . and so now, amazingly, mirrors *us* just as we mirror Him—a glorious broken God for a broken people. God forsaken by God for us. No one can know pain as He knows pain . . . To reach us, to reach across the chasm, to make a way back to Himself and to Truth, God broke Himself."

He was intrigued, enraptured, and it gave him a great surge of hope.

"But why? What kind of God does that?"

He held his breath, and the universe held its breath because somehow the answer seemed to really matter, not just to them, but to all men and women everywhere in every time and place; and also because, perhaps deep down, he and the universe already knew the answer, for it is written into every strand of being, which whispers it in the deep and shouts it into the void.

"One who is Love."

He looked at her and this time she did not avert her eyes but bathed in his gaze. Her face was luminous. Adam drank deeply from that eternal pool of her eyes. It was as if they were locked into a moment beyond time, trying to read each other's souls.

"Every heart . . ." murmured Adam softly, half to himself, remembering the fractured beauty of the Japanese bowl, "every heart to Love must come . . . But like a refugee."

The theologian of love

Little wonder, muses Alwin, that Augustine should
Be called the great advocate and theologian of Love.
He charts his journey to the place of peace
As a relentless pursuit by the passionate hound of heaven—
From his long student days in Carthage,
When he fell in love with the idea of being in love,
Through all his addiction to carnal lust,
His strong affection for friends, his deep desire for wisdom—
It is always love that enthralled and thrilled his heart,
Pursuing him back to the true source,
The relentless agent of that divine Love, the great Lover,
Revealed at last as the triune Holy Spirit of Christ
Who poured the love and righteousness of God into his heart.

His discourses of Truth have also kept from Alwin's mind
The tempting, treacherous heresy of Pelagius,
As himself, British born, but believing
We have in ourselves power to choose
What or when to love,
And that living by the law is enough
For lasting godliness and salvation, understanding not
That Love is the whole heart of gospel hope.
For we know, if candid with ourselves,
We cannot keep the law of works or achieve
That absolute perfection required by a holy God
Of burning brightness and searing purity,
But must rather from his presence be banished,
Like our first fallen parents from paradise.
But what glorious blessing to grasp, Augustine argues,
That our will is governed by our affections; by what we love.
Thus, without the Spirit, in our fallen selves

We freely choose to love our sin, but
By his saving work within us He frees our wills
To love the only object worthy of our love,
Our Creator who fashioned us for Himself
To bathe in the beauty of light eternal
And find our fullness and rest in Him.
For the truest, purest love
Is enjoyment of God for His own sake,
Insatiable satisfaction, sweeter than all pleasure,
A love that yearns and longs legitimately for fulfilment
As well as to give adoration and afford obedient worship;
And thus we love Him,
Desiring only to be rewarded with Him
And dwell eternally in His divine presence,
For He is the beginning and end of Love.

Annunciation

"I don't believe you're any more in love with me than any other tolerably attractive woman!" she exclaimed. "Not really!"

She felt cross and perverse this evening and wanted to goad him into an admission, one way or the other. After their strange and intense encounter last night he had abruptly turned and left, leaving her confused, a little hurt and utterly spent. She could not know he had been protecting her from those forces he knew neither of them would have been able to control if he had stayed any longer, true to his silent vow. He couldn't expect a second reprieve. And he couldn't explain it all to her, not yet. He still didn't really fully understand himself all that had taken place in his internal landscape last night, he just knew that the significance was immense. To her, however, he had seemed to go from fire to ice in the blinking of an eye. She didn't know of his inner battles or revelations. She still suspected his sincerity and yet she now craved his affirmation, craved his touch. But she was determined, completely determined, that she would not be his plaything. His attempts to make himself part of her life over the last few months had frightened, irritated, flattered and amused her by turn. She could no longer pretend indifference. Last night he had seen into her soul. His sudden declaration of love for her today left her stranded between hope and doubt. Not just doubt of his truthfulness but doubt of herself and doubt of what was right, doubt of what was real.

He looked thoughtful.

"You may be right," he said slowly. "On one level anyway, I suppose I am half in love with every youngish, prettyish woman I meet! Well, not love, love is definitely the wrong word. I'm sorry, it's just the way I am. I don't know how to be any different. Are all men like me, I wonder? There have been times when I've felt so full of passion that I might explode!"

He paused and winced. *Why must he always sink into such ridiculous hyperbole? Why did he speak as if the world must accommodate his excesses? How absurd and pretentious he was!* He carried on hurriedly, "But you, you *are* different all the same. You have something, something in yourself that

I want, that I want more than anything else, that drives me on relentlessly. I can't stop trying . . . "

He looked quizzically at her, trying to understand and articulate the feelings that had been steadily rising inside him and becoming ever more complex, since that day when everything changed. And then with sudden clarity, "And do you know what it is, Lucy, despite everything, you have peace, true peace, rest, like Augustine speaks of, and . . . and substance and *reality*, like the sensation in the church, like the images in the window . . . you are a little piece of truth."

She looked at him for a long time. She didn't know whether to feel offended or glad.

"I want peace, your reality, your rest. And I want you, with your peace, to be part of it . . . "

She turned away abruptly. She felt deeply troubled, and her pride was hurt. She had been taken aback by his honest frankness. It wasn't his usual way or the reply she'd expected when she'd challenged him. She realized in a sudden flash of self-knowledge that for all the discomfort, she had been increasingly enjoying his attentions over the last few months.

She hadn't really been posing a serious challenge; she had just wanted him to flatter her. *Beware asking the question to which we don't really want the answer!* she thought, angry with herself.

"Come to church with me if you like," she said rather coldly. She knew she should be pleased that he perceived her as different and was pursuing her company for the deepest reasons, but she now realized she also wanted to be desired, desired passionately for herself too, in that special, particular way. She felt confused. Was it wrong to feel this? She had thought at first she didn't want his flirtations, had felt irritated by his pursuit. She was disturbed by the feelings he'd awoken in her, but she was also now full of desperate longing.

"Maybe I will . . . but Lucy, I'm sorry, I've upset you. What have I done?"

"Nothing. Nothing at all!" She tried to smile.

"Ok," he said, a little perturbed. He looked at her wistfully. "You know, I feel I can talk to you about anything, honestly, in a way that I can talk to no one else. I don't have to pretend or put on an act, although that's fun sometimes . . . I can be my real self," he winced, "for what that's worth. You have no idea what a relief that is," he mused, "after years of pretence, years of running. It's like, like coming home . . . Aren't we strange creatures, working on so many levels and so oblivious to our own deepest needs and desires, only glimpsing them sometimes in our dreams or the shadows of our dreams, until love, true Love, intervenes . . . "

He thought of the words he had been translating only that morning, words from Augustine, the "Theologian of Love", that our wills are turned towards and governed by what we love. He didn't fully understand it but had some vague notion that this sudden conviction of his love for Lucy was a movement in the right direction, a movement towards the source. *A love that yearns rightly, legitimately for fulfilment as well as to give adoration* . . . it was focusing in on her and yet in doing so promised the opening of a great and wide vista, beyond anything he had ever known or could have before conceived.

She was looking at him intently now, a besieged city whose walls have been suddenly breached. She did not know how close she had come to real peril last night when she had hovered on the edge of the void. She couldn't say anything for a moment, but a new warmth was ignited in her heart.

"I didn't know it 'til just now either," she said eventually, "but I like, really like, being with you too . . . I didn't know until you said you could desire almost anybody that I wanted you to desire—to be in love with—me, just me."

She blushed. She couldn't believe she was saying these things. She gave a shaky laugh. He tried to grab her hand, but she evaded him.

"To my shame you are the only person I *have* ever properly loved." He continued, "But I believe—I know—you are beginning to change all that, have taught me and will help me from now on to love everyone more and more."

She looked at him, a little flummoxed, struggling to keep up with the febrile pace of his admissions, his agitated declarations.

And suddenly with joyful animation, "Come with me, come with me now and I will feast you like a queen! Let me cherish you and celebrate you, us, Love . . . I *will* take you out! You can't turn me down again after what you've just confessed to me, you beautiful, strange creature! It *is* just you, and yet so much more too. Don't you understand? There's no conflict! It's more that you—you and I together—are the first step to something richer, so much richer and more glorious. I can't really explain it, I feel I am at the limit of language . . . it's, it's like the light glimpsed from the corner of an eye but when we turn it's retreated even further back, or like the hint of a memory of a long-forgotten path. You are like a gateway, or the key to the door, or maybe even just a glimpse through the keyhole. You are everything I'm not and hold everything I need—a sight into a different world, a whole new way of being."

"And I couldn't be just anyone right now? Any woman I mean, the means to an end to fill an empty night?" she queried.

She still couldn't quite throw off her suspicion. She needed reassurance, was tentatively reaching out to him across the abyss of her self-doubt and his past.

"You still don't really understand, do you?" he smiled tenderly, poignantly. "It's not just more of the same order, or even more of the same in greater measure. That serpent has already been faced and somehow, amazingly, resisted. Yes, there is desire, you know . . . I know you also have known . . . the overwhelming potency of it, but the feelings are so, so much bigger than even that, although they encompass that too. My love reaches out to you, consuming my whole being, because . . . because in and through you I feel I am—we are—reaching out towards something immeasurably greater. My desire does not converge on you as a means to an end, in the old shallow, limiting way, that eventually binds us and makes us slaves to our own lusts, but my love *expands* towards you as a journey to a new beginning, an ever-opening vista. You are the moon that draws my tide, my lodestar. I don't just *want* you, Lucy, I *need* you . . . I need you so much that it's breaking my heart."

Through a mist of tears she slowly, tentatively reached out her hand and breached the gulf. Letting go, finally, of the few brittle, prosaic threads that still tied him to the old country he grasped it rapturously. So small and fragile it felt and yet with an underlying strength beyond his own. He was flooded with a sense of freedom and relief. Without a backward look and without a word he led her out into the star-strewn night.

His own life entered the realm of poetry, his whole being sliding in with the ease and grace of a swimmer, who after battling rapids and rocks, dark stagnant pools and muddy estuaries, finally breaks out into the clear expanse of an ocean of light.

We do not want to be peaceful, nor do we wish to be parted.
War is for ever between us, yet with arms that are yielding;
Peace established below, and therefore the battle quiescent:
Each from the other one guiltless always plucking the harvest.

Hwaetbert

Imago Dei

A feast fit for a queen
candlelight glistening
through pale ambers and deep reds
wine illuminating
bread of life
seared fish
fresh from the sea
the cream and the honey
the jewel-like fruits
music melodious
filled with deep longing
touched with poignancy
floating
man and woman
locked in the intensity
of each other's gaze
rapturous
feasting on each other's eyes and company
as on the beautiful bountiful food
drinking deeply at the well of joy.

They are as if alone
in a world of perfect delight
sensuous and spiritual
every level of their beings
basking gloriously in mutual meeting
recognition.
Peace in war
and war in peace.

Afterwards the two spill out together
indistinguishable shadows
onto the moonlit sand
dark water lapping gently
shell-strewn edges
silvery shimmering matching
cold frosty stars
keeping their watch overhead
singing their ancient
imperceptible harmony.

Hours dissolve
as they talk and walk
along the pale edge of the world
between shore and sea
day and night
sun and moon
hand in hand
two polarities straining
towards each other
wanting to understand
finding in their extremity
perfect and ultimate proximity
that balance of reflection
most closely resembling
the essence of being.

At length
the silver beauty of the night welcomes
the rose-gold salutations of the day
the western sky spreads with dusky purple
the velvet couch for the virgin moon
while the bridegroom sun
casts his gleaming garments

across the luminous eastern sky
as he rises in burning naked splendour
from the shimmering horizon
to meet her.

And so it is
that the two human creatures
as if in miniature re-enactment
of the great celestial and terrestrial dance
between moon and sun
shoreline and sea
the fine silken strands of their lives
drawn irresistibly
into the great pattern of being
find themselves standing
together
where day and night
sand and water
meet
always advancing
always retreating
battle quiescent
the line in the sand
for ever breached
ever embracing
ever yielding
also welcoming
the coming of dawn.

City of God

Approaching through a goodly country, well-tended,
Of sheep on soft green hills and sun-baked roads,
Lined by shady cypresses, curling towards the azure sky,
Fruitful vineyards and dappled olive groves,
At last the grateful travellers reach the holy city;
Great and glorious Rome, the goal of their strivings
And place of temporal rest, but in truth, simply
A small human expression of that great heavenly city
Where God eternally sits enthroned.
Alwin is awash with wonder at the spectacle of all this glory,
This manifestation of human skill and splendour,
But his ardour is checked by his aged companion
Who, though himself touched by the beauty
Of this pinnacle of artistic endeavour,
Reminds him gently that all this majesty
Is to be regarded as but a dim reflection
Of the true heavenly city, that New Jerusalem,
The blood-bought bride of Christ, spoken of by Saint John
As he raised his eyes to the last revelation.
So easy for our longing eyes to linger on lesser things
And to begin to believe they are themselves the end;
To forget to see beyond the sign to the substance,
To become enamoured with the mere picture
And fail to embrace the reality to which they point.
For in such lies the essence of idolatry,
That peril that will ever haunt the human heart,
That the truth of God be exchanged for a lie
And worship of the creature for that of the Creator.

Biscop speaks of the time, four hundred and ten summers
Since the blessed incarnation of our Lord,

When Alaric's barbarous Visigoths sacked this great city,
The beating heart of the glorious empire,
And even Jerome in his dismay wrote:
"If Rome be lost, where shall we look for help?"
How Augustine, in response to those pagan refugees—
Who had escaped to Hippo in his native North Africa,
And who claimed the great city that had stood
Unbreached eight hundred years was lost
Because the old ways and gods were cast aside—
Had conceived another masterful work,
His massive and magnificent theology
Of all things historical and political
That Biscop and Alwin have also lately acquired.
The City of God: a monument
To the great truth and substance of reality
Towards which the human heart cannot help but strain
Even when it knows it not. Those refugees,
Augustine writes, hankering after their home city,
The high and unsurpassable Rome, the wonder of the world,
Hunger aright in that they earnestly desire
A return to their honoured homeland and kindred dear
And yet, even this is but a shadow, and faint echo
Of the haunting yearning, deep within each human heart,
For in the end, they err in their longing for the wrong city,
That which is but a picture or a type of the true
And heavenly home, the city of the triune God.
For while this world's vain empires rise and fall,
God's kingdom ever grows and fills the earth,
As the tumultuous waters cover the sea.
And those who indeed espouse Christ as their Sovereign
Are those who truly understand,
As refugees, pilgrims and strangers in this world,
Who ever yearn and strain through faith
For their true and eternal heavenly home,

Those of whom the world is not worthy,
Those who seek a city not built with human hands
But one whose builder and architect is God Himself:
A great and complex creation comprised
Of all that is good and beautiful and true,
Not just a return to a garden, pure and undefiled,
Incubating, nurturing all the seeds of nature
And human progress in its nascent soil,
But a great monument and fulfilment
Of all the course of history and human endeavour,
The hope and treasures of the nations refined and gathered in;
A perfect testimony to redemptive Love,
Where from simple evil has been wrestled and wrested
Wide and complex good, devastating beauty.
For all human history, he writes, from the beginning of time,
From the first fall from grace in Eden of our primal parents,
Has been a conflict between the City of Man,
Built on the false, cruel and idolatrous love of self,
And the City of God,
Built on the true and righteous covenant love of God,
The sovereign Creator of all,
Who alone is worthy of worship.

This is not some new narrative,
Augustine argues to his Roman audience,
But from our first father Adam has been ever thus,
And to the end of this creation, will always be our human story.
And so must our allegiance never be to merely men,
Man-made monuments, monarchies, movements or signs,
For to confuse these insubstantial pictures
With the real truths towards which they point,
Is pernicious folly and fatal insanity. For all good gifts
Given here below are granted by His grace to open our eyes
And to draw us into His everlasting embrace

And to help us understand something
Of His great love for us, unworthy though we be.
But often, in our folly, we fashion into idols
These gracious gifts, not only rejecting and forsaking
The great Giver but are even tempted to twist,
To disfigure, what He has created good
And turn it into a negation of that true intent.
For the first and greatest tempter,
That ancient serpent and father of lies,
Can create nothing of himself but merely corrupt,
Distort and pervert what God has made.
And if we, like the first Adam,
Embrace the lie in place of divine truth,
We will be for ever lost and perish perpetually.
For though the City of Man promises the earth,
It delivers only death.
For this fallen world is not worth one single human soul,
And to barter with the snake of old and sire of falsehood
Is futile folly and yields nothing but dust.
But the City of God remains ever growing,
Glowing in glory and substance throughout all eternity.
And to those who surrender gladly
All these vacuous, vain and vanishing things,
Counting them but worthless mortal dross,
And take hold and cling to Christ,
The Word that spoke all things into being,
Who was made flesh to bear our human sins
And died to break the power of death,
To them is given a crown of life eternal
And to live for ever in love and light perpetual
And full of glory.

And so, concludes Biscop, these man-made marvels
Are both everything and yet nothing at all.

Yes, they are magnificent creations rightly inspiring us
To exercise God's good gifts in us,
Pictures pointing through our image-bearing passions,
Our created capacities and capabilities,
To the great Creator and true Architect of all,
And all His blessings are to be received with gratitude,
But even the sacred sacraments are but truths enacted,
"Visible words", and words themselves are but
A type of sign, pointing us to greater truths,
And Scripture, as very Word of God, the greatest sign,
Yet made up of all these little words,
All pointing to the wondrous Word-made-flesh,
Even the incarnate Son of God.
And when we faithfully follow the signs
Of sacrament and word by believing,
We receive the sublime substance
Of the gift of grace to which they point.
But if we fail to raise our eyes from gift,
However beguiling, to great Giver,
We cannot receive that glorious grace
Intended by our gracious Lord,
Who is author of all goodness
And Himself the precious prize,
The only peace and consummation
To truly content the restless human heart.

Alwin bows his head and begins to understand,
Beseeching the Lord of light to cast His sanctifying ray
Into the natural darkness of his heart,
To illuminate all that is erroneous and evil
And to help him to love aright
All that is good and beautiful and true.

Confession

As they had sat, side by side in his car, retracing as if in pilgrimage, Adam's first, momentous flight northwards to the sea, the day his brittle world had been shattered apart, they had talked of their different lives. They had tried to grasp tentatively the beginnings of an understanding of one another, to piece together each other's stories. It is hard to paint a full and faithful portrait, fill in the gaps from fragments and scraps of memories shared, hopes and fears confided, even when desiring to be honest. But wanting to know and be known does help, help overcome the instinct to hide and deceive.

He had told her about his boarding school, the abject misery of separation from his mother when he was only seven. Before then he had been at a small prep-school, where his memories seemed to be all of fighting other small boys outside in the mud, shorts in all weathers, with a little bit of Latin and Greek thrown in; tales of wars and exploits which seemed to blend in his mind with their own exciting, brutal games . . . He could hardly remember anything before that, except a single fragment of exquisite peace and happiness, sitting on his mother's lap under a tree, looking up at the pattern of golden leaves and branches against an azure sky.

Then there had been a hazy baby sister, who had appeared then disappeared just as suddenly in a painful cloud of confusion and despair. His mother had not been the same afterwards and he had learnt later that the loss of her infant daughter had plunged her into a deep depression, making her incapable, for a while, of anything. It had seemed best to his parents to send him to school. His father, although grieving in his own way, he supposed, had not known how to reach out to his son or his wife. His work at the Foreign Office meant he was often away. He couldn't care for a child, he had told himself and was glad of the excuse to escape whenever possible the empty scene of sorrow and devastation his home had become. He had tried, in his way, to comfort his wife, but had given it up as hopeless far too quickly, finding comfort and distraction for himself instead in the glamorous, treacherous world he inhabited.

All that Adam could really remember about him was that he was always terribly formal. He even used to say "Good morning" to the cat.

He had died after a brief but severe illness, which no one explained, when Adam was 21; a stranger whom he hardly knew. He told Lucy how he had sat by his bedside in the hospital, staring at all the tubes and screens. He had been there at the end. Neither of them could think of a single thing to say. They had sat in blank, empty silence and then he had died, without a murmur or even a pressure of the hand. And Adam had felt absolutely nothing. The scene, he said, had kept replaying in his mind, and sometimes even now in his dreams, and every time he sought for some kind of emotion, some kind of meaning, but never found any.

He and his mother had gradually rebuilt their relationship in the brief punctuations of school holidays. She still lived in Windsor, where he had been born. They now had a fragile but workable kind of relationship. "But I've never understood her," he had said, "and I don't think my father ever could either. That's one of the problems of spending so much time in an all-male environment. Not everything about school was bad, by any means, I mainly enjoyed it once I had got used to it. Some of it was wonderful fun, and the English teacher was inspiring. I learned to love poetry, particularly the epic kind. I've always tried, wanted, to write my own, but the words would never come. Perhaps now they will . . .

"I wasn't bullied or anything either, although I'm afraid I did probably bully a little myself, without even realizing it at the time. I was popular and confident by then and had achieved a sort of admired notoriety for my wild spirits and pranks. Even the teachers at those kinds of schools seem to approve of that kind of thing; it's an odd world. I don't suppose it did much for my ego—I must have been unbearable really. Probably still am—no, don't say anything! There were great opportunities, and temptations, all the usual, petty, grubby stuff, I'll spare you the details. It was certainly a great eye opener of a kind, but I was only ever with chaps, you see. It's not a very full education or balanced preparation for life, particularly if you don't have any sisters or know any normal people. I know I sound like

I'm making excuses for how I am, but I'm not, honestly, I suppose I'm just trying to explain, give some sort of account of myself."

She instinctively had reached across and squeezed his leg in a gesture of sympathy and acceptance. They had shot forward a little more quickly as his other foot had jerked on the accelerator. She had quickly drawn back her hand, embarrassed, and stared straight ahead, her cheeks colouring invisibly in the dark.

After a pregnant pause he had carried on.

"And then I'm afraid it gets worse . . . I suppose you need to know what kind of person I really am, even though I'm sure you know enough already from your own experience to put you off.

"I met Cynthia while I was at Cambridge. We were really quite young. She wasn't studying there but was the sister of one of my friends. They often had weekend parties at their pile in the country, rather splendid affairs. She was just back from Switzerland, where she'd been 'finished off', as she liked to put it. Although I think she had a rather better time there than later on."

Lucy hadn't fully followed what he was talking about; some of it felt like a different language that she didn't understand, but she hadn't wanted to interrupt him to ask or display her ignorance. It sounded more like something out of a book than real life.

"She was stunning, maddeningly sexy," he had said, "sophisticated, witty even in her way, well connected, wealthy, and everyone wanted her. So I decided *I* had to have her! And I did. I was used to winning.

"Unsurprisingly I wasn't considered to be the most suitable candidate by her parents. But exerting her will in this matter enabled her to satisfy her need to feel rebellious. They acquiesced after a brief but polite resistance. They were easily pestered and charmed. I fear she has paid dearly to satisfy that particular whim . . . I must admit though, it was all a rather heady mix. I like to think that there was at least the relative innocence of pure desire in there somewhere, because I did completely lose my head too—but not my heart, I realized only too soon afterwards. Apart from a powerful animal attraction and mutual friends we had very little in common. Our marriage was always brittle, even in the early days of physical intoxication. She had no real interest in my work or passions, and I suppose I didn't have much interest in hers, although I'm still not really sure what they are—she seemed mainly concerned with making sure she was outdoing friends with the latest whatever, the carefully played game, all performed, of course with impeccable taste and elegance. She always seemed so much more interested in how things looked than what they really were. Even then that puzzled and perturbed me, although I suppose I wasn't immune to it myself. The social game is deadly and once you start playing it's almost impossible to extricate yourself. It's a kind of addiction, and the goal of being beyond danger and unassailable—utterly unobtainable. There is always another peak just when you achieve the ridge. And if you ever do reach the pinnacle, for a brief flash of glory, there's nothing waiting but emptiness, because there's nothing there. The promised Valhalla is simply a myth. To win at the social game is the greatest curse of all. At least the striving keeps you going. And even if you do manage to break free, you find for all those years of ceaseless labouring you've got nothing left. Society is a cruel taskmaster, particularly to those who abandon her and won't play anymore. All that you've worked towards, all your supposed friendships, your career, your hard-won status and sense of worth simply melt away, like frost on a spring morning.

"Well, perhaps I was already getting a bit disillusioned with it all. I think I always knew, deep down there had to be more than this flimsy 'success', although I didn't know what it was. We moved to Durham when I took up my post-doctoral position at the university. I was in the fortunate position of not really needing to earn a living—mainly thanks to marrying Cynthia, I suppose—and with my work I've been pleasing myself and, as she said, just 'doing what I damn well liked' instead of following a 'proper' and more prestigious career. But it was the only thing in my life which seemed to have real meaning. The books and poems I read, studied, taught, seemed to have a much greater substance somehow than the world I was living in. Cynthia used to mock my 'disingenuous romanticism', as she called it, wasting my time on the words of the long-dead. Particularly as she said I couldn't be less chivalrous towards the living if I tried. She said I was just a phoney, repulsive hypocrite. And of course she was right!

"But she always wanted to keep up the pretence of happy families. When the children came along—the perfect boy and girl, in the correct order—there was a temporary lull in hostilities, and I suppose for a few years a brief period of fragile contentment. For the first time we had a real mutual affection and a shared interest.

"But it didn't last. As the children got older, we grew further apart. The brittle truce fractured more each year. We fell into a downward spiral of constant, mean jibes, snide sideswipes and recriminations. We both played that kind of game well, although I was better.

"Life lurched on. I enjoyed my work. I've always loved my work. I believed I was successful, happy even in a way. I even thought I was basically a good person! How could I ever have thought that? And all the time we were learning to slowly hate each other in that potent, creeping way you can only grow to hate someone or something that you have once worshipped and are still a little intoxicated by. I was awful . . . awful . . . so cruel, and I shrink from the memory of myself with my bitter, poisoned barbs. We squabbled and stung, carefully behind closed doors, thinking somehow the children, other people, wouldn't notice. In the end I always won and she always cried, although it sometimes took me a long time to get her to that point . . . She always hated showing emotion. It gave me a perverse satisfaction. We had turned subtle cruelty into a warped art form. She was good, but I was masterful. And I despised her even more each time, each time I broke her. But although I grew to hate her and was increasingly unfaithful—even though I expected, utterly unreasonably, that she should remain faithful to me—I never stopped desiring her, in some twisted, torturous way. And, I think, she me, because sometimes desire would grudgingly overcome spite. But it always made things worse, and we hated and despised each other even more afterwards. It was like we had poisoned the well but were still addicted to the water. We couldn't resist returning again and again, picking the scab, leaving ourselves more raw and bleeding every time. By the end, whenever I slept with someone else it was partly just to feel I was hurting and humiliating her—a sort of temporary relief. We were degrading and destroying one another little by little. Chipping, scratching away—a fraction of a hairsbreadth every second, every minute, every hour we spent together and even when we were apart—it was a horrible way of killing, of dying."

He had sighed deeply.

"But really she was just so miserably unhappy. I can see that now, that's why she was so vicious and bitter, and it was my fault, all my fault. And I was cruelly jealous and possessive; tormenting and tormented by my contempt and my desire. And she knew it, and used it against me, and in fairness it was the only really effective weapon she had. And she certainly used it to full effect! When she delivered that last, devastating death blow . . . I think it was planned. I think she wanted me to find her with that other chap, to see it. So I suppose in the end she won. But I can't blame her. I deserved it."

He had paused a moment, staring unseeing at the dark road ahead, the glinting cat's eyes flashing past. Then he had suddenly heaved a great sigh of relief, that sounded as if it had come up from the depths of his soul.

"But what's amazing is that I no longer even feel any animosity towards her. The poison fire has been completely quenched. I'm free and now I just feel pity for her and am so very sorry for how I've treated her. I've even been enabled to resurrect some long-forgotten tenderness for her, despite it all—thanks to you. Such a blessing and such a relief. I can't tell you . . . She was—is—a good mother. She's done a good job with the children. She was always there for them, through it all. I was not. I will never challenge her rights and custody. I've been useless, worse than useless, damaging. I deserve nothing and I must try to win back some respect and affection from them. I have no right to either. So, she's won. And—is it wrong to say this?—I'm so glad, so grateful, that she did. It was what finally smashed up my absurd ego, my stupid, stupid myth of myself, and then in the ruins, in that sudden dazzling beam of light, in that vision of transcendent, supernatural peace in front of the window, the scales fell from my eyes and afterwards I could suddenly see all the horror of my own darkness—not just in how I'd treated Cynthia but in how I had treated everyone, my whole way of living. It was all thrown into even sharper relief by the purity and beauty of that vision. Then the words I was translating seemed to spring into life, haunting me, my conscious thought and my dreams. There was no escape. And the brooding presence of some terrifying, irresistible force, always hovering over me, hounding me, pursuing me, towards—I sound mad!—but towards you. And through you, towards a whole new way of being—real, whole, untainted."

He had brushed away the tears beginning to well in his eyes with the back of his hand.

"But how can I put things right, sort out the mess? I know just how MacNeice felt. 'When all is told, I cannot beg for pardon . . . ' How can I possibly pay for the extent of the damage and pain I've caused?"

"You can't," she had replied quietly, "but He, Jesus, can. The second Adam! That's why He came, why He was born into this world—to live and die in our place. To do for us what we could not do for ourselves."

"Yes, yes!" His eyes had filled with tears again. Alwin's and Augustine's words once again resounding in his mind, blending with her quiet voice. "Grace! It's grace, isn't it? Grace alone. Amazing grace! I'm just beginning to grasp what it means—it's so vast and wonderful it almost frightens me."

They had driven on in silence for a while and Lucy had fought a fierce internal battle. Finally, she had said in a flat and strangely choked voice, dragging the unwilling words up like lead from the depth of the sea, "Do you think you should try to make things up with her? Repair your relationship? Wouldn't that be the right thing to do?"

There had been a long pause as he reflected. She had held her breath, not sure what the right answer should be but knowing desperately what she wanted it to be. Eventually he had replied with quiet conviction.

"No. No, I don't think so. I've thought a lot about this. Our marriage is dead. It's been dying for years. The death is a relief to us both. She doesn't want me back. She never will. And she's happy now, in her own way—well, as happy as she knows how to be. It would be cruel, wrong, to trouble her again now she's finally broken free. She's been very clear about what she wants. And I'll do everything I can to make sure she gets it as easily and as painlessly as possible."

Lucy had silently released her pent-up breath, her heart beating a little faster and tears leaking out of the corner of her eyes. She had no idea if it was right or wrong to feel achingly relieved, but she did.

They could now see the faint line of the sea, appearing like a silver thread in the distance.

"Now you really know what I'm like—what a monster I am—do you still want to be trapped in this car, stuck so close to me, heading into the middle of nowhere? Aren't you disgusted, afraid?"

"No," she had whispered, "not any more afraid than I sometimes am of myself . . . And love is stronger than fear."

"Love? You are a remarkable person, Lucy!" he had exclaimed. "You are the purest person I know and yet the least shockable and judgemental. How quietly and patiently you sit there and listen to my confession, without even a word of condemnation or a murmur of reproof."

"Not really so remarkable," she had replied quietly. "I am also acquainted with the human heart."

He had glanced across at her, so young and serious, with her softly lilting voice. He hadn't been able to help smiling a little.

"That sounds like it should be a quotation from somewhere! I can't imagine you ever doing anything wrong, well, not compared to me."

"Don't be so naive and, and foolish!" she had snapped back at him in sudden frustration. "It's patronizing, demeaning! You still think it's all about you, don't you? You with your highbrow sins! Do you not think that I am as human as you? That I have as full a heart as yours, with just as much capacity to fall?"

"I'm sorry!" he had said humbly, taken aback. No one had ever spoken to him like this before.

"What do you think I am?" she had demanded savagely. "Some kind of, of chintzy china angel for the top of the Christmas tree? I have also seen people driven to the brink of despair. Just because they couldn't express it in fancy words and posh voices doesn't mean they didn't feel it just the same. Maybe worse, because they didn't even have the words to help drain the poison.

"And do you think that I also don't know only too well the dark paths my own mind could follow? The twisted labyrinths I could lose myself in? That you are the only one to have tasted the darkness? I dare not even look in the direction of those shadows. It's not so much what I *have* done, it's what I'm capable of doing."

She had brooded long on these things in the lonely hours in her office and while performing her many mindless tasks.

"It is only ever grace that keeps any of us from the dark places where our fallen hearts would naturally stray, from the extremities and the terrible depths we are all capable of sinking to, if unrestrained. We are made in the image of God. The *image* of God! And we have all fallen . . . are falling. Every time we sin it's an assault on His image, a blasphemy against His character, a marring of the divine imprint we've been created to carry—a falling further and further into the abyss. Do you even *begin* to understand what that means, for all your lamenting and self-recriminations? Earth would be hell without grace, and we would *all* be monsters!"

He had marvelled at her silently, stunned by the sudden fire he had unwittingly unleashed. Such a fragile looking, enigmatic creature, so unsure of herself in so many ways and yet in others, having such conviction, such wisdom beyond her years and experience.

"Tell me about yourself," he had said quietly.

And so she had.

She had lived out her early years happy, carefree, secure, under the guardian shadow of the pit wheel and shaft, which for better and for worse had held sway over all their lives. It wasn't just a job but a way of life; their fortunes rose and fell together, wedded, inextricable.

Money had always been a bit tight, but it had never worried her when she was little. Although, she had said, she supposed it probably had caused a level of anxiety for her parents. "But they always made sure we never went without what we needed, what we needed, mind, not always what we wanted. I remember desperately wanting an electronic game when I was in primary school! And then when I was a teenager, I was very envious of a girl in my class for her pixie boots—burgundy, they were!"

She had laughed.

"I suppose it's too late to get you some now?"

"Yes, a decade too late, I'm afraid! Isn't it funny what seems important when you're a child! I also remember being so impressed when I was invited to a friend's house who had a video player. We watched *Star Wars* and *Superman* over and over again! Can you imagine! Our gran did get a telly though, in '81—a colour one!—to watch the Royal Wedding, and we all went round. We were so excited!

"We used to have one holiday a year, camping for two weeks in the Lakes or Northumberland. It was wonderful, but I did sometimes wish we could explore further afield. Some of the kids in my school used to go on holiday abroad. I've always wanted to travel, see the world. That's not something I've grown out of."

"Well, I may be able to do something about that!" he had interrupted again.

She had smiled. "Maybe . . . "

Then she had carried on quickly—mortified in case he thought she was hinting.

Life was a shared business. She had told him how she had played with her siblings and cousins and the children on her street, in and out of each other's homes, mostly outside whatever the weather, in the back alleys or the park, sometimes sharing a quarter of lemon sherbets or rhubarb and custards from the corner shop. And sometimes on a weekend they would take their bikes, the little ones balanced on the handlebars, and go down to the river or make dens in the woods. She remembered the winding Wear, so shallow in places you could walk across it from bank to bank and catch little fish in your net to carry home in jam jars, the bluebells in the spring falling away in a glorious carpet of blue down the steep woodland banks, punctuated in places by the white stars of the wild garlic.

"Sometimes we used to eat the flowers and leaves," she had said, laughing, "and then we'd smell awful for days! The first poem I wrote was about the bluebells. I lay on my back, looking up through those intense blue flowers, through the young pale green beech leaves and the web of thin branches, to the brilliant blue sky beyond. I had a little notebook I would write them in. I had another one for stories. But I never got round to finishing any stories."

Then there was the igloo they had built in '82, the year of the big freeze, when there had been all the snow. It was so cold that parts of the Wear and the Tyne had frozen solid, and even some parts of the North Sea, near Berwick. The fuel even froze in the buses and snowploughs and the temperature had dipped to below minus twenty in some places. Eighteen people across the region had died from hypothermia and exposure to the cold. They had all helped dig out paths from each house and along the pavements, the kids fetching the groceries for the old folk, making sure they all had enough coal, and everyone kept the fires burning day and night. Everyone pulled together. It was a closeknit community. We all knew we needed each other, she had said.

"Our friends were always welcome in our home, and anyone else too for that matter. There was hardly a day when we didn't have a few waifs and strays squeezed round our dining table. And if the portions were all a little smaller than might have been ideal, that was just the way it was. And anyway, there was always porridge before bed for anyone who was still hungry.

"We went to church every Sunday, of course. Our chapel is just down the hill in the village, next to the Co-op. I loved the words of the hymns we sang—Wesley, Newton, Watts, Cowper—the wonderful poetry and ideas, and I loved the cadences of the Bible as it was read—the Authorised Version always—long before I think I understood what it meant. It always seemed to have a sort of richness and resonance and weight beyond ordinary words. I always believed in God—actually I suspect all children do, until the world beats it out of them—but when I was nine a visiting preacher came, and in that sermon, I suddenly understood that *all* humanity had fallen, all. And as I was part of humanity that meant me too, even if as yet the worst things I could think of that I'd done were sometimes being mean to my friends, once stealing some of my brother's sweets, disobeying my mum and dad . . . It didn't matter if it seemed small because it was enough—enough to fall short of perfection. Enough to separate me from a holy God. It was then that I realized I needed Jesus just as much as any murderer. Our sins are just a matter of degree. If you fall short by an inch or by a mile, you still fall short. You are still lost. It didn't matter if I *felt* like a sinner or not, it was just an irrefutable fact. People always think young children can't understand, but I think children understand much more than people think, or like to think. And of course, once your eyes have been opened, the older you get the more you see the infection of sin in every part of you. It's not just what you do, but what you *are*—but of course, thank God, we're back to grace again! Saving grace, that washes you clean and begins to transform you from the inside out.

"I'm sure hearing the Bible each week in church, reading it together at home—my dad always read and prayed with us after tea, round the table—singing the great hymns, is what began my love of words, and poetry and great stories. I discovered Shakespeare at school. Once we travelled in a bus up to Newcastle to watch *A Midsummer Night's Dream* at the Theatre Royal . . . " A dreamy quality had entered her voice. "Oh, it was wonderful, magical. I remember sitting there transfixed. It was so beautiful to look at and to hear.

"I had always loved reading. We had the *Narnia Chronicles* at home, and *Peter Pan* and the *Jungle Book*, *Lord of the Rings*—and I read and read them, over and over again. I remember borrowing *Swallows and Amazons* from the library and I loved Enid Blyton—used to save up my pocket money and my dad would take me into town to the bookshop and I would spend ages choosing a new one. I wasn't very discerning back then! I just loved the way you could lose yourself in a book; it was like going into a different world, although none of the children in those books were very like me or had lives like mine. But it didn't matter. In some ways it made them more interesting. Whenever I wasn't outside or doing chores or homework I was reading. My grandad used to come for his tea every Thursday night and he'd say, 'Always got your nose in a book!' and shake his head, but with a twinkle in his eye. And then he'd always slip me 50p to help save up for the next one! I kind of jumped straight from the children's books into the Brontës, Jane Austen, George Eliot in my mid-teens. All so thrilling. I felt I learned more about what it meant to be human, what it meant to be a woman, from those books than anything I'd learnt in school. And then a bit later, during my A levels, I discovered Tennyson, Christina Rossetti, Emily Dickinson, Wordsworth, Coleridge, Keats and Shelley, Milton, Chaucer . . . It was like discovering an enchanted garden. The librarian at school was really nice. She used to let me borrow more books than I was really allowed. My bag was so heavy! I devoured everything I could lay my hands on. I couldn't get enough. And I kept writing myself. It was—is—a kind of compulsion, I suppose."

There had been one boyfriend a few years back. Her parents had liked him. He was sweet and a real gentleman, she had said. He went to her church too. He used to bring her flowers—unusual—and hold her hand in the cinema—not so unusual—but although she was very fond of him, she had realized eventually that she didn't want to do any more than hold his hand. "He felt more like a brother really than a boyfriend," she had said, "and he wasn't interested in the same things, although we shared our faith—the most important thing—but not enough, not enough for a marriage. I wanted a soulmate. I always have."

"And have you found one?" he had asked in a low voice.

"Perhaps I have!" She had smiled. "You keep interrupting me!"

"Sorry!"

"As I was saying, it was a little sad when I broke it off, but we had nothing to reproach one another with, so no real harm done, just surface scratches, easily healed. He still lives on my parents' street, with his now-wife and baby. We're still friends."

Inevitably, as she had grown older the clouds had gathered. First there had been the miners' strikes in '84 and '85. "To start with," she had said, "us kids thought it was all quite exciting. It was on the six o'clock news on the telly when we had our tea at gran's! Usually, it was people with posh accents from different places on the telly. But then it went on, and on. We all pulled together in the community as always; mam helped in the soup kitchen, but it got bad. I remember some children with their toes sticking out of their shoes because that was all they had and they'd got too small and had to be cut open at the front. In the winter they were purple with chilblains and cold. The teacher would let us warm our milk on the stove in the middle of the classroom. School was the warmest place to be. There was a family down our street . . . their baby died just a couple of weeks after he was born. They couldn't afford a funeral. And because his dad was striking, they couldn't get a government grant either. The undertaker had to ask around the relatives of people who had recently died to see if the baby could be buried in the coffin with one of them. Their baby was buried in the coffin of a stranger. They couldn't even bear going to the funeral; they were so humiliated and heartbroken."

She had sat silently for a while, sunk in thought, slipping back to a place he could not follow her. Then she had heaved a deep sigh.

"It's what Regan wanted to ask me about."

And then her thoughts had taken a brief side turn. "You know," shooting him a quick sideways glance, "I thought that maybe you and she . . . ? Oh well, it doesn't matter now . . . If you really want to know all about those days, you can ask her. Why is it that no one outside our communities is interested, except someone from another country? It was a terrible time. *Then* we knew what it was like to be hungry and cold and frightened. But much worse, a whole way of life was destroyed—people's livelihoods, and heritage and pride. We have never recovered, our communities—and no one seems to care. They tore out the heart of our lives and never put anything in its place. Everything we have is taken away."

Then her mam had been diagnosed with cancer. She had to endure chemotherapy, then radiotherapy, as well as an operation. "She was so poorly," she had said, the memory jolting a different kind of tears from her eyes. "I tried to help as much as I could with the younger ones. They were still at school. I had just finished. I had hoped, really wanted, to go to uni. I had even got a place to read English at Leeds. My teacher was really pleased, and was told I would be able to get a grant, but they needed me. I needed to stay at home and keep things going. Dad had found some work in a factory—long hours, low pay. He never complained, but he used to come back exhausted in a way he had never been from the pit, diminished somehow. And I suppose, although I knew it was the right thing to do, and although I loved them so much, I still resented it, having to stay home, all of it, and I resented God for letting it happen. But I couldn't really admit to myself how I felt. I still find it difficult to accept—that time.

"I remember my dad standing at the kitchen sink, with mum's pinny on, the soapy water dripping down onto his old slippers, trying to do the washing up and then suddenly breaking down and crying. I had never seen him cry before. And I couldn't say anything. Nothing would come out. I have always wished I'd been able to show him how much I cared, how much I loved him, them, in that moment. But I couldn't. I think I coped with the whole thing by part of me becoming a kind of robot, just thinking about the next practical thing that had to be done and not letting myself think or feel anything, like one me was kind of detached from the other. But I'm worried I seemed heartless, as if I wasn't bothered. I just don't think I could even let myself consider the possibility that we might lose her, along with all the other things we had lost. I couldn't cry because that would have been a kind of acceptance that we might.

"She did eventually recover, but she was weakened. The others finished school and did various things, all stayed local. It's really nice because we all see each other a lot.

"It seemed too late to try for uni again and I needed to get a job. I felt I should provide for myself and wanted to get a place of my own, to take some of the pressure off mam and dad and ease the crowdedness of the house. I worked in the Co-op for a while. That's when I started renting the flat in Bowburn. I suppose I also wanted to feel I was making my own way in the world, even if it was in a different way from what I had hoped for. I was so excited when the job in the Uni English department came up and I got it. I think I stupidly thought it would help make up for what I had missed. Well, how wrong I was! It seemed to make what I was really passionate about even more out of reach. The one good thing is being able to borrow books from the library. It's a wonderful library, but the librarians here always look disapprovingly at me, like I shouldn't be in there, sometimes pretending not to hear me when I ask questions.

"I realized pretty soon that I was definitely on the second tier of existence—relegated to the role of convenient dogsbody, useful for filing and answering the phone, logging essay results—I sometimes glance at the introductions, sometimes I know I could have done them better—making tea and arranging meetings for the important people, and lectures and tutorials for the lucky ones—like a kitchen maid who never gets to taste the food, or . . . or the scullery maid who gets to light the fires but never to warm herself by them."

Her voice had risen inadvertently with indignation and frustration, her imagery coloured by her diet of Victorian novels.

At another time this might have tempted him to laugh a little. But now it just made it all even more poignant. A lump had risen in his throat.

It was still a sore point with her and she couldn't conceal it anymore, didn't see why she should have to.

"It's bad enough being ignored; it's even worse being mocked and slighted. And when I did dare speak out and try to do some good, try to help someone, well, you know what happened! Sorry, I suppose that's unfair of me—you've already said sorry—but it's not just you, it's all of them, the whole system. It makes me feel like a second-class citizen, although I have just as much right to the words, the knowledge, as anyone else, and I bet more passion for them than some. I may not be as educated, but I have a mind and a heart and feelings too! And I'm not ignorant or stupid either!"

Her eyes had flashed in the darkness, angry tears sliding down her cheeks.

His eyes had also filled, with tears of remorse and regret.

"Oh Lucy! I'm so sorry. There's nothing I can say. It's a rotten, toxic system. But this I promise you, whatever happens about us, I will make sure you get to study, one way or another—if you still want to. I'll teach you myself if you like—you should see some of the soulless creatures that pass for undergraduates these days: no imagination, no inspiration, only interested in partying! I always partied, but I always worked too. I have always loved my subject. It would be such a privilege, such a delight to teach someone like you. And it's nothing, nothing compared to what you're teaching me! I won't let them keep treating you the way they do. Can you forgive me for how I used to treat you?"

"Yes," she had whispered, her sudden anger spent.

He had reached out to her, as she had to him earlier, in an impulse of contrition, compassion, yearning. And his hand had felt like a burning coal against her leg. She had sat as rigid as a statue, unable to move or speak, holding her breath. Partly out of habit and instinct, partly out of desire, but mainly out of a confused and stricken sense of wanting to make things right, to affirm—to bring comfort in the only way he knew how—his hand had begun to slide up her thigh, leaving a burning trail. With a great effort of will she had wrenched herself out of the dizzying entrancement and, as his hand reached the hem of her blue dress, had placed hers over his and gently removed it, placing it back on the wheel.

"Not yet, Adam, not yet . . . " she had breathed, almost inaudibly, and then with a shaky giggle, as they swerved slightly, "and anyway, I think you need both hands on the wheel at the moment if we're ever going to get there!"

She had blushed at the double meaning, feeling rather shocked at herself and the peculiar situation she had suddenly found herself in. And for a brief moment, detached from the little microcosm of churning passion within the small, hurtling metal box with its miniscule human occupants, she had looked down as if seeing things from outside, like the unblinking guardians of the night as they watched silently overhead.

He had laughed and they had sped on, through the night and the stars, towards the widening thread of water, the full, luminous moon racing along beside them, skimming through the flying clouds.

And then had come the glorious meal, and although not consciously thinking about what she was eating, she had, even so, been more aware than ever of the textures and the tastes and the fragrance. And he, so gratified that at last he'd been able to give her something, begin to make things up to her, that she had accepted a gift from his hand, however small, basked in the delight of sharing with her this simple, ancient human ritual of good faith and fellowship.

Afterwards, as they had walked and talked the night away, barefoot along the glistening sand, their ecstasy had slowly given way to a peaceful, contented exhaustion. And as the sun rose, turning dusky silver to fiery gold, they had found themselves standing, hand in hand, looking out to sea, with the fresh Northumbrian breeze blowing in their faces and the first rays of dawn caressing their tired, aching skin.

It was very early in the morning on the first day of the week.

Homeward

And so, after many days of gathering artifacts of worth,
And wisdom, which is a treasure beyond price,
Biscop and Alwin turn to wend their long and winding way
Back to their humble abbey home, collecting as they go
The precious hoard held in trusted hands
And also bring Sabinus and his companions
To sojourn with them a while in wild Northumbria,
To work their magic with stone and sand and fire,
To reteach the skills of weaving liquid light
And binding broken fragments in their net of lead,
To beautify the holy houses with luminous panes
Stained to catch the rainbow's hue;
To build from precious gleanings
A vast vista of glorious truth,
And piece by piece
The great story of salvation tell.

And, Alwin finds, as blessed Biscop had foreseen,
He has traversed more than miles
On this momentous journey
And has learned to better understand
The sacred signs vouchsafed to man
To lead him to his Creator, if he has eyes to see
And heart to understand.
And he determines that the great window
He has been entrusted to conceive and oversee will,
Through Sabinus' skill and his own sacred vision,
Be a testimony to all his soul has learnt
This extraordinary year
And if God so please, become itself a sign
To point to the beautiful truth and real reality
Of God's great and gracious story of salvation.

What though the sea with waves continuall
Doe eate the earth, it is no more at all;
Ne is the earth the lesse, or loseth ought:
For whatsoever from one place doth fall
Is with the tyde unto another brought:
For there is nothing lost, that may be found if sought.

Edmund Spenser, The Faerie Queene

Eden revisited

Adam bent down and picked a small shining gem from the wet sand and held it, glistening in the palm of his hand for Lucy to see.

"Sea glass! Hundreds of years in the making, smoothed by a thousand tides, saturated by a thousand northern suns . . . " he murmured, with a faraway look in his eyes. "The children used to love to come here and collect it when they were little . . . I can almost see them now, with their buckets, squatting down in the sand, foraging for treasure.

"This piece of soft turquoise is the oldest kind, and I've been told that whatever colour it starts out, the glass always ends up as this translucent aquamarine in the end. It must be the most enduring pigment, or maybe it's somehow that little by little it yields its own colours into the vastness of the ocean, so eventually is completely in harmony with the nature and hue of the sea itself."

"It's the colour of your name," she murmured.

"Eh?"

"I always think of names as having colours. Don't you?"

"No, but I can see it's exactly how you would see them!" He smiled at her, then surveying the beach again, sighed.

"Even this has changed. There used to be a lot more to find, so many younger colours too, deep reds, dark blues, bright greens. The kids loved it, and they really did look like jewels scattered on the beach, catching the morning sun. So many people make jewellery from it now and collect it on an almost industrial scale, like trawler fishing. Do you know it's technically illegal to take anything from a British beach above the high-water line? Something to do with wreckers, I think! Not that that seems to stop anyone. There was so much of it on these beaches because of the old glass works . . . And hundreds of years before that too, they say glaziers were brought over from France to reteach us the craft in the so-called dark ages. What an ironic name! They have been the light ages to me. How amazing the painting with light must have seemed back then. I've been able to see it through their eyes as I've translated their story. Over the centuries it's washed up here, softened and caressed by the sea, jagged fragments smoothed into things of beauty.

"Nothing is ever really lost, is it? Forgotten knowledge can always be reawakened, the flame of truth rekindled, drawn up from the darkest depths, if only we are willing.' . . . *For there's nothing lost that may be found, if sought . . .*'"

She looked at his face, softened beyond any expression she'd seen before. "And lost things can not only be found, they can also be transformed . . . ," she whispered.

Without warning he dropped to his knees in the sand, his palm still stretched out towards her with the tiny sea gem cradled in the hollow of his hand. The dawn rays caught his face, wet with sudden tears.

"Marry me, Lucy? Join your life to mine . . . Complete the sea-change in me?"

His voice was quiet, urgent.

She stood rooted to the spot, strangely aware of herself as a static point in that ever-moving landscape, occupying her miniscule piece of space and time. She could hear the waves lapping backwards and forwards and the gulls swirling, taste the salt on her lips and feel the sand being gently sucked from beneath her feet. Even the breeze lifting her hair from her forehead possessed a movement and enduring she felt denied.

He was speaking again, now more quickly and frenetically.

"I know it seems sudden and no doubt I'd be judged by everyone else for being absurdly irresponsible, but you know, the irony is that asking you is the first truly responsible action of my entire life! When the whole parameter of your reality shifts irrevocably and everything you thought was real is false and everything you thought was false turns out to be real, well, you realize how much time you've already wasted on fakes. Not of course that the people are fakes, but just my perceptions of everything. What's the point of wasting any more time?"

She had the absurd sense of being caught up in some existential game of "stuck in the mud". If she could just reach out and touch him, she could free them both from that static confinement, liberate them both to fully be, and love and live. As if from the depths of an enchanted sleep she found herself closing her hand over his and heard her own voice, sounding very very far away, saying, "If I say yes, make this sea gem into a ring for me, to remind us always of this moment."

And then properly awake and back in the present with a sudden sickening wave of realization and anxiety, "But how can I say yes? We have such a long road ahead of us before we can even get to that point, haven't we? For so many reasons . . . Can you be patient? I don't feel as if I can bear to be patient, not now . . . ; it's like having the cup dashed from my lips, but it must be that way . . . I think it must, even though it tears my heart."

He stared at her, transfixed for a moment, then passed his hand across his eyes.

"I'm sorry! What am I thinking? What am I saying? I am not free. I'm still in the prison of my own making . . . I must serve the rest of my time before I can be disentangled, even legally, for it to be possible to begin again, to even offer my pitiful hand to you."

He groaned as reality delivered blow after blow.

"And you can't even live with me in the meantime, can you, while we figure it all out? Of course you can't! I had forgotten . . . It's been so long since I have made myself wait for anything, I had forgotten . . . "

She looked long and hard into his eyes, questioningly, finally speaking.

"And even if we get there, reach our heart's desire, can you, in the end, when the dust settles, really be satisfied with me, just me as I am, for ever, you ravenous man? You lap at the shoreline of my being more greedily than these waves!"

She smiled wanly.

"I am not a piece of poetry, you know! Oh dear, I feel—apart from anything else—oh, I don't know . . . so inadequate. I'm only a secretary. You're so clever, so worldly wise! What if you get bored with me?"

"Oh Lucy! How can you even ask? I have a little knowledge maybe, a heap of words, but what's that to you, to what you hold? You are inspired, you have wisdom, you are light!

"You would be worth waiting for for ever. It can take as long as it takes if you will just walk with me, through the mess. But how can it be untangled? I cannot put it right. My shame must first be paraded through the courts and I must denounce myself in the public square. And I deserve it, every bit of it! But how can I drag a pure thing like you through the mire with me?"

She shot him a warning look, but he was too taken up with his conflicting emotions to be restrained.

"I should not even ask it of you, but I am aching for you, body and soul. I cannot give up the hope of you. I *will* learn patience. I *will*! But can you? Should you? I have not been fair to you. It grieves me that I must burden you with my penance. I am a wretchedly selfish being, though and I cannot let you go voluntarily. I could not blame you for walking away, but I can't promise I wouldn't pursue you . . . I feel I can bear anything if you are by my side. I need you and I am blinded by my own need. I have pursued you with little thought of your own needs and convictions and desires. Forgive me! I will learn. I promise I will learn. But even so, I do feel—believe me when I say—that I have also been pursued, hounded towards you by a greater force than either of our fears or desires . . . I have tried resisting it and have tried to hide from it, but I can no longer resist, no longer want to resist. And how utterly futile it would be anyway! I want to embrace it, all of it—to be embraced, to be welcomed home—and you, like a messenger of light, have, without maybe even knowing it, been showing me the way . . . "

The tears poured down his cheeks. He had cried so much over these last few months, more than he ever had as a child. It was as if years of pent up, unacknowledged, even unknown, emotion had been finally released. He would have felt embarrassed before anyone else. But with her it didn't seem to matter. It was such a relief; a kind of blessed purging.

"Every day with you the sky grows bigger, the view grows wider, the light grows brighter. I have gorged myself on the junk food of the world and find myself as empty and shrivelled as a rotten husk. But you . . . you are like wafers made with honey to me, my manna in the wilderness. But how can *you* put up with such tawdry second-hand goods as me? I want to pour all the jewels of Heaven into your lap, but all I have to offer are the soiled fragments of my pitiful, stained soul and my life in tatters around me."

She put her hand in his. She was crying now too.

"Because I *love* you, Adam Hunter! I couldn't walk away from you now, even if I wanted to. My life feels bound up in yours. And I'm no different, not really. How can I make you see it? In the end we all come with empty hands. The world is broken and we are broken. We are both soiled and stained and need washing and clothing in the light. But it's not all mountain tops and dreams and visions, you know! Most of the time it's just hard work and the daily grind of faithfulness."

He pressed her hand to his cheek, all wet with salty tears.

"Try as hard as you like to bring me down to earth! But earth will be like heaven if you will be with me, by my side. I will eat the bread of angels! My appetite will grow with the eating. And when we have endured and finally obtained, I will feast on your love. I will love you wildly, passionately. You will be my light in the darkness, my own pure burning angel of light and every day you will shine brighter. You'll save me from myself, you'll . . . "

She pulled away in alarm.

"Don't Adam! Don't keep setting me up too high. It frightens me because . . . because then the only way is down. We all have feet of clay . . . "

He knew it. He grabbed both her hands and pressed them to his heart.

"I will never, never let you go, and if you should fall like lightning from the heights, you will take me with you and be my broken idol, my fallen angel, my light still, however deep we plunge. You would light the darkest chambers of Hades, you . . . "

She shook him in alarm.

"Stop Adam, stop! You don't know what you're saying . . . It sounds romantic to be sure, but don't . . . don't tempt me! It's what went wrong the first time, right at the beginning, in the garden . . . Don't make an idol of me. I will so easily break! Idolatry isn't love anyway, not really, even if it's sort of flattering. Really it's just a distorted selfish projection. I don't *want* to be your idol; I *want* to be myself! Even though I'm nothing special, I am me and I will become all I'm intended to be, and . . . and I won't give it up! I won't be . . . be eroded or consumed by you or by anybody else.

"I can't save you! I can't even save myself. I can give you neither knowledge nor truth. Even the best of us are nothing more than fractured reflections of God's glory. I've been thinking about what you said last night, what you said again just now in fact, about me guiding you, about feeling your way in me, glimpsing the light through me—it is because you're glimpsing, reaching out to Him. You must understand, I'm nothing, non-existent, without Him; and you must know Him if you're even to really know me. You must know the One who hounds you! And when we feel our way to the end . . . to the limits of our little human love, and have been smoothed and refined by our knowing, only then we are ready, ready to be fully known, launched into that vast, immeasurable sea of divine love."

"Well, teach me then, show me, lead me slowly to that shoreline and *'purge my mortal grossness . . .'*"

He winced. He was doing it again! Why must he always stray into the realm of melodrama? Why this absurd self-importance, imagining himself the subject of all epithets? Why did he never learn? Could his own contrived or borrowed narratives either before or after his strange epiphany be better than the real story he was just beginning to discover? The words of Augustine, that he'd translated but not been able to comprehend, those words mediated by Alwin, mediated by that unknown mediaeval poet, flooded his mind in new understanding and light. Not idolatry but *love*, wonderful love. He began to glimpse that there need be no contradiction between self-sacrifice and self-fulfilment, no dichotomy, both flowing out of one another, the two sides of the same coin. Paradoxically not the loss of self but the fulfilment of self in the giving of oneself wholly to another, in sacrifice if necessary. And moreover, in recognizing the source of all love, and in submitting to that glorious worship of the One who alone can truly be worshipped. As Alwin had learnt to understand, so Adam felt himself beginning to understand. Not just sign but substance. Pure, simple, but the hardest thing in the world.

He looked at Lucy tenderly. Who did he think he was that his path must be strewn with angels and saints and demons? This ordinary human girl, this remarkable human woman, had, even so, truly been sent to him as a divine gift and guide in his baseness and folly. And wasn't she enough?

Despite everything Lucy found herself laughing as well as crying. This had to be the strangest proposal ever.

"You can't help showing off, even now! Must I even be wooed in other people's words?"

He smiled too. A different kind of smile from any she'd seen before. His whole face lit up like the suddenness of the bright midday sun when it pierces the clouds and sends the shadows flying. His eyes blazed through his tears.

"Occupational hazard of consorting with an English literature lecturer I'm afraid! All those words . . . " He shook his head in wonderment. "My work for so many years, heaped up like a treasure trove over the centuries, the writers, the prophets, the poets . . . who have been whispering to my heart all my life and yet only now are beginning to really live for me, to sing! No longer just black on white, but infused with every colour and hue, the complex beautiful harmonies, each word a little piece more of the picture, another silken thread in the great tapestry . . . Perhaps all of our lives we are just telling and telling the story, not changing it but enriching, adding depth, one life at a time. But . . . "

Stumbling to his feet he pulled her so tight to him that she could hardly breathe. The shock of his intensity momentarily took her breath away.

"My own words do feel too base, too tainted for you, my own beautiful Lucy! They run in the old ruts and grooves of my mind, and it is so hard, so hard, to carve new patterns of thought, of being. Oh Lucy, I am as sick with longing for you, every part of you, as I'm sick of myself. I need to lose myself in the exquisite brightness of your being, burn away my shrivelled and twisted dross. I must possess what you possess. You must be my pattern, my map. This is alien territory for me. I'm lost without you. I need to lose myself in you . . . but no, I know even that is not it. I know in the very core of my being that you're right, what I tried to articulate yesterday is right, what I just said about being pursued, this is all part of something bigger, much bigger than either of us. It's not about losing myself, is it? Even though that sounds like blessed relief, it's about the hard work and patience and courage of finding, of remaking in the mess, in the crucible of the ruins, however painful and however long it takes."

He had taken her face in his hands, gazing rapturously into her eyes, and now he exclaimed with sudden urgency, "Come now, come and see the window. Then you'll understand what I've been trying to explain. I know you think it's all a bit weird and crazy, but I know what was unleashed then has led me . . . hounded me into your arms so that literally nowhere else was tolerable, even as I have been pursuing you, and now it will, I really believe, lead us, both of us together, to something greater still . . . I will prove it to you. I must show you. Come now, it is time . . . "

Grabbing her hand, he eagerly turned towards the direction of the monastery.

"I don't need to see it, Adam," she said quietly. "I believe you. You don't need to prove anything."

He stared at her.

"I feel in my heart," she said slowly, "that what you saw in that place, what you may see and experience now, is for you and you alone."

"You will take me on trust?"

"I will."

He wiped the tears from his face and gazed at her in wonderment.

It had been growing brighter around them as they'd paced the sand and then the stained concrete and rusty metal, as far as they could reach; and now they stood there, at the end of the pier, the end of the world. A fine briny fret rolled in towards them from the sea. The dawn rays shone through it, turning the gossamer mist into a translucent golden haze.

"You'd better have my raincoat if you're going to stay here."

He tenderly wrapped the long grey coat around her shoulders and turned and walked back up the length of the pier while she stood at the end looking out to sea. He looked back and for an instant she appeared to be floating, weightless in the swirling glory, then the curtain of mist closed around her. By the time he had reached the path he could no longer see her, but he knew she was there, somewhere in that luminous mist.

Alwin's prayer

"As I bask in the beauty of the window,
Bathed in its comforting colour and liquid light,
I pray the Spirit that it might speak
And soothe the hearts of men for many years yet to come,
My dearest desire that the first fruits of my labour
Flown forth in physical form,
My mind's eye made manifest in magnificent matter,
Might be a blessing in this battered broken world and be
Some small sign to set the suffering seeker on his way.
As I am myself an image-bearing creature of the great Creator,
I have sought to spill my soul into a work of wonder,
Sounding the seasons of sorrow and of joy,
Delving into the deepest depths
Of human heart and mind which You have made
That I may give You glory in a humble grateful gift,
Even though it be a poor reflection
Of real reality that resides in You alone, yet
It remains the fruit of the gifting granted by Your grace,
Through which a glimmer of glory may be glimpsed.
And although the glass be dark, the veil drawn down,
I pray that the presence of Your precious peace
Pervading this personal offering,
From conception through creation to completion,
May yet, though temporal, flow forth into the future,
Moving out beyond my own mortal miniscule
Pinprick in time and space,
Stretching, straining beyond myself,
As waves washing onto some distant shore.
I long that my labour of love formed
Within the constraints of time may yet prove to be
Perpetual precious foundations,

Radiant jewels, solid stones
Stained with sacred light for all eternity,
Not chaff and dross, on that great and dreadful day of doom
When from the four corners of the globe are gathered in
All the toils and treasures of the nations,
Forged in hope and fear,
When human history is harvested
And all our wavering works are winnowed,
Flung into the flames, the furnace of refining,
Tested, and if worthy, wrought anew.
I pray that the precious offering of my poured-out soul,
My love's labour, may never lure away from light or be a snare;
For if there comes a time when truth is turned aside
And mere object has obscured the Word
Instead of wooing weary wanderers back to You,
Image become an idol, a false friend and fiendish foe;
Then tear it out, though it be the dearest treasure
Of my true heart, and as an erring eye or lascivious limb
May it be cast away and lost. For it is better
To bear the loss of a deceptive beauty that betrays,
Crush the counterfeit creation that has erroneously enticed,
And thus to enter eye-less into life eternal
Than to abandon the soul to everlasting suffering and strife.
For if we focus on the form in favour of the Former
Or crave the creature, crowning it above its Creator,
If that beauty, which is merely a borrowed beam,
A poor reflection of the real radiance,
Seduce us from that sacred sun, our Saviour,
Scourged and scarred for our sins,
We taint its truth, turning it into a tarnished, shrivelled thing,
Degrading it down to a dark and distorted device,
Narcissus' fatal pool, a deceitful glass in which
To gaze and glorify our own fraudulent reflection,
Instead of a window through which to better see
The beauty of Him who is All in All."

Ebb tide

She stood there at the end of the pier, wrapped in Adam's coat and mantled by the golden mist, with her eyes closed, listening to the quiet sounds of the sea until it seemed to enter into her tired, overwrought, excited mind and exhausted body, and she into it, allowing herself to be cradled in its calming, hypnotic embrace. The fret had become heavier and the gentle patter of light rain joined in the watery melody. Her undulating feelings were mirrored in the ripples that broke rhythmically, endlessly, alternately sucking and lapping at the worn concrete beneath her feet and the continual regular brush of the little droplets against her cheeks; the ecstasy and the anxiety, the love and the fear, the ebb and the flow of contrary emotions lapping against her, caressingly, relentlessly, irresistibly.

As she was drawn back and forth, contrasting scenes, imagined scenarios, flashed across her mind's eye. There was her home, where they had all lived and thrived in simple, threadbare, crowded chaos; her dad, in his old patched cardigan, with his worried eyes looking at her, honest, kind, wise, straightforward . . . The scene switched, there was Adam and all the intense complexity; the brilliant light and the dark shadows. The long struggle, the temptations, the possibility of bliss, but gained by illicit or sanctified means? And even if they were able eventually to marry, would he really be capable of faithfulness, of enduring kindness even? It is a fearful thing to commit your life into the hands of another person.

She was thrown back and forth, tossed on the tide of her thoughts and anxieties. How could these two disparate worlds be brought together, different in every way? It was not only Adam who would have to navigate a whole new existence; it would be her too. Although they lived in the same city and worked in the same place, his world could not be more alien to her if he came from a different continent. How could she negotiate it when she felt so ill equipped? But he was also opening up a whole new world of ideas and experience for her, which she was soaking up hungrily; had broken into her life, which had seemed to be shrinking in around her, and opened up great and liberating vistas of possibility.

How would Adam look, sitting at her parents' tatty dining table over the worn carpet in front of the two-bar gas fire? (Her dad would never burn coal since the pit had closed.) It wasn't that she was embarrassed—she was proud of her family and heritage—but it seemed so incongruous. And how would *she* look, squirming and awkward amongst his highbrow friends, looking askance at her, amused, possibly disdainful, if she dared to open her mouth, displaying her accent and her ignorance? And his, their, colleagues? The increased hostility and contempt—for all his heroic avowals to make things right. She didn't even want to think about their reaction!

And what would his mother think of her? His children? But his children were nice—that was a really big thing—but actually, when she thought about it, not so very much younger than herself, which felt weird and uncomfortable. She would like to be able to have children of her own one day . . .

Imagine having to stay with his family or friends! Would they ever really accept her? But if she could creep into his arms at the end of each day, worth it, infinitely worth it . . .

And above all, she knew that he would understand her, understand her in a way that no one she had before met, or could imagine meeting, could understand her. He had touched her on the plane of the mind, not just on that of the body and soul. And this, she sensed, was rare and precious.

She exhaled a long breath . . . But how on earth would she explain it all to her dad? He would be stunned, shocked, probably horrified—but perhaps only at first . . . And her mam? Gentle, patient, bewildered, disappointed maybe, definitely flustered, but always trusting others to know and understand better, even though they rarely did . . . Surely there always had to be a way to breach the gulf between worlds if the people really wanted to reach one another enough? Yes, and they also believed in the possibility of redemption. With time and with evidence of good faith, she believed her parents, her own family at least, would understand and open their arms in blessing, even if feeling comfortable with it all took a lot longer to come.

She now forced herself to do the thing she had been avoiding for so long, terrified of what she might find. She made herself at last take a long, hard, honest look into her own heart. Did she *really* believe there had been a sea-change in Adam? Or was it just convenient, what she wanted to believe in the face of her desperate longing?

With a wave of overwhelming relief she knew, with sudden conviction. Yes, she really did believe there had been, at least the beginnings of genuine transformation. The Spirit was hovering over the face of the deep. She had been unconsciously holding her breath and she now released it, gulping back a great, rising sob of gratitude and relief, a wave so powerful that for the time being it swallowed the lesser fears and anxieties.

She opened her eyes and saw the luminous curtain of fret, woven now with rainbow hues, gradually rising, taking the drizzle with it, inch by inch as if it was lifting onto the first scene of a new act in her life. It was a strange and awe-inspiring sight. Her feet were clear first, pooled in light, as the dawn poured under the white-gold cloud, then the fine mist gradually crept up her legs to her waist, her shoulders and then finally her head was out and she stood facing the rising sun, the warmth of its beams caressing her face, her whole body, her heart simultaneously opening, unfurling to the light. She prayed but without knowing exactly what. In fact, she couldn't help but pray as she basked in the brightness of all that created glory, more aware in this moment than ever before of her Maker, her Redeemer, the source and the end of love. And she knew, deep within her soul that somewhere, in that inland mist, Adam was also worshipping. She looked along the rippled pathway made by the sun as it shimmered across the vast expanse of the sea, disappearing into the vanishing point of the horizon. There was always a way and the plans, however hard, were always good—plans for hope and a future. There was no need to give way to fear and be afraid of the intense beauty and the pain, the loss and the love. She would be enabled to do and bear whatever was needed. The words from St Paul's first letter to the Corinthians, so often read at marriage services, although perhaps little understood, flooded her mind as the sun flooded her body and grace flooded her heart:

Love bears all things, believes all things, hopes all things, endures all things.

Love never ends. As for prophecies, they will pass away; as for tongues, they will cease; as for knowledge it will pass away . . . So faith, hope and love abide, these three; but the greatest of these is love.

Fear of beauty

"But as I, Alwin—lowly and unworthy servant
Of the living Lord and Father of Lights—
Have travelled through this wide world,
And all the winding ways of my own mind,
I have also come to see that ofttimes it is unfounded fear,
Though zealous and seeming free, that tempts us
To distrust truth taught us through true beauty
And mesh again in lines of law that lovely liberty
Which He laid down his life to loose
And so degrade and destroy what we dare
To dearly love aright. For it is not fierce hate
That is the antipode of love, but mortal fear;
And fear gives birth to hate, hatred
Of the unheard and unknown, hatred of the infinite,
Hatred of the testing, searing trial of truth.
For Your beauty bares our pitiful poverty
To which we cling for counterfeit comfort,
And in our paltry pedantic folly, pretend is piety.
But as there is no value or virtue
In vain glory or vile ambition, so also nothing divine
In the lukewarm, the indifferent; in dullness,
Despondent ugliness, self-deprecation, despair. Our fear
May fly from infinite beauty and what is finely wrought
And seek to slink behind the second-rate and shabby
To hide our soul's sad and sinful shame, but our actions
Only obscure the image of God in us, impotent,
Ineffectual covering, degrading not perfecting,
As the lifeless leaves lashed to our first parents
In lost paradise.

No, we must take courage to claim and embrace
The entirety of all He has created and redeemed,
All that He has pronounced 'very good',
And gladly with the giftings He has granted us,
In the purity of joy and delight, dare
To design dangerously, create courageously,
Love unreservedly, offer all of ourselves extravagantly
On the altar of His exceeding great glory,
Lest returning, He finds we have buried
Our talents in the soil, sealed from the sight of the sun.
No, let us rather gaze into the full brightness of His glory
And be not afraid of its blinding splendour,
For all that is truly beautiful speaks to us of God,
The Author of all beauty, the Word made flesh,
Broken to buy back his beloved bride,
Beautified, bathed by His atoning blood;
It is the climax, the consummation
Of his costly, creative, redemptive love;
For perfect, Incarnate Love casts out fear."

Benediction

The fine mist had turned to a drizzle. He was glad he had given Lucy his coat. As he hurried through the ruins, he felt his legs could not move fast enough. His hands fumbled on the ring of the church door with all the frustration and fervour of an impatient lover. He was through, pacing once again the stone flags that he had so many times trod in his mind's eye and his dreams. The pale light and colours cast on the stone floor led him on eagerly. He reached the place and rapturously raised his eyes to the window. What he saw almost physically threw him backwards with the violence of his dismay and disappointment. His worst fears and doubts had been realized. All there was in that circular space was a chaos of broken coloured fragments, arranged, it appeared, at random. No unifying vision. No completeness. No consummation.

He staggered to a pillar and leant against it. It felt cold to his shaking hand. Nausea swept through his exhausted body. He leant his head on the clammy, hard stone and wept, as he'd never wept before. Not the relieving tears of recent weeks, but the stifling, suffocating, throbbing tears of crushing anguish, tearing themselves up from the pit of his stomach. He felt as if all the grief and despair of all the world was coursing through his veins and forcing its way out of his eyes. He sank to his knees there in the broken light, himself utterly broken.

No truth after all. No purpose. No hope. He was just going mad, that was all, as everyone had said. And what on earth was he going to say to Lucy. What did his feelings for Lucy even mean now at the end of everything?

He did not know how long he knelt there, in the sway of his brutal lachrymal, head resting on the cold stone, contorted with the spasms of his passion. His exhausted mind, body and soul slowly succumbed to a trancelike state, like that of a young child who has cried himself to sleep under the weight of a great burden of sorrow and finally achieved a deep and disconsonant calm. As the violence of his grief had thus gradually spent itself, he had become simultaneously aware of a growing sense of the presence of another near him, emitting an irresistible impression of peace. He was no longer alone.

Out of the corner of his eye it seemed to Adam that he could see an old, stooped man watching him quietly. His body, still wracked with the echoes of his heaving sobs, attempted to stumble to its feet and turn to face the man, but it felt so heavy, or the air felt so thick, that it was like trying to wade through treacle and he found he could not move. Under normal circumstances, part of his mind seemed to be thinking, he would have been ashamed to be observed so undone by a stranger, but now nothing, particularly his pathetic dignity, mattered anymore. The old man drew closer, and Adam saw that his old face too was streaked with tears.

"I really believed I'd understood," he heard himself saying, as if from down a long tunnel.

The man said nothing, just stood next to him, and it seemed to Adam that he also wept.

"I wanted to see that window again more than I've ever wanted anything else in my whole life, more even than I wanted her. It made sense of everything. It gave me hope, even for someone like me . . . " Adam heard his own voice trail off.

"But," he found himself casting around for words, grasping them with difficulty from the cloying, honeyed air, thick with light, "it is different now, it's just a mess, no coherence. It's just like the world I thought I'd escaped from, just like myself. It's the worst thing I could see. I must be mad, or perhaps before I just saw what I wanted to see and now, like a bad joke, the sordid old world is holding the mirror the other way round, mocking my folly."

He heard himself let out a hollow, echoing laugh, that rebounded off the stone walls.

"What a bloody fool I've been."

The old man, however, seemed unmoved by his outburst. He just continued standing quietly, neither condemning nor comforting, but still he wept silently.

"You see, sir," Adam felt somehow that he must try to explain himself, and spoke on with effort, slurred like when one has had too much to drink or is inordinately tired, "I thought—I really believed—that when I stumbled in here, that other time, out of the storm, into this tremendous calm, that I saw, saw my whole life—and not just the whole of *my* life, you understand, but the whole of life itself, of meaning—stretched out in, encompassed by that window, in that space; and the most tremendous sense of awe, of my own smallness—almost nothingness—in the face of something, someone so much bigger, greater. A kind of awe, a dread of something utterly beyond me, but in a good way—the inexpressible relief of being in my right place at last, a miniscule grain of dust in a vast universe of light, so bright and unapproachable, and yet also, somehow personal. I know it sounds mad. I see that now. How could a picture in a window ever portray such a panorama of meaning in any case? And without the extremity of that profound, that blank wonder, I don't suppose I would ever have felt it did. Of course, it makes no sense. But nothing made any sense then, except this momentous image and this feeling of utter and absolute Otherness. And now—oh, how can I bear it—now the very thing that seemed the only real certainty in the world that I could hang on to, the moment I thought I had awakened from my, my facile *charade* of life, is revealed to me again as simply a mocking reflection of my own madness and of the terrible chaos that engulfs me, engulfs us all."

His own voice—or had he only been thinking the words?—cracked once again into great heaving, exhausting sobs.

The man stretched out a gnarled hand towards Adam's arm and it seemed as if he was trying to touch him, to speak, pondering, as if carefully measuring words. But he was fading, mingling with the beam of sun-specked dust in which he stood.

Adam tried to reach out and grasp hold of him, but his fingers closed on empty light. The words followed slightly after, as if breathed into that radiant, opaque air after the image itself had vanished, echoing in the stillness.

"*Tolle lege . . .* "

Take up and read—Read what?

He found his eyes were closed, but the red intensity of light through the film of eyelid, that thin veil of flesh, was rousing him from his dream-like state, the words still echoing in the stillness. Adam's hand automatically reached into his pocket to draw out his notebook, in which he had been keeping a copy of his translation. It had become such an essential part of his life these last weeks he did not want to have it ever far from reach. Having it there, almost touching his skin, made him feel rooted. That sense that it contained the life-giving clues and pointers he needed to begin to understand this strange new world had grown with the weeks; in a sense it felt the written, paper equivalent of Lucy. How strange that sounded! Perhaps he really was mad! And stumbling in here that first time, his vision of complete coherence and meaning, his awe and his wonder, his sudden and dread awareness of the great Other, that letting go, in that moment the most blessed, blessed relief he so desperately needed, perhaps had unknowingly been searching for—or avoiding—all his life; this is what had started it all. And here he was again, and the image was gone, had been broken. But the words remained.

He wanted to see that image again, that vision of meaning, with such strong, all-consuming desire. To see, with his eyes, to touch even, the great story, laid out before him, painted in light. The words were so much less immediate and took so much more time and effort of mind. He felt his desires, his needs, were being one by one thwarted, shattered and denied in this grand finale. A residual petulance rose within him. He began to have an argument in his head, possibly even out loud. With whom? God? Lucy? The Alwin of his translation?

I want to see it again, even if I'm mad and you *are mad* (he glanced at the book in his hand) *and she is mad and, and the whole world is mad. Although . . .*

He stifled a strange gulp, somewhere between a laugh and a sob, that ricocheted through his mind.

. . . that would be the cruellest joke of all if the mad things should have more meaning than the sane ones.

A pause. Time trickled slowly by.

His anger passed. He watched it ebbing away, as if from the outside, slowly like sand through an hourglass.

Settling himself more comfortably, back propped against the stone pillar, Adam sighed and opened the precious notebook, yielding to the inevitable. In the last few days he had been translating Alwin's final prayer and warning. There had also been a few other fragments of text which did not seem to quite fit with the main narrative, one of which he had already placed quite near the beginning as it continued the "Sparrow and the Hall" motif from the opening, speaking of the famous conversion of King Edwin. Then there was another section that extended and rounded off the "sparrow" metaphor and this appeared to be a natural conclusion to the whole story, so he had placed it at the end—bringing the narrative full circle, bringing the "winter sparrows" in from the cold and incorporating a wider plea to a beloved people in danger of losing its first love and light.

But there had been, in addition to this, another piece that was certainly older than the rest, like the lost piece from a jigsaw puzzle that has ended up in the wrong box. It was part of a much older text even than the Middle English poem, the lettering extremely faded. It had been penned on a quite different, coarser type of vellum and it was written in Latin prose, not Middle English poetry, perhaps part of a letter. Adam realized now, with a sudden flash of inspiration, as he looked over his scribbled translation again, that it must have been written by Alwin himself, the real Alwin, a much older Alwin perhaps than had appeared, fictionalized in the poem, to someone else, probably someone younger, maybe a scholar, possibly someone denied, like Sabinus, a holy, monastic calling. Someone, maybe, who could even have been a contemporary of Bede himself, he thought with growing excitement. And it was borne in on him how very remarkable it was to think that they too, all those hundreds and hundreds of years ago had been where he now was, in this same sacred place, also looking on, speaking of, touching the beauty wrought in stone and glass, speaking and writing of truth and love; so far away in time, and yet, in the light of eternity, perhaps no more distant than the space of a heartbeat. In this incomplete scrap he realized that Alwin was speaking again of his window, *this* window, of his own hopes and desires, of the power and yet limitations of art, and of human experience in the light of a greater truth. It was almost like an elegy, a love song to this fallen world, in all its brokenness and all its beauty.

Perhaps, Adam thought with another thrill of excitement, this fragment of text was actually part of the inspiration for his Middle English poet. Perhaps it was the lost key to the whole narrative. That would explain why it was found with the, relatively speaking, much younger manuscript. There was no context, what had come previously and afterwards must have slipped away and been buried in the vast vaults of time. Adam turned to the page where he had jotted down this last broken fragment and read again fervently and with new meaning:

> . . . *sometimes things, people, need to be broken before they can be made whole, transformed. The rock must be crushed to become sand. The sand must endure the furnace to become glass. Truth, you must understand my son, is so much more than a collection of facts, the brittle, flimsy grains of time and space . . .*

Then the words had been too smudged and faded to read, only the phrase, " . . . *Time is a great mystery, but Eternity an even greater one . . .* " had been able to be made out.

Then the legible text resumed:

> . . . *You say you have been vouchsafed a vision and have been granted to perceive something marvellous in the glass. I believe I also know something of what you have seen, for it was, in a manner of speaking, of my own conception and I know the great intentions and prayers of the maker, his struggles and sorrows too. But as with all our works and devices, it has only ever been a window, a dim reflection in a glass.*
>
> *Windows are for looking through, not just for looking at. They are only gateways to the light, not the light itself. There are many windows in this world, windows for different ages and indeed as many as there are eyes to see. Many windows but only one way.*

I could try to tell you the story of this window, as you ask and it is, I believe, the first and foremost of its kind. But with regards to its substance, and its meaning, that you must judge for yourself.

However, there are better storytellers than me and greater artists. It is better to speak with the supreme artist and to listen to the great storyteller, who not only wrote the story but is the story. But I will tell you something, give you a picture to help you understand.

While travelling with my former Bishop and Father in the faith, the late lamented and much blessed Benedict, to gather artefacts of beauty, worth and facility for our revered houses, I was gifted a wondrous gem, by an ancient holy brother who resided between the azure sky and sea of the southern sunlit climes. (He has no doubt now attained to even brighter plains.) He pressed it into my hand the day we left his cloistered home. He said it had once belonged to a great King and I have pondered its bright beauty many times since to try to find its meaning. It is unlike anything else I have beheld. I have not seen its equal before or since. Perhaps it is an epitome for such a time as this.

Think then, if you will, of this marvellous diamond, this jewel of greatest price. It has many facets, all equally part of the same stone. So, there is only one real story, my son, just many ways of telling it. Or think of it another way. This stone is like Truth—a perfectly cut prism which can both fragment and converge. It holds all colour, all diversity within its perfect white unity. It is the hardest thing on earth and utterly inflexible. Anything that comes against it will be shattered. Did you know it can only be cut by its own dust? It is as sharp as a two-edged sword. But it is beautiful, radiant, good. It is perfectly clear, clear as glass, and yet when I hold it up to the light, it scatters rainbows. Rainbows are His gift, His promise, to a broken world. And yet what love, what unsurpassable love, that from our brokenness should be contrived such beauty. All the rainbows of all the world are woven together, silken strands upon silken strands to create the complete picture, and even that is only a veil, a type or pattern of the real thing, a dark and imperfect reflection of the

*beauty of the real Truth. It is too great and too wonderful for us
to bear now, but we will, when all things are bound up together in
perfect Love, and fully known and fully knowing we will see Him
face to face.*

*But for now, your path lies out there, in the world beyond the
window, and you must learn to embrace it in all its tainted beauty.
Strange to need to say this to you, you man of words, but now
image must give way to word, The Word made flesh, the great lover.
Perhaps you begin to understand. Fear has driven you to its polarity,
to Love. Love in all its fullness. Now perfect Love, redeeming Love, is
casting out fear. It is time to put off childish things, the dreams and
the nightmares. Remember what I have told you and think much
on these things . . .*

That was all. There the text broke off. What came before or after Adam
didn't know, didn't need to know. But it was enough. Whoever it was
originally written for, Adam had no doubt that it was also written for him,
for him in this moment. For after all, every word that has ever been spoken
is still out there somewhere, reverberating through the ever-expanding
vastness of the universe. Every word ever written remains, even if no
longer able to be held in the hand or recalled from brittle human memory
or the great vaults of time. And we will each answer for all our words,
for good or for ill. The great Author is also the great Steward and there
is no waste. None of His words, or the words of His image-bearers, ever
return to Him empty, but accomplish all His purposes and He knows,
knew from the very beginning, before any were spoken or penned, all
that would come of them, of all their meanings for every person, in every
age. Nothing is lost. Truth can always be found, if sought. Adam closed
his eyes. The warmth and light penetrated his whole being: body, mind
and soul. The whole atmosphere felt heavy with collective being, as if all
the ages were condensed into this space, suspended in the radiance. It felt
strangely timeless, as if the thin one-dimensional experience of ordinary
existence was suddenly full and fat. He felt his withered soul within him
expanding, burgeoning, filling his emptiness, nourished by the weight

of this light, greedily soaking in its abundant synergy. Maybe he slept again. Maybe he dreamt. Maybe he dreamt of Alwin, the Alwin of his translation, the Alwin of the letter, the Alwin of his imagination, of the body behind the words. And then he dreamt of Lucy, girdled in light. And then he dreamt of others, all in their way heralds, messengers, companions even. And then in ways beyond words he dreamt of the great Source, the great Father of Lights. He was not alone; he would never again be alone. In fact he never had been. But he would always now know, really know, that he was part of something bigger, something so much bigger that he could not grasp it. A small stone in a vast building, a humble dwelling in an immeasurable city, a tiny member of a great body, a little word, a miniscule character on the vast canvas of history. But with a part to play and words to speak and love to give.

His dream shifted and returned to the strange and yet familiar old man.

"Who are you sir?" he heard himself asking.

The man seemed to smile. For a moment, body and voice were united— words and substance together.

"I think you already know. We have spoken many times—and you have been writing *my* story, Adam!"

"You know my name!"

"As you know mine."

As he spoke his old face looked almost beautiful, reflecting the golden light. And it seemed to Adam that a sudden and inexplicable fragrance filled the air. The smell of spring.

Adam saw the old man (and yet he somehow now did not look so very old) standing with his arm raised as if in benediction. The light streamed through the broken fragments of the window, illuminating his frail form, almost seeming to dissolve and absorb it and yet the impression was strangely of a great substance of radiance, and all the former grief and despair were swallowed up in that exceeding weight of glory.

And then he was gone.

Adam opened his heavy eyes and stared a long time at the luminous space in the archway where the man had seemed to stand, reorienting himself, as if dragging himself out of a deep well of golden sleep, his head still resting against the cool, smooth pillar.

Had he ever been there or had everything just taken place inside his own head?

It didn't matter. It was still true. All of it. The images of his dreams, the words he had heard, had read. For hadn't Alwin, through the unknown poet, through his, Adam's, own translated words already been speaking to him for months across the gulf of the centuries? Was it, after all, so surprising that he, along with a multitude of others—all human beings, all image-bearing creators—should still be speaking through their art and through their love, into the minds and experience of others? For both have the power to leave a mark for good on the world. And anyway, hadn't all his life, the weavers of the rough magic of letters, through the heaped up treasuries of their words, in their many and varied lights and colours, added each a new voice to the heavenly music, that chorus that echoes through the ages, speaking truth, reflecting reality—sometimes even despite themselves—creating beauty, whispering love to the world and to his own hardened soul?

Words everywhere, often conveying truth beyond even the author's intention. *Because words have a life of their own*, he thought, *and though cracked and crazed, are little vessels of light*. The key thing was to see, to listen, to hear. He was finally able to hear. His own heart resonated with both the broken and the holy praise.

But if this was so, it really was time, as Alwin and Lucy had both entreated, that he sought out the Living Word who was the true Author of all and who was redeeming all those little words. Alwin knew him, Lucy knew him. He must, like Augustine, *Tolle lege* . . . *Take and read*. Take hold of the Word made Flesh and follow wherever He would lead. All the other little words were merely the signposts and symbols, only the introduction or the prologue to the real, the great story.

And now, thanks to Alwin and Biscop and Sabinus, and indeed the poet who had written of their endeavours, he also could return bearing the gifts they and so many others had bestowed. Gifts of beauty and words and light. He could return to Lucy, his own great gift, and with her, together discover more and more of the greatest gift of all: the one who is both ultimate gift and giver, the Divine Lover and embodied Love.

He got up and walked to the front of the church, where the great Bible on the lectern was open at the beginning of the Gospel of St John. It now struck him as strange that he had not turned to this book of books before. Perhaps something in him had been innately resistant or perhaps it was simply because he had thought he already knew what it said, as Augustine had thought before him, and rejected as childish tales. *"To look at a thing is very different from seeing a thing. One does not see anything until one sees its beauty."* How true those words of Oscar Wilde were. How blind and deaf we can be; always looking but never perceiving, always talking but never listening or understanding, dulled and hardened to beauty and truth. His eyes and ears had been wonderfully opened. He could now see and hear. And the beauty of it thrilled his heart. He stood, back to the window, face towards the open door, with the golden dawn spilling through, and read the familiar passage, but with new eyes:

> *In the beginning was the Word, and the Word was with God, and the Word was God. He was in the beginning with God. All things were made through Him, and without Him nothing was made that was made. In Him was life, and the life was the light of men. And the light shines in the darkness, and the darkness did not comprehend it . . . And the Word became flesh and dwelt among us, and we beheld His glory, the glory as of the only begotten of the Father, full of grace and truth.*

He turned over a few pages and read again:

> *Jesus said to him, "I am the way, the truth and the life. No one comes to the Father except through me..."*

The rain had stopped, and he walked through the ancient door and out into the glorious light of an Easter morning; the sun breaking through the darker hues of mist and cloud and the daffodils dancing joyously in the morning breeze. A vivid rainbow once again stretched across the sky. But this time he saw it. And he thought to himself, as he looked upon its beauty, that without the brokenness, the fallenness, the pain, there would be no rainbows; no beautiful, broken light. How can we mortals know what to feel in such moments? They are utterly beyond us. Could we wish things another way? We can do nothing but shut our mouths, bow our heads and worship in the presence of the Maker. Adam looked along the many-coloured arch as it rose and then plunged beyond the shining blue horizon of the sea. It was like a bridge, indeed a pathway, a long road that must be trod, through the rain and the sun. The next stage of the journey. There are not many Enochs and Elijahs. Very few simply get to climb through the window, and indeed who could ever be ready, who could ever approach on their own terms, the purity of that uncreated, unmediated, holy white light?

He passed a hand across his eyes. How long a road would be necessary for such as him? But it was alright. Journeys can be good things, he thought, exciting even, as long as we carry the light and know the way and the destination. *And He is the way*, he thought, *as well as the destination and the light*. We are not wandering alone and aimless in the dark but are part of a great cloud of witnesses, a great throng of fellow pilgrims and travellers, some who have walked before us, some who walk alongside and some who will follow after—until there is "time no longer".

He passed a crumbling tombstone and stopped, kneeling down to brush away the moss and dead leaves that obscured its faded and weather-beaten Latin text. It bore, under a text from Ecclesiastes, a double inscription. He translated as he read:

> *He has made everything beautiful in its time.*
> *Also he has put eternity into the hearts of men.*

> *Alwin, Servant of God, DCCVXI*

> *For now we see through a glass, darkly; but then face to face: now I know in part: but then shall I know even as also I am known.*

Sabinus, Master Artisan, DCCVXI

In your light do we see light.

He smiled. The spikes of fresh green blazed with purple and saffron crocuses and pale primroses peeped from where he had cleared the dead leaves. He could smell the warm damp earth mingled with the salty tang, and the birds were singing. The winter was truly over. Brushing the dust from his knees he set off towards the sea, where the tide was turning and the girl in the blue dress was waiting for him at the end of the pier.

The sparrows' rest

And so came the sparrows in from the cold
And the cruel wilderness of winter
To find a hearth and a home and dwelt
In the light of hallowed life.
And a favoured place was found for them
To build their nest and raise their young
Within the heavenly courts,
Even by the holy altar of the Lord of Hosts,
Not now the ephemeral respite of their former kin
But the everlasting welcome of Eternal Love,
A room of their own in the many mansions
Of their God and Maker, to Whom,
Though simple, slight and humble,
They are yet precious in His sight. For though
Two small sparrows may for a penny be sold,
Not one falls to the ground without our Father,
Who knows and cares and wills,
And Who will establish all His works,
And not one word will come back void
Or without substance, but accomplish all His purpose.
So not one single drop of ink or blood or human tears
Is shed in vain but stored up in His jars of clay
Against that day when the dread books are opened wide
And all, both great and small, are brought
Before His throne of judgement and of grace
To give account for all our weeks and days and hours
Upon this weeping, wondrous earth.

Our light is now dwindling
And the deep darkness comes on a-pace,
We dwell within the twilight of our race

And soon, maybe, our sun will set.
But we have been here before it seems,
So many times, on history's spinning wheel,
Seeming abandoned to the darkness
And deserted to our doom,
Our tide ebbing and our sand spread thin,
Strewn across the shoreline of retreating Time.
We, if we but will, His heirs of light,
Redeemed with precious costly blood,
This our gift and heritage, will we even now,
Without lament, lose ourselves again
To lengthening shadows and creeping gloom;
Cast ourselves once more, without a backward glance,
Into that cold and cruel abyss,
The black holes of our absences and voids,
Bereft of all of substance, beauty, hope and truth
And as the great betrayer, turn from all that blessed light
To go blithely, gently to the deceiver and the night?
Will we willingly walk in winter bleakness
Or will we rage against the dying of the light,
And fight with all we have to hold
The sacred flame aloft and plead for heavenly aid?
For a smouldering wick he will not snuff,
Nor snap nor shun the broken flax,
But bind up all in Love.
For even through these mortal throes
And torturous travail of the soul,
Resurrection Life is born anew,
And from the womb of dust and ashes
Will rise the real and wonderful world,
Crafted and cradled in the crucible of New Creation,
Life's rainbows cast upon Heaven's white stones.
For Time's twilight is but Eternity's timeless dawning,
The bright and morning star that rises in our hearts;

But until day breaks and shadows flee away,
May this gospel lamp of Love by God's good grace
Ever burn on blessed Britain's shores,
And though much in peril and hard-pressed,
May the flame of Truth be never quenched
Or utterly silenced in Arthur's ancient Albion;
May it rather ever shine and speak
While sun and stars endure
And moons and tides and seasons
Run their course.

Amen.

Epilogue

Adam sighed and laid down his pen. His sense of his own abilities, like everything else, had taken a serious knock over these last few months. He was not satisfied with his translation. It lacked the precision, balance and beauty of the original. What mastery those old poets had achieved, aspiring to heights almost impossible for the flabby modern mind to grasp. But, he supposed, at some point one simply has to stop and accept whatever stage of imperfection has been reached. There was no point in editing for ever. He looked through the pages of his own neatly penned writing wistfully. Despite its imperfections and limitations, it still had real value, he was sure of that. It had certainly conveyed light to him, even though the words had passed through the broken prism of his own mind. He could now see that his gifts were not remarkable, simply serviceable. In a way, though, the recognition and acceptance of this was quite a relief. He felt strangely lightened. It is, after all, a wearisome business constantly trying to prop up the illusion of one's own genius! *But Lucy . . .* he reflected; Lucy was quite a different matter; living proof that inspiration still existed. In a sense she was, of everyone he knew, the person with the most substance, and yet, paradoxically, also the most transparent, if that was the right word to use of flesh and blood. She was herself like a window through which the light poured in an unsullied stream, sparkling, joyful; pure inspired poetry. How incredible it was that she should wish to share it with him. Smiling, he closed the folder containing all those little words and hard-won truths; his imperfect offering. Serviceable was enough.

Once it had been duly typed up, by Lucy in fact, a true labour of love on her part, and sent off to the publishers, Adam gave her his handwritten translation of Alwin's story, as a sort of pledge, beautifully bound in soft blue leather. He also kept the gem of sea-glass safe in the hope that he could one day use it.

He had never spoken of his strange experience in the church, other than to say she had been right. And Lucy never asked. It formed a sort of wordless bond between them. It was enough to know that they were now travelling the same path together, and however winding and dark it might be, were united in their faith that it would in the end lead them home.

And she, along with many private works of her own composition, written for him alone, had given him a pocket-sized Bible and a copy of Francis Thompson's *The Hound of Heaven*; one of those small, slim Edwardian volumes of yellowing pages, bound in faded olive-green leather embossed with gold. How many hands, she had wondered, as her fingers gently ran over the soft, worn cover, had held it down through the years? She had only recently discovered the poem; had found it with great excitement, for a few pounds, in the Aladdin's cave of the Cathedral's second-hand bookshop, hiding between two larger books, and, as she said eagerly, with her characteristic blend of mischief and seriousness, it really did seem to sum things up so well.

"Listen, Adam . . . " she said, as they sat once again on their beach, watching the sea, their backs resting against a dune with its spiky scrags of silvery marram grass. They had returned there often and watched the many different faces of the water, through the changing seasons; sometimes turbulent, sometimes expectant, sometimes wild and splendid, sometimes peaceful, sometimes alive with heartbreaking beauty.

"Listen, if you ever need an epitaph, here is one for you!"

. . . Fear wist not to evade, as Love wist to pursue . . .

He smiled at her. "I hope I don't need it too soon!"

"So do I!" she exclaimed with a sudden frown. "How hard to accept that there always must be that tearing apart before the final making new."

She gripped his hand harder. "But we must not be afraid. He will carry us through the waters and it will be better the other side, even though it's so hard to imagine when the shadows can seem so sweet and full of promise. But then there is so much here that is broken and can't be mended, isn't there? It would be terrible really if it all went on for ever as it is. Time needs to be swallowed up in eternity if we are ever to know that complete fullness and renewal and healing. Nothing will be lost, just transformed, into the real thing—the apostle Paul again, I suppose. I love

Paul's letters. '*When the perishable puts on the imperishable, and the mortal puts on immortality, then shall come to pass the saying that is written: "Death is swallowed up in victory."*' All the waiting and the longing and the pain, it *will* be worth it, now and for ever . . . "

She brooded a while and he stared, through misted eyes, at the broken horizon, out upon that uniquely northeastern paradox of wild nature and heavy industry, marred one might say, but real and robust and beautiful.

She leant across and gently kissed his damp cheek and he turned and put his arm around her, pulling her close and twisting his fingers meditatively in her hair. She nestled into his shoulder.

"Listen, I will read you some of the poem," she whispered. And, opening the little book, she began, her voice shaking slightly:

> *I FLED Him, down the nights and down the days;*
> *I fled Him, down the arches of the years;*
> *I fled Him, down the labyrinthine ways*
> *Of my own mind; and in the mist of tears*
> *I hid from Him, and under running laughter*
> *Up vistaed hopes I sped;*
> *And shot, precipitated,*
> *Adown Titanic glooms of chasmèd fears,*
> *From those strong Feet that followed, followed after.*
> *But with unhurrying chase,*
> *And unperturbèd pace,*
> *Deliberate speed, majestic instancy,*
> *They beat—and a Voice beat*
> *More instant than the Feet—*
> *'All things betray thee, who betrayest Me . . . '*

She skipped ahead a few pages. "This is the bit I really think you should hear!"

. . . Now of that long pursuit
Comes on at hand the bruit;
That Voice is round me like a bursting sea:
'And is thy earth so marred,
Shattered in shard on shard?
Lo, all things fly thee, for thou fliest Me!
Strange, piteous, futile thing!
Wherefore should any set thee love apart?
Seeing none but I makes much of naught' (He said),
'And human love needs human meriting:
How hast thou merited—
Of all man's clotted clay the dingiest clot?
Alack, thou knowest not
How little worthy of any love thou art!
Whom wilt thou find to love ignoble thee,
Save Me, save only Me? . . .'

"Is it necessary to read that part with quite so much relish?" he interrupted with a wry grin, giving her a quick shove.

She laughed and the cloud lifted. She carried on, this time with confidence and conviction:

'. . . All which I took from thee I did but take,
Not for thy harms,
But just that thou might'st seek it in My arms.
All which thy child's mistake
Fancies as lost, I have stored for thee at home:
Rise, clasp My hand, and come!'
Halts by me that footfall:
Is my gloom, after all,
Shade of His hand, outstretched caressingly?
'Ah, fondest, blindest, weakest,
I am He Whom thou seekest!
Thou dravest love from thee, who dravest Me.'

Dedicated to my dear mum Jane
(7 November 1952 – 7 April 2024)

and my dear friend Alison
(27 October 1971 – 7 November 2022)

*who both loved stories and who I miss so much but also remember
with gratitude before God, with all those who rejoice with us,
but upon another shore, and in a greater light, that multitude
which no man can number, whose hope was in the Word made
flesh, and with whom in the Lord Jesus we are for ever one.*

References

Preface
John Keats, *Endymion*.

A sparrow in winter
Bede, *A History of the English Church and People* 2:13.

Beginnings

> From twin shells in the blue sea I was born,
> And by my hairy body turn soft wool
> A tawny red. Lo, gorgeous robes I give,
> And of my flesh provide men food besides:
> A double tribute thus I pay to Fate.
>
> *Aldhelm (639–709)*

Bede, *A History of the English Church and People* 1:1.
Bede, *Lives of Benedict, Ceolfrid, Eosterwine, Sigfrid and Huetbert*.

Translation
Bede, *A History of the English Church and People* 2:13.

Rekindling
Bede, *A History of the English Church and People* 2:13.

"Mene, Mene, Tekel, Upharsin"
Daniel 5:25–27.
Michelangelo, *The Creation of Adam*.

Alwin

C. S. Lewis, Introduction to *On the Incarnation* by Athanasius (London: Centenary, 1944); Psalm 19:1–4; John 8:6–8; Romans 5:1–11; Philippians 3:16; Genesis 22:17; Revelation 21:6–7; 1 Corinthians 1:25–31; 1 Samuel 1:11.

Revelations

Thomas Hobbes, *Leviathan* (1651).

Commission

Revelation 1:1–3; Revelation 5:5; 1 Peter 1:19; Judges 16; Exodus 12; Hebrews 3:17; Exodus 32:4; Numbers 21:9; Exodus 33:11; Genesis 3. Bede, *Lives of Benedict, Ceolfrid, Eosterwine, Sigfrid and Huetbert*, p. 67. Ephesians 6:10–20.

Vision

Hebrews 12:2; Revelation 22:13; Philippians 2:6; Genesis 3:15; John 10:11; Ecclesiastes 4:9–12.

"More things in heaven and earth . . . "

William Shakespeare, *Hamlet* 1:5.
Dante Alighieri, *Inferno*.

The dream

Luke 10:25–37.

> *The cry of the gannet was all my gladness,*
> *The call of the curlew, not the laughter of men,*
> *The mewing gull, not the sweetness of mead.*
> *There, storms echoed off the rocky cliffs; the icy-feathered tern*
> *Answered them; and often the eagle,*
> *Dewy-winged, screeched overhead.*
> > *Old Northumbrian Poem, tr. K. Crossley-Holland,*
> > *cited in Northumbria in the days of Bede.*

The Exeter Book (*c*.970).

> *Upheaved, swiftly I run, but leave not my home when I bear things,*
> *Tenuous, vagrant I am, conveying abundance of burdens;*
> *Snow does not cover, nor hail strike, nor does frost overcome me,*
> *Less from above am I pressed, than by what lie hidden within me.*
>   *Old Jarrow Riddle, cited in Northumbria in the days of Bede.*

Acts 27.
Hunter Blair, *Northumbria in the Day of Bede*, Chapter 4.

Foreign soil
Acts 21:5–6.
Christina Rossetti, *A Better Resurrection*.

Kintsukuroi
C. Bartlett, "A Tearoom View of Mended Ceramics", in *The Aesthetics of Mended Japanese Ceramics* (New York: Cornell University Press, 2008).
Christina Rossetti, *A Better Resurrection*.
Leonard Cohen, *Anthem*.

Painting on silence
William Shakespeare, *A Midsummer Night's Dream* 5:1.
Malcom Guite, *The Word Within the Words*.
P. Hunter Blair, *Northumbria in the Days of Bede*, p. 150.

Augustine
Augustine, *Confessions* 1 and 2
Michael Reeves, *The Breeze of the Centuries*, Chapter 4.
Attributed to Augustine in *Select Proverbs of All Nations* (1824) by "Thomas Fielding" (John Wade), (London, Longman, Hurst, Rees, Orme, Brown and Green), p. 216.

Other fruits, other gardens
William Shakespeare, *King Lear* 3: 7.

Love in Carthage
Augustine, *Confessions* 3 and 4.
Acts 17:22–31.

Touching the void
Ecclesiastes 1:2.
Oscar Wilde, *An Ideal Husband* (1895).
William Shakespeare, *Romeo and Juliet* 2:2.
William Shakespeare, *Twelfth Night* 2:4.

Privation
Augustine, *Confessions* 5.

The rising
Augustine, *Confessions* 6, 7 and 8.

Magi
Numbers 24:17; Matthew 2:1.

The book of memory and dreams
Augustine, *Confessions* 10.
1 Chronicles 29:14–17.

Beatitude
Augustine, *Confessions* 13.

Dead white men
Evelyn Waugh, *Brideshead Revisited: The Sacred and Profane Memories of Captain Charles Ryder* (London: Chapman & Hall, 1945).
William Shakespeare, *Richard II* 2:1.
Matthew Arnold, *Dover Beach*.

William Shakespeare, *Hamlet* 1:5.
Jane Austen, *Pride and Prejudice*.
Luke 12:48.
William Shakespeare, *A Midsummer Night's Dream* 5:1.

The ways of love
Genesis 2:24.

Elegy
William Shakespeare, *Hamlet* 2:2.
Leonard Cohen, *Suzanne*.
Johann Strauss, *Die Fledermaus*.
Andrew Marvell, *To His Coy Mistress*.

The lighthouse of Ostia
1 Peter 5:8; Psalm 74:20; John 10:1–18; John 14:6; Hebrews 12:2;
    Ephesians 5:27.

Animae dimidium meae?
William Shakespeare, *Twelfth Night* 5:1.
Claude Baudelaire, *Les Sept Vieillards (The Seven Old Men)*.

Monica
Tr. D. Boin, "Church of Sant'Aurea". <https://ostia-antica.org/>, accessed
    30 October 2023.
Augustine, *Confessions* 9.
Matthew 25:23.

Knowledge of the evil and of the good
Genesis 3.
John Keats, *Ode on a Grecian Urn*.
1 John 4:8; Psalm 19.
Leonard Cohen, *Anthem*.

The theologian of love

Michael Reeves, *The Breeze of the Centuries*, p. 98.

Augustine, *On Christian Doctrine* 3.10.16.

City of God

Revelation 21:2.

Jerome, Letter 123.

Augustine, *City of God* 1–7.

Habakkuk 2:14; Hebrews 11:38; Hebrews 11:8–16; Revelation 21; Haggai
    2:7; Romans 5:20; Genesis 3:4–5; Mark 8:36; John 1:1–4; James 1:12.

Confession

L. MacNeice, *The Sunlight on the Garden* (1936), in *The Earth Compels*
    (London: Faber and Faber, 1938).

1 Corinthians 15:42–9.

Eden revisited

Edmund Spenser, *The Faerie Queene* (1590).

> *Nothing of him that doth fade,*
> *But doth suffer a sea-change*
> *Into something rich and strange.*

William Shakespeare, *The Tempest* 1:2.

> How art thou lost, how on a sudden lost…?
> And mee with thee hath ruind, for with thee
> Certain my resolution is to Die;
> How can I live without thee, how forgoe
> Thy sweet Converse and Love so dearly joyn'd,
> To live again in these wilde Woods forlorn?
>
> *John Milton, Paradise Lost, Book IX.*

William Shakespeare, *A Midsummer Night's Dream* 3:1.

Alwin's prayer
Genesis 1:26; 1 Corinthians 3:12–15; Mark 9:47; Romans 1:25; Isaiah
   53:5; Romans 11:36.

Ebb tide
1 Corinthians 13 (RSV).

Fear of beauty
Galatians 2:15–21; Genesis 3:7; Genesis 1:31; Matthew 25:14–30;
   Revelation 7:14; 1 John 4:18.

Benediction
2 Corinthians 4:17.
William Shakespeare, *The Tempest*, 5:1.
Leonard Cohen, *Hallelujah*.
Oscar Wilde, *An Ideal Husband* (1895).
John 1:1–3; John 14:6; Luke 20:18; Hebrews 4:12; Genesis 9:13; 5:24;
   Kings 2:11; Hebrews 12:1; 2; Revelation 10:6; Ecclesiastes 3:11
   (ESV); 1 Corinthians 13:12 (ESV); Psalm 36:9 (ESV).

The sparrows' rest
Psalm 84:3; John 14:2; Matthew 10:29; Isaiah 55:11; Psalm 56:8; Romans
   14:12; John 9:4; Hebrews 9:12; John 13:30.
Dylan Thomas, *Do not go gentle into that good night*.
Matthew 12:20; Revelation 22:16; Song of Songs 4:6.

Epilogue
Francis Thompson, *The Hound of Heaven*.
1 Corinthians 15:50–58.

Dedication
From the first prayer in the *Nine Lessons and Carols Service*, King's
   College, Cambridge.

Bibliography

Aldhelm, The Riddles of (639–709), tr. J. H. Pitman (New Haven, CT: Yale University Press, 1925).

Augustine, *The Confessions of Saint Augustine*, tr. J. G. Pilkington (London: The Christian Literature Company, 1886).

Augustine, *Confessions*, tr. R. S. Pine-Coffin (Harmondsworth: Penguin Classics, an imprint of Penguin Books, 1961).

Augustine, *City of God*, tr. Henry Bettenson, revised edition (Harmondsworth: Penguin Classics, 2003).

Bede, *Lives of the First Five Abbots of Wearmouth and Jarrow*, tr. Rev. Peter Wilcock (originally published by Hills & Company, 19 Fawcett Street, Sunderland, 1910, reproduced by Franklin Classics, an imprint of Creative Media Partners).

Bede, *A History of the English Church and People*, tr. Leo Sherley-Price, revised by R. E. Latham (Harmondsworth: Penguin Books, 1955).

Bede, *Bede's Ecclesiastical History of England*, A Revised Translation, With Introduction, Life, and Notes, By A. M. Sellar, Late Vice-Principal of Lady Margaret Hall (Oxford and London: George Bell & Sons, 1907).

Blair, P. B., *Northumbria in the Days of Bede* (London: The Camelot Press Ltd., Victor Gollancz Ltd., 1976).

Greene, G., *A Sort of Life* (London: The Bodley Head, 1971).

Greene, G., *Ways of Escape* (London: The Bodley Head, 1980).

Guite, M., *The Word Within the Words: My Theology* (London: Darton, Longman & Todd, 2021).

Needham, N. R., *2000 Years of Christ's Power, Part One* (London: Grace Publications Trust, 1998).

Reeves, M., *The Breeze of the Centuries* (Downers Grove, IL: InterVarsity Press, 2010).

Thompson, F., *The Hound of Heaven* (New York: Dodd, Mead & company, 1926).

Milton Keynes UK
Ingram Content Group UK Ltd.
UKHW011847040724
445175UK00039B/183

9 781789 593525